No Breaking
My Heart

Read more Kate Angell

Sweet Spot (Richmond Rogues)

No Tan Lines (Barefoot William)

Unwrapped (Anthology)

He's the One (Anthology)

No Strings Attached (Barefoot William)

No Sunshine When She's Gone (Barefoot William)

The Sugar Cookie Sweethearts Swap (Anthology)

No One Like You (Barefoot William)

No Breaking My Heart

KATE ANGELL

KENSINGTON PUBLISHING CORP.
www.kensingtonbooks.com

KENSINGTON BOOKS are published by

Kensington Publishing Corp.
119 West 40th Street
New York, NY 10018

All Kensington titles, imprints, and distributed lines are available at special quantity discounts for bulk purchases for sales promotions, premiums, fund-raising, educational, or institutional use.

Special book excerpts or customized printings can also be created to fit specific needs. For details, write or phone the office of the Kensington sales manager: Kensington Publishing Corp., 119 West 40th Street, New York, NY 10018, attn: Sales Department; phone 1-800-221-2647.

KENSINGTON and the K logo are Reg. U.S. Pat. & TM Off.

ISBN-13: 978-1-4967-0366-8
ISBN-10: 1-4967-0366-9

First Kensington Trade Paperback Printing: August 2016

10 9 8 7 6 5 4 3 2 1

Printed in the United States of America

First Electronic Edition: August 2016

ISBN-13: 978-1-4967-0367-5
ISBN-10: 1-4967-0367-7

Alicia Condon, Editorial Director. I appreciate you.

Debbie Roome, my very best friend for so many years.
You've always been there for me.

Laura Hamilton Sanders, Landon Kane was written for you.

To Mugster-Pugster . . . my favorite pug.

RICHMOND ROGUES
Starting Lineup

28 – RF – Halo Todd
19 – C – Hank Jacoby
13 – 3B – Landon Kane
22 – CF – Rylan Cates
6 – SS – Brody Jones
17 – 1B – Jake Packer
45 – LF – Joe Zooker
3 – 2B – Sam Matthews
55 – P – Will Ridgeway

One

"**B**e my boyfriend for one hour."

Halo Todd stared at the woman dressed in the chicken costume. At least, he assumed she was female. Feminine voice. Short in stature. Indeterminable age. She wore a padded yellow, feathered jumpsuit with orange leg covers and spiky chicken toes. The head cover had a red wattle. A sharp black beak.

Six-fifteen a.m. on a Monday morning, and she paced outside Jacy's Java, a popular coffee shop in historic Richmond, Virginia. Brick buildings and sidewalks. Gas streetlights and narrow avenues. A hint of dawn was on the horizon.

He'd purchased a double espresso in preparation for his drive south. The Rogues were about to begin spring training in Barefoot William, Florida. He played right field. It was the second week in February. Pitchers and catchers had already reported. Position players had another week.

The morning was chill. Fifty degrees. Overcast skies. A stiff wind blew from the north, ruffling the chicken's feathers.

Who the hell was she? He scratched his head, asked, "Do I know you?" He had, on occasion, slept with women and not known their names. He would have remembered a chicken.

She shook her head, and the red wattle beneath her chin quivered. "We've never met."

"Why me?" he asked. Amused. He wondered if his teammate Landon Kane was pranking him. But there was no one on the street corner other than him and the chick. No one hiding behind a parked car. No one recording a video for YouTube, as far as he could tell.

The woman clapped her hands, stomped her feet. Shivered. A few feathers flew. Apparently, the costume wasn't as warm as it appeared. "My boyfriend broke up with me last night," she said on a sigh.

Her man must not be into chickens.

Achoo. Her whole body shook. "I'm allergic to feathers."

Her jumpsuit was all feathers.

A second sneeze, and she went on to say, "You're the biggest guy to walk down the street. The last male costume for matching couples at Masquerade was an extra-large rooster. Cock-a-doodle-do me?"

His mind went to the gutter. Cock-a-doodle-do her sounded kinky. He had no idea what she looked like. Other than that the eyes visible through the slits appeared green. Her mouth was hidden beneath the beak. His curiosity got the better of him. "What's with the costume?" he asked.

"*Go Big or Go Home.*"

"The game show?" No way, José.

"I have tickets. I stood in line for three days."

Go Big or Go Home was a popular television show. He'd watched it on occasion, during the off-season. While seated on the sofa, sipping a beer. The show got funnier as he worked his way through a six-pack. He'd be cheering for his favorite contestant when he crushed the last can in his hand.

Challengers lost their inhibitions. They made spectacles

of themselves. Jumping, shouting, and waving signs to get the host's attention. Alex Xander encouraged them to riot. The louder, the crazier, the more out of control, the better. The costumed guests fed into the frenzy.

Halo had been born restless. There was no peace in his soul. He was familiar with wild and foolish. Raising hell. Sleeping around. Calling a friend for bail money. He lived in the moment. Just when he thought he'd reached the bottom of his craziness, he found there was a crazy underground garage.

Team Captain Rylan Cates constantly urged him to tone it down. To grow up. Halo had complete respect for Ry. He'd made the occasional effort. Yet acting normal never lasted long. More times than not his inner child came out to play. That kid played hard. Still, he kept at it. He'd made it an entire week without slipping. He felt mature. Momentarily sane.

A game show would flip his competitive switch. Winning was important to him, in all aspects of his life. He would have to abide by their rules. He'd have no say in the matter. The show was based on challenges as the contestants competed against each other playing various games. Some were mental; others physical.

Each day had a different theme, which varied from midway at the fair to three-ring circus, haunted house, rodeo, and jungle safari. No one knew the activity until the curtain went up. He'd be at the host's mercy. He had better things to do than parade around as a rooster.

"So, what do you say?" the chicken pressed, sounding hopeful. "Sixty quick minutes."

Quick minutes? It would be the longest hour of his life. One he could never get back.

"The television studio is six blocks east." She rolled back the orange mitt on her hand, glanced at her watch. A big-faced Minnie Mouse on a red band. She had a Disney heart. "The show films in the morning and airs in the afternoon. We have less than an hour to sign in. As it is, we'll be stuck standing in the back row."

The last row wasn't far enough away for him. "Sorry, I can't help you."

"Can't or won't?" she challenged, standing up to him. Chicken was brave.

"Won't." He was honest with her.

She pointed a hand claw at him, said, "The show's in its tenth season. This is anniversary week. Friday is for couples only. Winners in each segment take home cars, jewelry, and dream vacations. Fifty thousand dollars is the grand prize." She spread her arms wide and her chest puffed. He glimpsed the outline of her breasts for half a second. Small, high, and firm. A-cups. "Anything you'd ever want," she tempted him.

Halo wanted for nothing. He was set for life. Professional baseball had been good to him. He had a fat bank account and shrewd financial advisor. He owned the renovated lumberyard warehouse he called home. Unconventional, but comfortable, and party central for his teammates.

Construction had centered on the freight elevator that rose to the second floor. A wide balcony overlooked the lower level. He'd transformed the upper office space to bedrooms. Six total. A contractor had knocked out a section of cement wall that faced the James River and installed an enormous plate-glass window. Halo converted the loading dock to a four-car garage which housed his Hummer, TerraStar pickup truck, a 1955 red Roadster Corvette, and a forklift. His dad's forklift.

Generations of Todds had owned the lumberyard. His old man wanted Halo to manage the warehouse out of high school. Halo had resisted. He was a jock. A damn fine ballplayer. He liked the praise and attention that came with athletic ability. His sights were set on the major league.

He and his dad had argued. Their voices bounced off walls, echoed down hallways, and raised the roof. Lyle believed in legacy and family loyalty. Halo believed in himself.

He graduated high school, nabbing a sports scholarship to UCLA. The Rogues later scouted him, drafting him fourth round. He'd signed the contract. His father was livid. His only son had let him down. His mother called him selfish. Silence and separation took their toll.

In Halo's rookie year, his father had suffered a heart attack. The team was on the road, deep in a three-game series against the Tampa Bay Rays. Lyle passed away before Halo made it home. His mother laid blame on him. According to her, Lyle had worked himself to death. Despite his best efforts, the lumberyard was in debt when he died. Deeply so.

Halo couldn't go back; he could only move forward. He'd paid off the warehouse mortgage and all outstanding bills, then sold off the inventory. The scent of cedar and white pine, redwood and oak, were no more than a memory.

Deed in hand, he'd taken up residence. Richmond treated him well, even though his mother still held him at arm's length. The beach was his favorite vacation spot. Barefoot William on the Gulf Coast did it for him. That's where he was headed now, with a stopover in Atlanta, as soon as he walked away from the chicken.

He took a step back.

She moved forward, bobbed her head, as if to peck him.

He held up one hand, palm out, stopping her. "I'm leaving town, and have a long drive ahead."

She exhaled, shrugged, and her shoulders slumped. Defeated. Her voice was soft when she said, "Safe travels."

She turned then, left him. The bottom of her orange leg covers dragged on the uneven brick sidewalk. The hem snagged on a rough, raised corner.

An unidentifiable guilt walked with him to his Hummer. He couldn't shake it. Why he felt blameworthy was beyond him, yet a part of him felt bad for her. A small, nagging part. She had tickets that would go to waste if she didn't find a partner. Couples Day was a big deal. He'd seen the advertisements on TV. The anticipation was huge.

Halo scrubbed his knuckles over the stubble on his chin. Shaving was not a priority. Not first thing in the morning. Not at noon. Not even before sex. His lovers never complained about his beard burn. He gave good orgasms. Satisfaction eased the redness on their breasts and inner thighs.

He picked up his pace as he crossed the street and climbed into his Hummer. The chicken was still visible from the corner of his eye when he keyed the engine. Then he drilled his fingers on the leather-covered steering wheel. Why was he procrastinating? That was unlike him. He made decisions on the spot. Some without forethought or consideration of possible consequences. He stuck to them.

Shifting into reverse, he backed from his parking place. Instead of heading south as he had planned, he turned east at the stoplight. Minimal traffic, so he was easily able to follow the chicken to her car.

She slowed beside a white Dodge Dart, rested her tail feathers against the hood. She leaned back, looked to the sky, appearing to pray for a hero.

Halo was no hero. Not even close. The game show would delay him. He had plans in Atlanta tonight that involved a female pilot and the penthouse suite at the Four Seasons.

He'd met Captain Susan Nolan when the Rogues

played the Braves the previous season. His team and her flight crew had stayed at the same hotel. One night of hot sex, and they now hooked up whenever her flight plan crossed his. They left their clothes at the door. Walked around naked. Twenty-four hour in-house dining allowed them never to leave their room. They burned up the sheets. Checkout, and they took the elevator to the lobby. Sated, satisfied. Smiling. No strings attached.

His thoughts scrolled back to the chicken. He had his own mental game to ease his conscience. He played it now. He would circle the block, and if she were gone with his second pass, he wouldn't think twice about her. She'd be out of his life. If she still leaned against her car . . . well, shit, he might reconsider wearing that rooster costume. Might.

He drove so slowly, killing time, that the cars behind him honked. More horns blared when he sat too long at a stop sign. He needed to give the chicken a chance to leave. Ten minutes later, he was certain she would be gone.

The coffee shop sat on the corner of the next block. He tapped the brake, stretching out the moment even farther. He slitted his gaze when he took a right at the light, not fully certain he wanted to witness the outcome.

A Caravan had pulled in behind the spot where her Dart had been parked. It blocked his visibility. He didn't see her immediately. In those seconds he felt an odd sense of loss, as if he'd missed out on something. Something he hadn't initially wanted, but did now. Because he couldn't have it. That was his way.

There was a flash of yellow feathers as the chicken squeezed between her vehicle and the minivan. Her costume added a roundness to her body that made it difficult to maneuver. She left feathers on the front bumper.

Relief rushed through him. Unexpected and undefined. Halo pulled his Hummer alongside her. Let it idle. The engine rumbled. He rolled down the passenger window. "Chicken," he called to her.

She glanced his way, was unimpressed. "You, again?"

"Yeah, me," he hated to admit.

"Are you lost?"

He'd found her. "Just passing by."

"This is your second pass."

She was observant. "You haven't found a partner." More a statement than a question.

She rested her feathered hip against her car door. "I've tried. I've been called silly, crazy, and told to get plucked." She sounded disappointed. "Game shows aren't for everyone. My loss."

He could help her win. There was something about this situation that sucked him in. He said, "Grab my costume and get in. I'll cock-a-doodle-do you."

She was so startled, she flapped her wings. "Why the change of heart?" she asked, as she opened her car door. She swung it wide, nearly scraping the side of his Hummer.

"Who the fuck knows?" he mumbled.

"It's a sixty-forty split, whatever we win," she said over her shoulder.

Chicken was screwing him. That didn't set well. He was about to make a fool of himself and wanted his fair share. "Why should you get more than me?" he wanted to know.

"I have the tickets." That said, she collected the rooster suit, locked her Dart, and climbed in beside him. "Gun it, Buster."

Buster? No one called him Buster

"There's a parking lot behind the studio building," she directed. "Take a left at the next alley."

The lot was packed. They circled the rows. Twice. The only remaining spaces were for compact cars. His Hummer would take up two. He'd get fined. Beside him, the chick now bounced on the passenger seat. Nervous and excited. Her feathers flew, floated to the floor mat. She sneezed. Twice.

"A van's pulling out two rows over," she noted.

He drove in that direction. Another car had also seen the parking spot. They were both headed toward it now. The Smart Car was closer. . . .

Halo turned on the blinker, indicating the spot was his. The Hummer was big and intimidating. The Smart Car, small. Halo could see the whites of the man's eyes when he motioned Halo to take the space.

Halo pulled in, cut the engine. Then jumped out and shut the door. He flagged down the man, grabbed his wallet, and gave him fifty dollars. "Sorry, dude," he said. "Game show, and we're late."

The man stared at him. Recognition prompted his smile. "Halo Todd?" he asked.

Halo nodded, feeling uneasy. He'd hoped to enter the building, change into his costume, without any witnesses. Richmond was baseball central. The Rogues were visible in the community. He valued his fans. They paid his salary.

The man riffled through a stack of papers on the passenger seat. He passed Halo a blank envelope. "Can I get a quick autograph?" he requested.

Halo signed, *Thanks for the parking place*, along with his name. The man was pleased. "There are spots for compact cars near handicapped parking," he said. The man gave him a salute and headed in that direction.

The chicken was struggling to get out of his Hummer. She'd gotten in with a high hop, but it was a long step down in a bulky costume. He went to her. His hands at her waist, he lifted her to the pavement. She was a lightweight. He released her.

"Here," she said, handing him the rooster suit. "There are backstage dressing rooms inside."

He followed her into the building. Chickie walked with a purpose. Lady had wiggle. She sneezed every other step. She left a trail of tail feathers. A sign for the game show pointed toward a side door. The dressing rooms were at the end of a long hallway. Men's and Women's.

A pirate exited just as Halo entered. He dipped his head, not wanting to be spotted a second time. It dawned on him then that the chicken hadn't recognized him. Perhaps she couldn't clearly see him through her eye slits. That was a possibility. Or perhaps she didn't follow sports. A sin in his eyes. Baseball was All-American.

What did it matter? They were a couple for one hour. No more. No less. They had no plans to see each other after the show. Still, he wondered what she looked like without her costume. Male curiosity. He might never know. That bothered him a little.

A row of lockers lined the back wall in the room. He didn't need a locker. He would put on the costume over his clothes. A Henley pullover and jeans. He heel-toed his Nikes, slipped off his socks, then stepped into the white jumpsuit. Jerked it up. Grunted. It was lined and bulky. Cotton didn't stretch. He was six foot two and weighed two-fifteen. The rooster suit was too damn tight. The back zipper gapped several inches. Shit.

Off came the costume, followed by his clothes. He was fully exposed. That's when the door opened, and the chicken called in. "You ready? We only have ten minutes."

He clenched his back teeth. There was no point in her rushing him; he was going as fast as he could. "Almost there," he growled.

"No, you're not." She walked right in, inhaled sharply, but didn't avert her gaze. "You're standing there . . . naked."

That he was. Locker rooms were like home to him. Players frequently walked around in stages of undress. Nudity was as natural to him as breathing. Despite that, the moment turned awkward. His muscles flexed defensively. "The costume's snug," he grated. "I'm down to skin."

He looked good in his skin. Alyn Jayne's breath caught. She couldn't take her eyes off him. He was standing in profile to her. He was huge. Jacked diesel. Muscled shoulders and arms. Thick chest. Tight butt. Athletic legs. Big feet.

He turned slightly, and she saw the tattoo on his abdomen. Nothing small for this man. It read *Caution: Hard and Hot* in bold script. An accurate description. His sex was shadowed on his inner thigh. Impressive. He didn't have a shy or modest bone in his body.

She had no idea who he was. She hadn't asked his name or gotten a good look at him on the sidewalk. It was dark and her eye slits were narrow.

She wasn't always good at reading people, but seeing him now, he defined confidence. Arrogance. Heartbreaker. Rule breaker. Badass. She intuitively knew that wherever he went, he would dominate. Own the moment. Belong.

He had a sexy mouth. His lower lip was a little fuller than the upper. Sculpted for kissing. Women would fall fast and land horizontal. Men would envy him.

He made her nervous. So much so, she stammered, "I-I'll wait for you outside."

He smiled then. Slow and sinful. His voice was as deep as his dimples when he said, "No need to leave. You're my girlfriend, remember? Naked comes with my territory."

His gaze held hers as he gave his costume a second try. He got it up his legs, over his hips, then tucked his junk. He still looked ballsy. He worked the rooster suit across his chest. Then fitted his arms in the sleeves, and fought with the shoulder seams. His smile soon left him. "I can't fuck-in' breathe. There's no way I can sit down. I'd bust an ass seam."

"We'll be in the back," she assured him. "There aren't any chairs in the last row. We'll be standing." She crossed to him, and forced up the zipper. She swore the seams moaned.

"You look like Foghorn Leghorn on steroids," she noted, referring to the rooster cartoon character.

"I can't bend over to put on the red-and-white stock-ings and orange shoe covers," he complained.

Achoo. She hunkered down, and yellow feathers fol-lowed her to the floor. She drew on his stockings. His calves were thick, and the stockings didn't reach his knees. He then slid his feet into his untied Nikes. She hurriedly double-knotted the long laces on his shoes, then secured his orange polyfoam shoe covers, fastening them behind his ankles with Velcro strips. She struggled to get up, stag-gered sideways. He hooked his hand under her arm, steadying her.

They stood so close, she poked him in the chest with her beak. Her feathered roundness brushed his abdomen. He set her away from him, and made one final male ad-justment. His red rooster mitts barely covered his palms. His mask also came up short. It left his lower lip and stub-bled chin exposed. His too-long black hair showed in the back. He blew out a disgusted breath, and his red comb and black rubber beak bobbed.

She scooped up his clothes, passed them to him. He stuffed them in the locker, removed the key, placing it in a small pocket over his left hip. "Let's do this before I change my mind," he threatened.

She beat him to the door. The hallway was empty. They made fast tracks to the stage entrance. A red light blinked a warning that the show was about to start. Alyn produced

NO BREAKING MY HEART 13

their tickets, and a security guard motioned them inside. A woman with a clipboard was making identification tags. She held a black magic marker. "Name?" she asked, ready to write.

"Alyn," she was quick to say.

The rooster hesitated. "Ha-rold," he said.

Alyn blinked. The man didn't look like a Harold. More like a Kane or Hudson. Ryker or Sutter. Did his friends call him Harry? She would never know. Still, she wondered.

The lady stuck their tags to their chests, stating, "Back row, standing room only. You're at the top of the roost," she joked.

Alyn smiled. Harold did not.

They took their places among the costumed contestants. Her game-show boyfriend was on her right; King Kong, on her left. The ape wasn't as big as her rooster, but he was more active. Kong bumped her every time he raised his arms and beat his chest. His partner was dressed as a sock monkey. A retro and nostalgic toy. Her cream jumpsuit had a knit-stitch print. A long stuffed tail.

Anticipation put everyone on edge. The air buzzed with craziness. Participants needed to be noticed. To be picked for the challenges. To win the grand prizes.

Alyn's heart raced. She slapped her palms against her thighs. Antsy. She lost a few more feathers. Cameras panned the crowd. Contestants were bouncing, screaming, waving their banners and signs.

She raised her voice, said, "I wish we had a sign."

"I'm glad we don't." Harold's tone was flat. He slumped over, tucked his head to his chest. Tried to make himself small, which was difficult for a man his size.

She jabbed him with her elbow. "Stand up straight. We need to draw attention to ourselves. Maybe you could crow at the top of your lungs."

He snorted. "Or maybe not."

"It's a game show. You need to participate."

The corner of his mouth that was visible curled. "I'm here, what more do you want?"

"Go big or go home," she reminded him.

The stage manager hand-signaled the start of the show. Applause signs flashed on both sides of the stage, and heart-pounding intro music bounced off the walls. The audience welcomed their host Alex Xander with an insanity that blew her mind. The curtains parted, and he walked out. A tall man with short brown hair and thick eyebrows. He wore a dark blue suit, bowtie, and wide smile.

"Welcome!" Alex shouted into his microphone. "Impress me!" He began walking the aisles, the cameraman close behind.

A belly dancer in a sexy red chiffon top and sheer pants stepped into the aisle, drawing the host's attention. The gold-tone coins and beads sewed into the outfit sparkled beneath the overhead lights. Alex gave her a thumbs-up.

Harold admired her, too. "Nice hips."

Not to be outdone, a ballerina in a pink leotard and rainbow tutu pirouetted one row above the belly dancer. She whirled about on one ballet slipper for so long Alyn got dizzy.

A roaring twenties couple joined the mix. They broke into the Charleston. The flapper's fringe swung wildly and her partner in a black-and-white Zoot suit lost his black fedora. Alex Xander picked it up, and put it on his head. Finders keepers. It was his now.

A moment later, a costumed king and queen waltzed down their row. A couple dressed as glittery as a disco ball did the hustle. An entire row of contestants connected for the Bunny Hop. Bugs Bunny led the line. Jessica Rabbit brought up the rear.

Harold looked down his rubber beak at the action below. "It's a dance off," he grumbled.

Alyn's mind raced. They had to participate. They needed to get noticed. She came up with, "Chicken dance?"

"Seriously?"

"Shake a tail feather."

She wiggled past him, and her hip pressed his package. She heard his sharp intake of breath, then air hissing through his teeth, right before he poked her. Harold had a hard-on.

An erection at a game show? Unbelievable. Now was not the time. She missed the top step and stumbled, colliding with Alex Xander. She was quick to apologize. The host was gracious. The rooster with a boner slowly joined them. Bowlegged and walking stiff.

The host raised an eyebrow at Harold, then went on to challenge Alyn, "Go big or go home."

Alyn chicken danced for him. She imagined the music, went with the beat. She held her arms up in front of her, pinching her fingers and thumbs together, forming beaks. She opened and closed the beaks four times. She then put her thumbs in her armpits and flapped her elbows. Again to the four-count. Bending her knees, she wiggled her hips four more times, getting her backside as close to the ground as possible. All the while she stretched her arms and hands behind her like tail feathers.

Harold followed her lead, then improvised. Raw and masculine. The man had moves. The crowd loved him. Men clapped and women whistled. He threw back his head and crowed. Deep-throated and sexy.

Alyn held her breath, afraid his butt seam would split when he waggled down. The cameras captured the twist of his hips on the televised screen above the stage. Harold had a very tight ass. Fortunately the seam held. Just barely.

Straightening, they next faced each other, and clapped four times. Then joining hands, they skipped around in a circle. Which was no easy feat. They bumped and jarred each other. They reversed their direction once, then ended the dance.

Harold still held her hand, and he raised it high. They both took a bow. The game show host nodded his approval. "Nice going."

Alex's gaze swept the audience, settling on the back row. On King Kong and the sock monkey. His grin flashed when he announced, "Barnyard versus the jungle, let's do it!"

Barnyard. Rooster and chicken. That would be them. Alyn was so stunned, she couldn't move. She'd hoped to get picked, prayed on it even, but to land the first matchup was beyond her wildest dreams. Should they win, they would progress to round two. Then on to three, for the grand prizes.

"On the stage," Alex directed. "Let's get acquainted."

The ape and monkey raced by, beating them down the stairs. Harold took her by the arm when she again tripped on the slanted walkway. "You up for this?" he asked her as they neared the stage.

Alyn knew the routine. One she now dreaded. Meeting the contestants. A Q&A. She knew nothing about her boyfriend. Other than the color of his hair and eyes. That he was built, had a major tattoo, and got hard in a heartbeat. At the most inopportune times.

Panic set in. Stage fright gripped her. She hadn't fully thought this through. There was a huge difference between daydreaming about the show and living the reality. She was here. The moment was now. The cameras were on her. The show was being taped. Late afternoon viewers would witness her attempt to win prizes. Her possible failure. She rubbed her throat, gagged, about to hyperventilate.

"Chicken?" Harold questioned her. "The stage."

She tried to take a step, but her body locked up. She sneezed. Six consecutive times.

"What the fuck?" Harold placed his big rooster body between her and the cameras. He gripped her shoulders, shook her. Hard enough to get her attention. His competitive tone chased away her fear. "You wanted this. You got it. So get it together. I can't carry you. We have to do this as a couple."

A couple. "I don't know you."

"I'm not that complicated. Wing it, babe."

Two

Harold nudged Alyn, and she made it onto the stage. King Kong continued to pound his chest, making ape noises. Harold bested him. He was charismatic, in a rooster sort of way. His challenging cock-a-doodle-do set him up as the contestant to beat. The crowd went nuts.

Alex Xander stood on their left. The main curtain soon parted, and a blonde in a silver satin camisole, black leather pants, and mile-high heels brought them each a wireless microphone. "My assistant, the beautiful Natalie," he introduced her.

Natalie was gorgeous. And instantly into Harold. She openly admired the fit of his costume. He packed it tight. There was little left to her imagination. To anyone's imagination. The model tapped his beak with a red manicured fingernail. Flirting with him. His lower lip was visible, and he gave her a half-smile. One that was far too sexy for a man in a serious relationship. Harold would stray. No doubt about it.

Alyn cleared her throat loudly enough to gain his attention. "You're with me," she reminded him. "Don't get distracted."

His smile faded. "Possessive chick."

The host looked into the camera and said, "Happy tenth

anniversary show! It's Couples Day. Our prizes are huge. Twin Mercedes Benzes, a Caribbean vacation, Rolex watches, and fifty-thousand dollars. We welcome King Kong Carl and sock monkey Mary. Harold the Rooster and Alyn the Chicken."

The audience applauded. Shouted out their favorite contestant. "Rooster" rose loud and clear. Harold pumped his yellow wing. Strutted in a circle. Crowed.

Alex went on to ask, "Carl and Mary, are you boyfriend/girlfriend, fiancés, or a married couple?"

Carl answered, "Boy/girlfriend."

Alex next turned to Harold and Alyn. "Your status?"

Alyn had the answer on the tip of her tongue, but it was Harold who said, "Fiancés."

Engaged. Her jaw dropped. He was writing his own script. He dipped his head, and his beak stuck in her ear when he whispered, "We one-upped them." That they had.

Alex kept the show rolling. "Carl and Mary, we all want to know, where did you first meet?"

Mary giggled. "At a University of Virginia football game. Go, Cavaliers!"

The crowd clapped and cheered. The state campus ranked high with them.

The host pointed to Alyn and Harold. "How about you two?"

They had met on the sidewalk outside Jacy's Java. The answer was straightforward and simple, yet Harold complicated the matter. "James River Stadium, a Rogues' baseball game."

His response brought the audience to their feet. Fanatic baseball fans jumped and shouted. Punched the air. Harold poked Alyn with his rooster wing. "Nailing it." He kept his voice low.

"Who's your favorite player?" Alex asked her.

Her breath caught in her throat. "Um-uh . . ." she faltered.

Harold curved his arm about her shoulders and once again spoke for her, "She loves Halo Todd," he said. "Makes me jealous when she wears his jersey."

"I cheer for the right fielder," a gypsy in the front row called out.

"Me, too." Women's voices rose in unison.

The rooster puffed his chest. Big and bold. Looking inordinately proud of himself.

What was that all about? Alyn wondered. Harold confused her. Made her uneasy. The man could exaggerate. Halo Todd meant nothing to her. Harold drew her deep into a relationship that didn't exist.

"Engagement ahead?" the host question King Kong and the sock monkey.

"Next month," Mary was quick to say.

Carl responded more slowly. "Two years."

Alex frowned for the camera. "Doesn't sound like they're on the same page." He then prodded Alyn and Harold. "Your plans?"

Harold crowed, then said, "She only has to set the date. I'm there. Today, tomorrow, whenever."

Woot-woot! The audience liked his answer.

Alyn rolled her eyes. Marriage wasn't in their future. The man was a crowd pleaser. She couldn't take him seriously. She had one purpose: to win the grand prize. She needed to stay focused, which was difficult with a loose cannon for a partner.

Natalie collected their microphones. She winked at Harold and he winked back. Alyn felt like a third wheel. She wanted to kick him in the shin with her spiky chicken toes. Barely resisted the urge.

Alex stepped to the center of the stage. "Let's get

started." The panels on the curtains swept back, revealing Midway at the Fair. "You'll face three tests. Funhouse Mirror Maze, Balloon Darts, and the Strongman. The ladies start with the mirrors, the men follow with the darts. You'll work as a couple, combining scores, with the Strength-O-Meter."

The host looked to the audience, cupped his hand behind his ear, and said, "Are we ready?"

The crowd responded at the top of their lungs, "Go big or go home!"

"Ladies, take your places at opposite ends of the maze," Alex stated. "The mirrors are tricky. Many of them are distorted and give unusual and confusing reflections. Some are humorous and others frightening. There are choices to make in direction. You may or may not pass each other. Whoever exits first wins!"

Harold tugged on Alyn's wing, pulled her close. He lowered his voice, said, "I've worked my way through mirrored mazes at state fairs. Stay left. Left," he emphasized.

She took his advice to heart. She'd never faced a network of mirrors. They looked intimidating.

Cameras were anchored above the maze, Alyn noticed, to catch the competitors' progression, their attempts and failures, as they maneuvered through the narrow glassed pathways. Natalie returned to the stage and led the ladies to their separate entrances. Alyn drew a deep, steadying breath.

"On your mark, get set, go!" Alex shouted.

Game on! Alyn felt a moment of panic as she wiggled her chicken body into the maze. She lost feathers along the way. Her sneezes were uncontrollable. Her eyes watered. Her whole body shook.

She found herself surrounded by mirrors. Her reflection made her blink. One mirror made her look thin, another blown out of proportion. Still another gave back an image of alien poultry. Very scary.

The paths split in several directions. She went left at every turn. She heard footsteps, and figured the sock monkey was coming her way. A loud bump, followed by a groan, indicated the monkey had walked into a mirror. Alyn pushed on. Encouraged by the audience's boisterous chant, "Chick, chick, chick!"

Seconds later, she rounded a corner and came face to face with Mary. "Out of my way." The sock monkey tried to push past her. There wasn't a lot of room. Alyn grunted when Mary elbowed her in the gut. Hard.

Pushing and shoving ensued. Alyn refused to give ground. Playing dirty, Mary ripped the red wattle from the chin on Alyn's headpiece. Then worming around her, Mary grabbed a handful of her tail feathers in an attempt to hold her back.

Alyn retaliated. She seized the monkey's long stuffed tail and gave it a tug. Mary stumbled. The tail fell off. Alyn dashed away before the monkey recovered.

Left, she continued on. Only to face a path that split straight or right. What now? She went straight, and hit a dead end. A waste of time. She backtracked, looped right, and finally caught sight of a blinking green light reflected in one of the mirrors. Her exit! She raced as fast as her chicken legs would carry her. She burst through the door a split-second before the monkey rushed out. Carrying her tail. The curtain sealed shut behind them.

She had won!

Harold rushed to her. His hug lifted her high off the stage. The man was strong. Her spiky costumed feet dangled near his rooster balls. She was careful not to jab him.

Alex Xander clapped his hands and congratulated her. "Chicken deserves a kiss, don't you think?" he asked the audience. The applause was deafening.

Harold set her down, then swooped low before she could step back. There was a wicked glint in his eyes when he angled his head and touched his visible lower lip to the slit at her mouth. She expected no more than a peck. She got tongue.

The man was a sexual catalyst. Sparks flicked her nipples and her breasts tightened. Her skin prickled. Heat spread between her thighs. Her knees weakened. She clutched his forearms for support.

Whistles, cheers, rose around them.

"Get a room!" the talk show host joked, breaking them apart.

Harold straightened, in his own good time. A small feather tipped the corner of his mouth. Alyn swatted at the feather; it fluttered to the stage.

His smile curved, sly and full of mischief. He no longer looked like a rooster, but a fox who had raided the chicken coop. Popular and appealing, he played to the crowd. They loved him. Loved them. They were a couple. Fiancés.

"Rooster, Kong, you're up next," Alex directed. "It's Balloon Darts." The curtain swept back, revealing a large wooden backdrop pinned with dozens of multicolored balloons.

Anticipation built as the host explained, "Players are given twelve darts. You'll stand behind the yellow line, and have ten seconds to break balloons. The contestant to pop the most will win the second round."

Natalie appeared with two plastic boxes of darts. She handed Harold the red set and Carl the blue. The ape tugged at his furry headpiece, but Alex stopped him. "You'll throw the darts in costume."

Kong complained, "The eye slits are narrow."

"Rooster can't see any better than you can," Alex stated.

Alyn held her breath. Harold had two strikes against

him, she realized. Her partner wore rounded hand mitts with little flexibility while the ape's gloves had separate finger sheaths. Kong could easily clutch the game darts. The rooster could not. Harold's costume pulled tight across his shoulders. There was no give. Tossing the darts would prove difficult.

Despite his disadvantages, Harold was all barnyard strut and cocksure when he crossed to the designated line. King Kong was close behind. The ape beat his chest, grunted his challenge. Harold crowed, deep and daunting. A warrior rooster.

"Go big or go home!" Alex called out.

Contest on. Ten seconds passed in the blink of an eye. Harold somehow managed to throw all his darts, but he only popped eight balloons. Carl beat him by one pop. The ape screeched his victory. Harold set his jaw, and one corner of his lower lip curled. He wasn't happy with his performance. The curtain closed, and the crowd bemoaned his fate.

Returning to Alyn's side, he scuffed the sole of one athletic shoe on the stage, leaving a mark. "Sorry, I thought we had it," he mumbled.

We. He spoke of them as a team. She liked that. Even if he had lost. She patted his arm. "Round three. We've got this." Or so she hoped. She crossed her fingers.

The producer cut to commercial, allowing those onstage to talk among themselves. Carl joined them. "We're tied."

"Not for long," said Harold.

"Think you're going to win?" came from Kong.

"Know it."

"Don't count your chickens before they hatch."

Mary laughed at her boyfriend's joke.

Alyn rolled her eyes. She didn't find him funny.

Neither did Harold. He made a rude noise.

Carl backed up a step.

The curtain soon swayed, separated, revealing the Strength-O-Meter. Alex Xander crossed to the tall vertical tower. "Which of you two is the Strongman?" he goaded the contestants as they stepped up and flexed their muscles. "You'll smash a red weight with a ten-pound rubber mallet to send a puck flying up the track. There are names and numerical values along the groove. Sissy Boy gets ten points. Ring the top bell, and Hercules receives one hundred. You'll each take a turn. We'll combine your couple score to determine the winner."

The host gave the participants a moment to let his words sink in before adding, "You're competing for more than a kewpie doll or Chinese finger trap. Winners, we've put together the best prizes of the season. Losers, it's a long walk back to your seats."

Natalie brought out the mallet. She presented it to Alex. "Ladies first," he said.

The sock monkey pushed by Alyn. "I'll go."

Alex handed her the mallet. "Go big or go home!"

Mary stood before the tower, and her hands visibly shook as she settled the long-handled hammer over her shoulder. She huffed and puffed. Shifted her weight from foot to foot. Nervous.

Harold nudged Alyn, and in a low voice said, "The most important factor is strike accuracy. Swing as you would to split wood."

"I've never split wood."

"Shit," he mumbled before counseling, "Hold the handle as near to the end as possible with both hands. Draw the mallet head directly over your own head, then swing down. You have to hit the pad directly in the center if you want to ring that bell. Got it?"

More or less. She hoped to make a better showing than the sock monkey. Mary lost her balance with her downward strike. The puck barely rose two feet.

"Weakling, twenty points," Alex shouted to the audience.

There were low moans of sympathy and pity.

The host motioned to Alyn. "Next."

Her heart was beating so fast she was sure it would burst through her chicken chest. She shuffled forward. Mary passed her the mallet with more force than she'd shown in her swing. Alyn staggered backwards. Alex was there to keep her upright.

The crowd got behind her. They chanted, "Chick, chick, chick."

The mallet was heavy, but nothing she couldn't handle. However seeing the launch pad proved a problem. Her eye slits tapered, and her rounded feathered stomach got in the way. She bobbed her head several times, gathering momentum, before she let the hammer fall. With all the power she could muster.

The puck rose to thirty points. Wimp. Still, she was ten points ahead of Mary. She prayed Harold would do well.

Alex took the hammer from Alyn and handed it to King Kong. "Manly pride is on the line. Ring that bell!"

Kong put his back into it. He growled, grunted, and slammed the mallet down. He earned ninety points. Powerhouse.

Expectancy surged when Harold took his turn. He side-mouthed Alyn, saying, "Kicking King Kong ass."

Taking his position, he crowed with barnyard fierceness. The audience crowed back. He stretched his arms over his head, and the seams along his shoulders split, baring thick muscles across his upper back. The smash of the mallet took down his zipper. All the way to his butt crack.

Instead of kicking ape ass, Harold showed his own. On

camera. To the viewing audience and all America. It was an image Alyn would never forget. Neither would the crowd. They went crazy. Oohing and awing. Whistling, cheering, and falling off their chairs, laughing.

Embarrassed for her partner, Alyn hustled to stand behind him. She tore off her mitts and tried to zip his costume. The teeth were off track. So she clutched the sides together, covering as much of him as was possible. Still, there were gaps. Wide gaps.

Harold twisted, looking over his shoulder. "What are you doing?"

"Keeping you modest."

He snorted. "I lost my modesty when I was six, and swam naked in the neighborhood kiddie pool."

"This is national television."

He shifted. "You're scratching my ass."

As she tightened her hold on him, her fingernails left red marks.

He pinned his gaze on The Strength-O-Meter. "The bell?"

It had not rung. Alex Xander announced their defeat. "Seventy points, rooster. Muscle Bound, but not enough to win."

Harold stilled. His jaw dropped. "We lost?"

"Carl and Mary beat you by ten points."

Harold swore beneath his breath. Berating himself.

Alyn couldn't find words to express her disappointment. She had wanted this win as much as she'd wanted anything in her life. Her stomach sank, and her dreams paled. Her future plans were once again put on hold.

She'd hoped to use the prize money to establish The Shy Lily. A boutique with antique and vintage heirlooms. She had scrimped, saved, and collected items over the years, attending public auctions, estate sales, bidding on storage units. The majority of the treasures was packed in a rental facility for safekeeping. The overflow landed at her mother's cottage, where space was minimal.

She'd waited patiently to lease a store in the historic district. Prime real estate. Space on the second floor of a large brick building had recently become available. It was within the same block as Jacy's Java. Lots of traffic and customers. Newfound success.

Sadly, a trusted friend had turned on her. Alyn's potential business partner had bailed a month earlier, cleaning out their joint bank account. She had seventy-two dollars and sixty-five cents to her name. With no immediate income in sight.

Her shop wasn't meant to be. Her heart hurt.

She wasn't the only one disillusioned by the outcome. A stunned silence hung over the studio audience. The applause sign flashed over the stage, but few people clapped. Harold was a charmer. A grandstander. The spectators took Alyn and his loss as their own.

The host motioned to Natalie to escort them offstage. The model curved her arm through the rooster's wing, pouted her condolences. Alyn clutched the back of Harold's costume as she shuffled behind them. The flex and ripple of his muscles tickled her fingertips. His skin was hot.

"You can go back to your seats or exit," Natalie told them at the stairs. She patted Harold's shoulder. "Sorry, big guy."

"I'm done here," Harold said when the model left.

Alyn agreed. "Me, too." They took the steps. Defeat walked them up the side aisle.

Alex kept the show rolling. "Who's next?" he called to the audience. The contestants got back into the spirit of the show. They bounced and cheered to get his attention. "Fifth row, Mr. and Mrs. Potato Head, go big or go home!"

The Potato Heads rushed passed Alyn and Harold to get to the stage. Mr. Potato Head lost an ear in his excitement. Alyn left a trail of feathers. She sneezed her way to the exit door.

"You can free my ass anytime," Harold said once they reached the hallway. She let go of his costume, and he turned to face her. He yanked off his rounded hand mitts, balled his fists. Scowled darkly. "We fuckin' lost. I let you down."

Alyn frowned. The man took their loss personally, even though they'd been a team. She'd picked him off the street. Chosen him for his size with no idea as to his abilities. She was disheartened, but not ashamed of their performance. They'd done their best. She couldn't ask for anything more.

Another time, another place, she'd turn her luck around.

"It was a game show." She spoke softly. "There were no guarantees."

He tugged off his rooster hood. His dark hair was mussed, spiked on one side, and he had a red mark over his nose were the beak had rubbed. His gaze was sharp. Hard. Intense. Ticked. "I came up short on Strongman. We should've won."

But they had not. She released him from all blame. "Your costume was tight and hindered your movements. We would've won had you been dressed as Tarzan or Adam."

"The Garden of Eden?" Had him thinking. "A leaf at the groin would've given me more freedom."

A very large leaf, she thought. The size of an elephant ear.

He rolled his shoulders, and his voice was tight in his throat when he said, "I'm not used to losing."

She wasn't used to winning.

He turned then, and pushed through the locker room door. "Give me five. I'll drive you back to your car," he tossed over his shoulder.

Halo Todd crossed to his locker, slammed the flat of his hand against the metal grate. Felt the sting from his wrist to his shoulder. He was not a good loser. He'd been crazy to participate in the first place. Yet there was something about Alyn that got to him. She'd appeared so forlorn on the sidewalk outside the coffee shop. A woman defeated before she'd even gotten to compete.

He rubbed the back of his neck, and rewound their time onstage. The chicken had done her part. She'd worked her way through the maze like a pro. He'd been proud of her. So pleased, in fact, that when goaded by the crowd, he'd kissed her. Her mouth was soft. Her taste, sweet innocence. Surprise had parted her lips, and his tongue had glanced off hers. He would've deepened the kiss had Alex Xander not broken them apart.

That single kiss had distracted him during Balloon Darts. The warmth of her mouth lingered. He'd missed easy shots. He'd hoped to redeem himself with the Strength-O-Meter. He worked out. Twice a day. He was he-man strong.

His costume was as snug as a second skin, but that hadn't hampered him. The seams gave way when he'd raised the mallet. He'd flashed his ass with the downward motion. He knew a second too late that his swing was off center. There'd been no time to make a correction. No do-over. He felt bad for Alyn. She'd had faith in him, and he'd failed her.

There was something about her light green eyes, optimistic attitude, and trail of feathers that got to him. He didn't like being gotten. It left him on edge.

The woman had guts, he had to admit. Approaching a stranger on the sidewalk to find a game-show partner. He wondered what she wanted out of life. What she would have done with the grand prizes, had they won. He might never know.

He took the small key from his side pocket, opened the locker. Then shook out his shirt and jeans. The rooster costume had seen better days. A shrug of his shoulders, and it fell off him. He kicked the costume aside.

He got dressed. Finger-combed his hair. He was as good as he was going to get. Scooping up the torn costume, he headed for the door. He would pay Alyn the rental and replacement cost. He was bigger than most roosters. He wouldn't stick her with the bill.

He found her in the hallway, leaning against the wall. Her chin dipped, and her shoulders slumped. She had yet to remove her costume, so he had no idea what she looked like.

Anonymity was sexy, he found.

She glanced up, and gave him a small smile. "You look more yourself now."

"I wasn't cut out to be a rooster."

Aachoo. She wasn't cut out to be a chicken.

They left the building. Her rounded body bumped him again and again as they walked toward his Hummer. A brush to his thigh, his side, his arm. Feathers fluttered to the ground. Awareness of the woman crept beneath his skin. He'd never been attracted to a chicken before, that was for sure.

He opened the passenger door and gave her a boost onto the seat. He pushed too hard. His hand on her bottom slipped between her thighs, and his fingers touched her inappropriately. She squirmed, thrust out a foot, and her spiky chicken toes kicked him in the balls.

Damn. He jerked back, adjusted himself, while she righted herself, and then sat all stiff and facing forward. He closed her door, rounded the wide hood, and climbed in beside her. He pulled his seat belt across his chest and buckled up. He keyed the engine, shifted into reverse. They rode the short distance in silence.

He circled the block, looking for a parking place. One opened behind her Dodge Dart. He pulled in, and she hopped out, without his assistance. She left a seatful of feathers. He passed her the torn rooster costume, then rolled his hip and removed his leather wallet from his back pocket. Sixty dollars should cover the replacement cost. "I want to pay—"

She never let him finish. Shutting the door, she waved him off. "I got it covered. You went above and beyond. Nice cock-a-doodle-do."

His mind went to the *cock* side of doodle-do.

He had a lot of crow left in him.

He glanced at his Oakley 12 Gauge Chronograph. The watch had been a gift to himself when he'd signed with the Rogues. Inspired by the gauges in the cockpit of a fighter jet, it had more functions than he'd ever use. Or had ever figured out how to use, even with the instructional booklet.

He worked his jaw. Time had gotten away from him. He'd lost ninety minutes of his day. His sex date with the pilot would be delayed. All because of a game show.

He collected Alyn's feathers from the floor and seat and tossed all but one in the glove compartment. The single feather went into his wallet. A reminder to avoid game shows. He'd have the vehicle washed and vacuumed when he reached Florida.

He let his Hummer idle until Alyn safely reached her car. Traffic had picked up. A line stretched out the door of Jacy's Java. Customers looking for their morning caffeine fix. People stared at her. A few pointed. One elderly man shook his head.

She tucked herself into her car. Which was no easy feat.

He waited for her to remove her chicken hood. She did not. He hoped she wouldn't get a ticket for impaired vision.

Smoke shot from her car muffler as she pulled from the curb. Then headed west. The Dart chugged like a tugboat. He noticed the bumper was rusted, a back taillight busted, and that the rear tires were bald. The vehicle had seen better days.

Halo rapped his knuckles on the steering wheel. Feeling restless and unsettled. As if a part of his life had slipped away from him. Unfinished.

Alyn had needed a boyfriend for an hour. He'd made her his fiancée. Their loss ended their relationship. Relationship? His wild side laughed at him. Called him crazy. Foolish. Sensitivity squeezed passed his laughter, nudging him to follow her. To be kind.

Why should he go after her? He ran one hand down his face. Sorted out his thoughts. That's when he realized he wanted to do something nice for her. He could turn their loss into a win with little effort. He could be a good guy when he tried. It would ease his conscience.

There was something else, too, that drove him to shift gears and ease into traffic. To follow the lingering gray smoke of her car muffler. His male curiosity had yet to be satisfied.

He hadn't seen her without her chicken costume.

She had seen him naked.

Three

Halo followed Alyn for thirty minutes. He kept a discreet distance between the vehicles. He thought he'd lost her at an intersection on the outskirts of town when he was forced to stop for a red light and she scooted through on yellow. He took two wrong turns as he entered an older neighborhood, but eventually caught sight of her Dodge Dart parked at the curb before a single-level cottage. The corner yard was fenced. There was a small outbuilding, yet no garage. No sign of the chicken, either. She must have gone inside.

He came to a stop, exited the Hummer, and locked it. He walked past the Dart, glancing inside. The baby carrier attached to the backseat gave him pause. As did the box of Pampers.

Once on the sidewalk, he looked around. The houses along the boulevard were all boxy, painted white with short porches. Mature bare-limbed trees stood out against an overcast sky. Snow was forecast. He was tired of winter.

He unlatched the gate, pushed through. It creaked as it closed behind him. A cement walkway led him to the porch. Blades of brown grass pushed between the cracks. Three wooden steps landed him at a door painted deep blue, the same hue as the wooden shutters on either side of the front windows. One narrow window was raised, drawing fresh air into the cottage.

He pushed the doorbell with his thumb and, seconds later, saw an eye through the peephole. He heard the slide of a dead bolt. A middle-aged woman peeked out. An inside safety chain crossed her nose as she peered up at him.

"Can I help you?" she asked.

He shoved his hands in his jean pockets and gave her his most charming smile. "I'm looking for—"

"Me!" A skinny young boy with shaggy brown hair came running. "It's Halo Todd. He picked my letter. I won. He's here for me."

Here for the boy? Halo blinked, taken aback. He caught a glimpse of a navy T-shirt ripped at the collar, sweat pants, and a short plaster arm cast, reaching from the kid's knuckles to just below his elbow.

Bouncing on his bare toes, the boy unhooked the chain. The door swung wide, and the kid charged Halo, giving him an enthusiastic hug. Then looking up, he grinned, revealing a missing front tooth, before turning to the woman behind him. "The contest. I'm going to spring training!"

Halo stiffened. Letter, spring training? What the hell?

The woman smiled at Halo, a warm, grateful smile. "I'm Martha Jayne, Danny's mother," she said. "Danny loves baseball. He gets on the computer every day after school and checks the Rogues' website. That's where he learned about the contest."

Halo's jaw worked. Realization slapped him upside the head, unsettling him. He was aware of the event, but had ignored it. Community liaison Jillian Mac-Cates had spoken to the players at the final team meeting of the previous season. She'd set up a contest where fans could write to their favorite players. Then, on a designated date, the starting lineup would stop by James River Stadium, scan

the letters, and each select a winner. They would personally notify and congratulate the winners.

Those who won would be flown to Barefoot William
for preseason. Ten days of ballgames, beach, and boardwalk. The players had benefitted from the positive press
coverage and photo ops. Everyone but Halo. Months had
passed. Time had gotten away from him. As it so often
did.

Jill's most recent text was a stern reminder to get his butt
in gear. He was the last player to pick a winner. He could
almost hear Jillian drumming her fingers. Tapping her
foot. He could picture her scowl. She was growing impatient. Plane tickets needed to be booked and accommoda-
tions reserved for the winners. Anyone under eighteen
would travel with a chaperone.

Last minute, and groaning inwardly, Halo had driven to
the complex. Better late than never. He figured the letters
could be read in under an hour. Maybe two at most. He
had been wrong.

The media room was stacked with huge boxes and
bulging mailbags. Garbage receptacles overflowed with
opened and tossed letters. He'd barely been able to squeeze
in. Walking anywhere but the perimeter had been impossible. The starting lineup had received a ton of mail. He
saw his name posted on the back wall. He found his entries piled in a corner, reaching all the way to the ceiling,
and spilling outside the emergency exit.

He'd sucked in air. Felt as overwhelmed as Santa Claus
at Christmas. Hemmed in, and claustrophobic, he'd
dropped onto a metal folding chair. Untying a mailbag,
he'd withdrawn a handful of letters. Opening each one,
he'd skimmed the contents. Men and women, boys and
girls of all ages had their hearts set on attending preseason.
Each entry was well-written, the words hopeful, but none

hit him on a gut level. He had no idea what he was looking for from his fans, but he wanted something beyond
praise of his career and the mention of how cool he was.

Three hours passed, and his eyes had crossed. He'd had
enough. No winner. Straightening, he'd stretched, then
left the room with every intention of returning the next
day. Needless to say, his well-intentioned plans never ma-
terialized. He got distracted easily.

A guys' night out with five of his teammates landed him
and his buddies at an after-hours men's club. On the darker
side of midnight, Halo had hooked up with one of the
hostesses. The sex had been wild. Had lasted three days.
She'd drained him.

Shame on him, but he'd never gotten back to the mail-
room. Despite that fact, a boy stood before him now, all
wide-eyed with hero worship, believing that he'd won. In
a roundabout way, Danny had saved his ass. The spring
training event was the last thing on his mind when he'd arrived at the cottage. Yet he'd found his winner. The boy
would get Jillian off his back. He went with it. A meant
to be, if he believed in destiny.

He figured the chicken was somewhere in the house.
The boy would get Halo's foot in the door. He extended
his hand. "Congratulations, Danny."

The boy grasped Halo's hand with both his own. His
cast rubbed roughly against Halo's wrist. "Thanks for
picking me."

"Thanks for writing a great letter."

Danny puffed out his chest. "What part did you like
best?"

"Uh—" Pause. "It was all good." That should satisfy the
boy. He eyed the kid's cast and changed the subject.
"How'd you break your arm?"

Danny's smile slipped. His shoulders slumped. He

sighed heavily. "I tried to save Quigley from getting hit by a car," he said. "It was all my fault. I left the side gate open. Quigs escaped."

"Quigley?" Halo asked.

"My daughter's dog," Martha explained. "Danny was pet sitting. The pug ran into the street. Into traffic. Danny took off after him. A car rounded the corner before he could reach Quiggie."

"I wasn't fast enough," the boy confessed.

Martha pressed a comforting hand to Danny's shoulder. "The driver slammed on the brakes. Too late. There were injuries. Fortunately, Danny and Quigley are both recovering."

The boy and his mother looked expectantly at Halo, waiting for him to say something. Anything. "It took courage to chase after the dog," he managed.

"You'd have done the same," Danny said. "I know you would have."

How could the kid know that? Halo wondered.

"My son admires you," Martha told him. "You're his role model."

Role model. Halo didn't stand well on a pedestal. He was far from perfect. But people saw what they would. He'd gotten by on his good looks and athletic ability for much of his life. He had flaws just like the next guy. And a few deep scars. He did have something in common with the kid, which he shared. "I broke my wrist and two fingers when I was your age. Monkey bars were not my friend."

"I'm eight." Danny then held up his cast. "Seg-seg—"

"Segmental fracture," came from his mother.

"Broken wrist and forearm. My cast comes off in five weeks. I'm healing a lot faster than Quigs." His voice broke. "He may never be the same."

Never be the same didn't sound good. Halo was about

to question Danny further when a commotion in the living room drew his attention. He raised an eyebrow as a black pug in a rear support dog wheelchair made his way around the corner of the couch. He carried a spiky-toed foot in his mouth. A foot stolen from the chicken costume. He struggled slightly around the end of a coffee table, moving as fast as his front legs would carry him. He wore a diaper. His back legs were supported in stirrups.

Feminine laughter flowed with the words, "I'm going to get you, little sneak." The pug was being chased by a woman on all fours. Long brown hair hid her face. Her shoulders scrunched beneath a white T-shirt. Her jeans were white seamed and ladder-ripped on one thigh. Her feet bare.

She crawled slowly, yet steadily, calling to the dog. Careening in his escape, the pug bumped into the base of a grandfather clock and tipped himself over. The chicken foot went flying. He lay on his side, panting, his front legs pawing the air.

Halo had a soft spot for animals. He wasn't certain what to do. His initial reaction was to go to the dog. To see if he was hurt. Instead, he took his cue from Danny and his mother. They stood still. Didn't interfere. They let the woman handle the situation.

Halo watched as she approached the pug. Reaching him, she shifted position, leaning back on her heels. "Thought you could outrun me, did you, Quigs?" she teased him. She next patted her thighs, directing him, "Up, Quigley. Rock the cart."

The dog's ears flickered. He did as she asked. He awkwardly rolled his shoulders, gathering momentum. His first two attempts failed. He barked, sounding annoyed. Then whined, pitifully.

The brunette bent forward, flattening her palms on the

hardwood floor near his head. "You can do this, Quiggie," she assured him. "You did it for your therapist yesterday, you can do it for me today. Up, boy."

Tough love? Halo's chest tightened. This was a scene he would never forget. The pug calmed, nuzzled her palm. "I'm here with you. Always," she encouraged.

Giving a deep, determined growl, Quigley threw his body into rising. He struggled, fought and, by determination alone, somehow managed to get his front paws under him, to roll and push up. To turn one short tire just enough that the wheelchair wobbled, yet righted itself. He was on solid ground once again.

The woman pulled the dog close; tucked him against her side. "You are brave and amazing," she praised, her voice watery. "So strong. I believe in you." The pug licked her face.

In the silence that followed, Halo heard Danny swallow hard, along with Martha's sniff as she wiped away a tear. He released a breath he hadn't realized he'd been holding. He wasn't an overly sensitive guy, yet the moment got to him. He'd never been around a disabled dog. The woman was patient, kind, and gave Quigley the encouragement to stand on his own. Definitely a survivor skill.

The brunette brushed back her hair and turned toward the door. That's when she realized she wasn't alone. Her gaze glanced off her brother and mother, and met Halo's own. She stared, and he stared back, recognizing her light green eyes.

She was his chicken.

In that moment, she knew that he knew who she was. She appeared confused, and not the least bit glad to see him. He was the last person she'd expected to darken her doorway.

She gave Quigley a final pat, and slowly rose. Halo took her in, and liked what he saw. Fresh-faced, delicate features, small-boned, almost fragile. A scripted *Hug a Pug* T-shirt was tucked into her jeans.

Damn, she was pretty. Far prettier than he had imagined.

His male animal instinctively evaluated every woman he met as a potential sexual partner. It was part of his DNA. He was a breathing boner. In his mind, a lady's smile flashed her availability and willingness. Her readiness for sex.

Alyn wasn't smiling. A vulnerability surrounded her. She didn't look all that trusting. Flight flickered in her eyes.

His heart slowed, and all sexual thoughts left him. He was here to make amends, not to make her anxious. What to say? What to do? He'd pretended his purpose at the cottage was to inform Danny he'd won the contest. No one knew he'd actually come looking for her.

"Harold?" she questioned.

Danny shook his head, corrected her. "Not Harold, but Halo. Halo Todd. Richmond Rogues' right fielder. Alyn's my sister. She's not into baseball."

Brother and sister? There was a significant age gap between the two, Halo noted. He guessed Alyn was close to his age, and Danny was eight. The boy had come along late in Martha's life. Perhaps a second-honeymoon baby. "Alyn." He gave a short nod, as if meeting her for the first time.

"Halo," she contemplated. "My mistake. I took you for someone else. You must have a twin."

"Everyone's said to have one."

"Yours is identical," she said pointedly. "Why are you here?"

Danny jumped in then, pumping his arm. "Because I won the spring training contest. Halo picked my letter. He notified me in person. I'm going to Barefoot William!"

"Lucky you," she congratulated her brother before giving Halo the eye, looking suspicious. "What were the
odds? One in a thousand?"

"One in ten thousand," Halo said. The pile of mail had
been daunting.

"Alyn checked my spelling and gave me a stamp," Danny
said. "She dropped off the letter at the post office so we
didn't have to wait for the mail carrier. She's the best."

"Definitely the best," Halo agreed.

Martha touched Halo's arm, and offered, "Can you stay
awhile? I have a fresh pot of coffee and a cinnamon coffee
cake right out of the oven, cooling on the kitchen table.
We could discuss the details of Danny's trip."

The specifics . . . he hadn't a clue. He'd thought he was
doing well finding a winner. He pulled his iPhone from
the side pocket of his jeans, texted Jillian, requesting travel
and hotel information. He figured she would get back to
him by the time he'd finished his first cup of coffee and
second piece of coffee cake.

"I have a few minutes," he said.

"I'll set out cups and plates." Martha went to do so.

The cottage didn't have an entryway. One step, and
Halo stood in the living room. He looked around. He'd
never seen so much furniture in such a small space. More
was not always better. Someone in the family was either a
pack rat or a collector. No wonder the dog had tipped his
cart. There was little room between the chairs, couches,
coffee and side tables. There were at least two, if not three,
of each type of furniture. The sofas were covered with
plastic.

How much light did a room need? he wondered,
counting ten sconces, eight table and six standing lamps.
All with fancy, heirloom shades. Decorated in pink silk
and matching roses, one shade reminded him of a birthday cake. He blinked against the brightness.

A dozen clocks counted the hour on a mantel above the brown brick fireplace. History surrounded him, Halo realized, as he moved toward the display. Identification tags described each vintage item, from the cherry wood tripod table and Chesterfield armchair, to the tufted Victorian blue velvet settee.

Once reaching the shelf, he examined the carriage clock and one that resembled a church steeple, with its triangle front and column-like sides. His great aunt had such a clock.

Danny joined him at the fireplace. "The banjo clock is my favorite," he said. "Alyn likes the Orm—" He pulled a face.

"Ormolu." Alyn pronounced the word for him.

"It's French," the boy said of the ornate bronze cube clock.

Halo looked down at the boy. "You're a smart kid."

Danny's chest puffed, but he remained modest. "I know a little; Alyn knows a lot. She wants to open an antique shop. Her business partner ripped her off. Left her dry and high—"

"High and dry," mused Halo.

"She's waiting for the money fairy."

"Danny," Alyn softly cautioned. "We don't share personal information, remember?" The boy scrunched his nose. "I'm sure Har- Halo isn't interested in my plans."

Oh, but he was. Money fairy, huh? "When were you planning to open your shop?"

"Not today, but someday."

Danny huffed, revealing more than he should once again. "She could've moved in this afternoon had she won *Go Big or Go Home*. She found space in a brick building downtown. She took Mommy and me to see it. There was a coffee shop on the corner. We had hot chocolate and cookies."

"What else?" asked Halo.

"The hot chocolate came in big mugs with marshmallows. Mom had an oatmeal raisin cookie. Alyn and I had peanut butter chocolate chip."

Halo grinned. The kid talked food when he wanted to hear about the game show. "*Go Big or Go Home?*" he nudged.

The boy shrugged. "Not much to tell. Her boyfriend dumped her. She didn't have a partner for Couples Day. She scrambled to find someone."

"Danny . . ." Alyn's voice was strained.

Her warning fell on deaf kid ears. He finished with, "She found a guy last minute, but it didn't go well. They lost. Had she played with you, Halo, she would've won."

"We don't know that for sure," said Alyn.

Danny disagreed. "Look at the man, sis. He's big and tall and would've played all-out. He'd have rung the bell on the Strength-O-Meter."

Alyn bit down on her bottom lip. "You think?"

"I know," Danny convinced her. "He's a ballplayer, all aim and power. Halo would've killed it."

She gazed fondly on her brother. Relented. "I'm certain he would have." She then crossed to the fireplace. The going was tight. Halo admired the twist of her body, the sway of her hips, as she maneuvered between two chairs. She bumped into the arm of a replica Queen Anne sofa, and rubbed her thigh. Pale skin peeked between the blue threads of torn denim. Nice.

Standing beside Danny, she ruffled his hair. He accepted her affection with rolled eyes and a groan. "Older sisters."

Despite his pained expression, Halo saw the slight shift of his body as he leaned into Alyn. It was obvious they were close, despite their age difference.

"Table's all set," Martha called from the kitchen.

Danny hopped away from Alyn. He motioned Halo to follow him. "Hey, do you like mirrors?"

Halo checked his reflection whenever he passed one. A natural reflex. "Sure, why not."

"They're on the walls in the hallway." Danny took off with Quigley on his heels. The dog stretched out his chest and pulled the cart like a pro. The small wheels clicked on the hardwood floor.

Halo was left alone with Alyn, who was sizing him up. She didn't come on to him. Didn't seem the least interested or impressed. She appeared troubled. Ill-at-ease.

"Cock-a-doodle-doo," was his icebreaker.

She didn't find him funny. She lowered her voice, said, "I can't believe you're here. Or that you're a ballplayer. How did this come about? The truth, Harold. Did you follow me home? Did Danny really win the contest?"

He was honest. "Total coincidence. I was looking for you, and found Danny. Your brother met me at the door and jumped to the conclusion he'd won the contest."

She clasped her hands together, chest high, as if in prayer. "You didn't tell him otherwise?"

"Who am I to disappoint a kid?"

"Did you even read his letter?"

"Does it matter?" He bent rules when it suited him.

She lowered her arms. Frowned. "More than you know. You are his hero. Danny worked on his letter for weeks. He wanted each word just right."

Weeks, huh. The kid had taken his time; put real thought into it. "You could tell me what it said."

"Or you could locate the letter and read it yourself."

He released a sharp breath. "There's not enough hours in the day to dig through thousands of entries to find his."

"Make time." She busted his balls.

"No can do. I need to be in Barefoot William by the

end of the week. I was late picking a winner. Danny saved my ass. He's my guy."

"You'd never take away his win, would you?" She looked as vulnerable as her words sounded.

He shook his head, surprised she thought so little of him.

"You better never let him down," she warned, putting him on notice. "Or you'll tangle with me."

Hell, he'd never hurt the kid, but he might like tangling with her. "Got it."

She hesitated before saying, "This is our secret then? Not a word to anyone."

No one had ever asked him to keep a secret. In this case, keeping quiet was to his benefit. "Deal."

They stared at each other for what could've been seconds or a minute. Maybe even two. Until she returned to her earlier question. "Why did you come after me?"

Admitting his mistake did not come easy. He jammed his hands in the pockets of his jeans. Stood taller. Said, "I owe you. I fucked up the Strength-O-Meter. I hit off-center. We lost. I'd like to make it up to you. Do something nice. Call it compensation."

Alyn shrugged a slender shoulder. "It wasn't my day to win. It was Danny's. He's very deserving. He plays baseball in his sleep. He's going to spring training in Barefoot William. Make that my reward."

She wanted nothing for herself, only for her brother. "He's under eighteen and will need a chaperone."

"My mother—"

"I was thinking of you."

"My mom needs a vacation more than I do."

Selfless was nice, but didn't work for him. Not in this case, anyway. He tried a different tactic. "Couples travel together."

"We're not a couple," she told him. "You were my pretend boyfriend—"

"Fiancé," he corrected.

"For an hour. That's hardly a relationship."

"You saw me raw."

Yes, she had, Alyn thought. He'd looked good without his clothes. Unforgettable, in fact. She had met him as Harold, man on the street. She now knew him as Halo Todd, elite athlete. Huge difference.

Her cheeks warmed when she said, "I'm not the first woman to see you naked, and I won't be the last. Once was enough for me."

"Once is never enough, babe." There was challenge in his tone. Arrogance and assuredness.

Her throat went dry. She could barely swallow. "We're done here."

"I don't consider us finished."

What more did the man want from her? She was afraid to consider the possibilities.

Bare feet on hardwood indicated Danny had returned. She was relieved by her brother's arrival. Danny slapped his arms against his sides, all restless kid energy and big appetite. "What's taking you guys so long?"

Halo improvised. He was good at it. "I was getting a lesson on the cuckoo clock," he said easily. "Your sister went on and on."

"She does that with me, too," said Danny. "She'll keep talking after I've stopped listening."

Alyn raised an eyebrow. "You tune me out?"

He squirmed. "Once, only once."

"One time isn't so bad." Halo took Danny's side.

Her brother grinned. Relieved.

Male bonding. Alyn didn't stand a chance.

Danny motioned to Halo. "Mom squeezed fresh orange juice for us guys. I think she snuck in a tangelo."

They headed for the kitchen then. Halo followed her. Way too close. He breathed down her neck. His arm brushed her own, and his thigh bumped her bottom. Twice.

The hallway of mirrors. She caught his profile in gilt-framed glass. He side-eyed her, too. With a look she didn't understand. Creased forehead. Slightly flared nostrils. Set jaw. Muscle tic. What was he thinking?

His slow smile spoke for him. His dimples, deep. There was a heated intensity and startling sexuality in his grin. He was pure testosterone. A man born for seduction, Alyn thought. He'd be good at it. That unsettled her most.

Her steps faltered, and Halo walked into her. The solid imprint of his chest and groin pressed her back. His knee slipped between her thighs.

She reached behind her, slapped at his hip. "Stop that," she rasped.

"Stop what?"

"Your knee's between my legs."

"Quit clenching me with your thighs."

"I'm not—" But she was. Her muscles squeezed him. Her cheeks heated. Her body had betrayed her. She died a slow death in the hallway.

He chuckled, deep and knowing. Irritating her even more. She released him. Stepped away. Her shoulders squared.

"You okay?" Danny stood at the end of the hall, his expression concerned. "I saw you trip."

"I'm fine," Alyn assured him.

"Did you see the Eagle Bull's-eye?" Danny asked Halo, referring to the convex Federal-style wall mirror. "Way cool."

Alyn turned slightly, pointed out, "Upper left."

Halo took a closer look. "I like."

So did Alyn. She'd found it at a garage sale. The couple was going through a divorce, and, while the husband was at work, the wife sold off his office fixtures for next to nothing. The man had been a collector.

Alyn had lucked out and also purchased a Remington Five typewriter, pirate's spyglass, and Bakelite telephone. She'd hooked up the black dial phone in her bedroom. She allowed Danny to play with the spyglass, as long as he was careful.

The scent of Columbia dark roast and warm coffee cake drew them into the kitchen. A small china cabinet held three complete sets of Wedgwood. Blue with white décor. A fourth set was minus the salad plate, which Danny had accidentally dropped. The cottage didn't have a formal dining room. The family ate in the kitchen.

Although short on space, her mother had believed in spoiling her husband after a hard day's work. She'd fix a nice meal and serve it on their best dishes. That had changed when Paul passed away. Paper plates replaced the Wedgwood. Plastic silverware was used instead of the English flatware.

Today a white Amazon lily decorated a vintage glass milk bottle placed in the middle of the floral-patterned table cover. Alyn's heart squeezed. Her mother had gone to the greenhouse, located behind the cottage. The glass structure had been her father's domain.

A landscaper by trade, Paul Jayne had specialized in exotic plants. Even in winter, he'd managed to coax orchids, birds of paradise, and angel-wing begonias to bloom. Bamboo was plentiful. He'd gifted his wife with fresh flowers. Daily. Alyn had thought it romantic. The cottage always smelled like a florist shop.

An unexpected heart attack had taken his life six months earlier. Holding on to his memory, Martha had kept the electricity on in the hothouse. She couldn't bear to turn it off. It was filled with equipment: screening installations, heating, cooling, and lighting, and an automatic watering system controlled by a computer to maximize potential growth.

Martha's trips to gather flowers were few and far between. The plants that survived grew wild. The greenhouse was a jungle. Another few months, and they'd need a machete to cut a path. Alyn made a mental note to do some pruning. Perhaps she'd be able to coax her mother to help her. Memories were therapeutic.

"Sit here." Danny drew Halo to the chair beside him.

Alyn wasn't certain the narrow ladder-back chair would hold the man's weight. It was meant for a smaller person. The chair creaked and the spindle legs bowed when he dropped down. She crossed her fingers they wouldn't break.

Quigley waited for her, his "snack face" expectant. She crossed to the counter and removed the lid from his treat jar, shaped like a pug. Three small Milk Bones in hand, she returned to the table. The dog barked excitedly. He spun his cart in a circle.

Alyn knelt, set the biscuits on the floor. She unhooked the straps on the wheelchair and lifted him out. He stretched on his belly, and she arranged his back legs in a position that was familiar to him, and would've made him comfortable had there been feeling in his lower spine. He nuzzled her hand. She rose, and he enjoyed his treats.

Halo looked down at the dog, asked her, "Can he crawl or scoot on his butt? Wag his tail?" Logical questions.

"No wagging." She missed the swish of his curly tail. "His chest and front legs are strong. He's quite fast at both. I try and change his position throughout the day. For circulation."

"Is the paralysis permanent?"

"Could be temporary, could be long-term," she told

him. "Two lower vertebrae were crushed in the accident. He's had surgery. The nerve endings haven't fully healed."

"*Pffft, pffft.*" Danny made a sparking sound. "The endings sometimes flicker like hot wires."

"He gets tingly," Alyn added. "His body twitches as if there's feeling. He's yet to put weight on his back legs. Still," she sighed, "we're hopeful."

"You should call him Sparky."

"Or not." Alyn stared at Halo. Was the man serious? Joking? She wasn't certain. He raised an eyebrow as if the name was a perfect fit. To him, anyway.

Martha got his humor, even if it fell flat with Alyn. Her mom's eyes twinkled, but she swallowed her smile. She added a spoonful of sugar to her coffee instead.

Danny liked Halo's suggestion. A lot. "How about Quiggie Sparks? What do you think, sis?"

Alyn was hesitant. She didn't want to dash their bonding moment, but neither did she want to consent to a name change. "Let me give it some thought. He responds to Quigley—"

"Quiggie Sparks," Danny called to the dog.

The pug barked back.

Danny pumped his arm. "He likes it."

So it seemed. Traitor. "Quigley for now," she gently said. Danny's disappointment was expressed in an apologetic whisper to Halo. A whisper Alyn couldn't help but hear. He didn't have a low indoor voice. "Do you mind that we stick with Quigs? He is Alyn's dog."

The man lowered his voice conspiratorially. "Alyn can keep Quigley, but he'll always be Quiggie Sparks to us guys."

"Us guys." Danny beamed.

The ballplayer had the power to shift alliances. She and Danny had always been tight, despite their age difference.

Yet Danny now looked and listened to Halo as if the man could do no wrong. No one was perfect, Alyn knew from experience. She'd been dumped by a lover who'd promised her the world. Further deceived by a close friend. She was not a good judge of character. She refused to let Halo charm her, as he had her brother and mother. They'd warmed to him immediately.

She had liked him better as Harold.

Alyn kept her eye on him as she took a seat between Danny and her mom. Halo stared openly back at her while Martha circled the table, pouring orange juice and coffee, then cutting the cinnamon coffee cake. She gave Halo a large piece. He turned his full attention to the morning treat. The Rogue took big bites. Ate hungrily. He must have missed breakfast. He held his plate out for seconds before Alyn was halfway through her own slice.

Danny imitated Halo, stuffing his mouth. Crumbs flecked his lips, and he choked. Halo thumped him on the back, then passed him a glass of orange juice. "Wash it down," he said.

Her brother drank deeply. He looked sheepish with his second bite. Much smaller this time.

"Better?" Halo asked him.

Danny nodded. "I could go for a second piece." He wanted to keep up with Halo.

His mother raised an eyebrow. "You haven't finished your first." Still, she cut him a small square. Danny was all smiles.

Alyn dabbed her forefinger along the edge of the plate, collecting the last of the cinnamon sugar. She licked her fingertip, happened to glance up, and found Halo's gaze on her. His green eyes were as dark as the leaf on an angel face rose. Yet his expression was anything but angelic.

Wicked came to mind. As did indecent. The slight

curve of his lip was a turn-on. His dimples flashed. His look alone promised racing hearts, sweat-slick bodies, and tangled sheets. Orgasms. He scared her breathless.

Self-conscious of the tightening of her nipples and the sweet heat between her thighs, she looked away. Concentrated on Danny instead. "Wipe your mouth." There were more crumbs on his face than coffee cake in his mouth.

He rolled his eyes, swiped a napkin. He missed a few crumbs. Alyn brushed them off his cheek with her thumb. Danny pulled a face.

Martha took a sip of her coffee, and requested, "Tell us about spring training, Halo."

Halo leaned back on his chair, tilting on two legs. He crossed his arms over his chest. Said, "The Rogues have a new facility in Barefoot William. Nice clubhouse—"

Danny bounced on his seat, all energy and excitement. "Will I get to see your locker?"

Halo nodded. "That can be arranged. We'll schedule a tour before practice starts. I'll take you out on the playing field—"

"Can I run the bases?" The boy's eyes were round, hopeful. "Slide into home?"

"Your cast," reminded his mother. "No sliding."

"What about the batting cages?" Danny wanted to know.

Halo's brow creased. "A one-handed hitter?"

"I'd manage," Danny reassured him. "I'd be real careful. Swear."

Halo gave it some thought. "The speed on the ball machine could be regulated. Maybe use wiffle balls instead of regulation baseballs," he added, tongue in cheek.

"Wiffle?" Danny gaped. His disappointment was evident. "I want fastballs. Power alley. I can burn 'em."

Halo ruffled the boy's hair. "We'll see when the time comes. I don't want you to reinjure your arm."

Danny sat up straighter, and assured him, "I'm getting stronger every day. My cast won't interfere with our fun."

"The beachside town has a great boardwalk, carnival rides, and an amusement arcade. There's something to do twenty-four-seven."

Danny's eyes widened. "I never have to sleep."

Halo put his hand on the boy's shoulder. "Even ballplayers catch a few hours each night."

Very few hours, Alyn imagined. Bars, women, sex. Halo wouldn't lack for entertainment.

"We'll be there for ten whole days." Clearly, it sounded like forever to Danny. He turned to Halo. "Can Mommy and Alyn come, too?"

"Only one of us," Alyn was quick to say. "Mom should chaperone."

"Me?" Surprise showed on Martha's face. "I was thinking you, Alyn."

"You go, Mom," she insisted. "When was the last time you had a vacation?"

Her mother looked thoughtful. "It's been a few years."

"A lot of years," Alyn reminded her. "Not since Danny was born."

Martha poured herself another cup of coffee. "I'm content at home. Truly, I am."

"You'd make me happy if you went with Danny." Alyn said, and meant it.

Halo's iPhone rang. *Dun dun da-da da-da*, the great white shark tone was realistic. Scary.

"*Jaws?*" asked Danny.

"No, Jillian Mac-Cates," Halo said. "She's the team's community liaison. Nice enough, when she's not trying to take a bite out of me."

"Does she bite hard?" From Danny.

"Hardest when I'm running late or not paying attention to her."

"That happens how often?" Alyn wondered aloud, certain it was a regular occurrence.

"Often enough." Halo was truthful. He tapped the screen. "She has travel details. Hold on." He dropped the chair back on four legs, rose, and took the call in the mirrored hallway.

Alyn was sitting closest to the hall, and she could hear parts of his conversation.

"Boy, age eight." Pause, followed by a clearing of his throat. "Three instead of two." Indistinguishable mumbling. "Give me a break." Some male finagling. "An alternative . . ." Next, "I'll take care of it." His voice lowered even more. "I need you to do me a favor. . . ."

He returned to the kitchen shortly thereafter. His expression was unreadable.

Danny hopped off his chair, and met Halo by the refrigerator. Curiosity and anticipation had him bouncing on his toes. "My mommy or my sister? Who gets to go?" he rushed to ask. "When do we leave? Are we flying? I've never been on an airplane."

Alyn sat very still. If truth be told, she would've loved to make the trip. However, her mother was a priority. She was still grieving her husband's death. She would for a long time to come. Alyn hoped the sunshine would lift her spirits. No one deserved it more.

She glanced at Halo, who was eyeing her. Or evaluating her, she thought. His brow was creased and his lips were pursed. She had no idea why. He went on to pinch the bridge of his nose with his thumb and forefinger, then rub the back of his neck before saying, "All three of you can come to spring training."

Danny whooped, pumped his good arm.

Grateful, Martha's eyes watered; her smile was soft.

Alyn contemplated his decision. When they'd spoken privately in the living room, Halo had indicated Danny and a chaperone would travel to Florida. Two people only. Yet now the entire family was headed south. How had he managed that?

He hadn't taken her dog into account. "I can't leave Quigley," she said.

Danny jumped in with, "Cadbury and Merlin would have to come, too."

Halo looked uneasy. "They are . . . ?"

"My bunny and goldfish," her brother was quick to say.

One corner of Halo's mouth tightened. Alyn figured he was getting in deeper than he'd expected with the trip. Family travel became a whole different ballgame with pets included. She cut him some slack. Gave him room to back out. "No worries. I'll stay behind, feed Cads and Merlin."

Halo shook his head. "I want you with us," ended their debate. He then took a moment and considered their options. "Airline won't accept a bunny or fish. So . . ."

"So . . ." Danny echoed him.

"How do you feel about a road trip?" was his solution.

Alyn did her best not to laugh out loud. Did this hotshot ballplayer have any idea what he was getting himself into? What it would be like traveling with three people he barely knew along with their pets?

A handicapped dog was very hands-on.

An eight-year-old boy couldn't sit still for more than a few hours at a time.

Her mother mapped out every rest stop.

His patience would be tested.

Four

Landon Kane, third baseman for the Richmond Rogues, impatiently paced the southern end of the Barefoot William boardwalk. "Where the hell is Halo?" he asked two of his teammates who leaned negligently against the blue metal railing that separated the boardwalk from the beach.

Left fielder Joe "Zoo" Zooker and pitcher Will Ridgeway were slow to respond. They were more interested in the bikinied babes who strolled the shoreline, and those stretched out on beach loungers, lying facedown with their tops untied. Their slender backs and thonged butt cheeks glistened with suntan oil. Their supple sun-warmed skin seduced a man. It was a pretty sight.

The ladies on the boardwalk were hot, too. Their side glances and sexy smiles showed a willingness to party. And so much more. A female with cropped dark hair, enormous sunglasses, and wearing a one-piece cutout swimsuit accidentally bumped into Landon. The brush of her full breast and curvy hip was an open invitation. He drew a breath; her scent was tropical fruit. Nice. He winked at her. She winked back. But he didn't pursue her. He had more important things on his mind. The woman sighed, walked on.

Zoo noticed their exchange. "Babe sent out her bat signal," he said.

"You should've gotten her number," agreed Will. "Saved her for later."

Land exhaled slowly. His teammates thought him fast and easy when it came to the ladies. And that he got laid often. That wasn't the case, even though he gave that impression. He'd lost interest in random sex. Quickies were no longer satisfying. Physical friction was fleeting.

He preferred romance. Flirting and foreplay. Long kisses. Lingering touches. Learning each other's bodies. The slow burn. Anticipation was a turn-on. The steadiness and growth of a relationship appealed to him most. He was always on the lookout for that special someone. She was out there. Somewhere. He would find her. Someday. When the time was right. Somehow.

His teammates would laugh their asses off if they knew the number of dates he'd left at the front door with only a hug or good-night kiss. Women frowned, pouted, and begged him to stay. Still, he left. Not wanting to lead anyone on. Honesty was important to him.

Partying with his buddies remained a big part of his life. The ballplayers were like brothers from different mothers. They'd planned a blowout tonight before the start of spring training. Blue Coconut and Lusty Oyster called their names. As did Boner's, a bar thirty miles north, outside the city limits, where shots were a buck and beer kegs ran free after two a.m. It was the last stop of the night for most, and many slept facedown on the bar, waking with a hangover. Good times.

The men had a few hours before their first drink. It was late afternoon, and tourists and townies enjoyed the moderate temperature and picturesque Gulf. The sky was a pale blue, almost white. The seagulls merged with low-hanging clouds. Fishermen collected on the pier. The water below glistened. Clear and turquoise. Waves rolled lazily onto the sugar sand.

The multicolored doors of the connected beachside shops were open, welcoming the stirring breeze and a breath of salt air. Food kiosks were numerous. Mobile metal carts served snacks and meals. He was tempted to order a basket of chili fries. But decided against it. He seldom ate between meals. He'd save room for supper.

Landon tugged his Rogues baseball cap low on his brow, protecting his eyes from the glare of the sun. He drew his Android Smartphone from the pocket of his khaki cargo shorts, then scrolled the texts from Halo. They made little sense. "It's Saturday. He's five fucking days late. No reason."

"He'll show," Zoo finally said. "He probably hooked up."

Land shook his head. "No hooks. Messages have him driving randomly. He's on and off Interstate 95. Taking in the sights."

Will scratched his chin. "Sounds like a road trip."

"Halo doesn't road trip." Landon was concerned. "He had one planned stop in Atlanta to see his pilot, then straight here."

Zoo snorted. "You're such a mom."

"You're a dick," Land growled. The Halo behind the texts wasn't the Halo that Landon knew. The two of them were close. People seldom saw one man without the other. They had each other's backs. No matter the circumstance or situation. If Halo got in trouble, Landon shouldered half the blame. They competed against each other during the season: hits, runs, errors. Then went on to celebrate their individual successes.

Zoo lowered his bronze lens Maui Jims, and side-eyed a blonde in a tight tank top and a tiny bikini bottom. She eyed him, too, checking out his T-shirt. She slowed, curled a finger in the cotton of his collar, and mouthed, "Top," as she passed him.

Zoo grinned. His navy tee was scripted with *Top or Bottom?* More than one woman had relayed her preference. He shoved his shades back up his nose. Pushing off the railing, he crossed to Landon. Will followed. They looked over Land's shoulder. "Run through Halo's texts," said Zoo.

Land skimmed back to the first post. He read, "'On my way.' That was sent early Tuesday morning as he left Richmond. I asked him to let me know when he got to Atlanta. Instead he responded with: 'Stopping in Smithfield, North Carolina. Shadowhawk.'"

"What's 'Shadowhawk'?" asked Zoo.

Landon had downloaded the website. "A replica of Wild Bill's Western town. Built by a retired actor, in his own backyard."

"A movie set, huh?" That interested Zoo. "Halo as a gunslinger, downing shots of whiskey in the saloon? Yeah, I can see it."

Will craned his neck, claimed the next text. "'Reached South of the Border.'" He rubbed his forehead. "I've been there. Rest stop and roadside attraction south of the North Carolina border. Adobe architecture and neon signs. Small amusement park, a mascot named Pedro, and a shitload of Mexican trinkets."

A further message confused them even more. "'Locating a pet-friendly hotel.'"

Will frowned. "Halo doesn't have a pet."

"Not unless he adopted a dog during off-season," said Zoo.

"He would've told me." Of that Landon was certain.

The men took turns reviewing the posts. "'Baseball water tower in Charlotte, South Carolina,'" Land continued. "Can't believe that would hold his interest."

Will rolled his eyes. "'UFO Welcome Station, Bowman, SC.'"

" 'Bee City, Town of Beehives, Cottageville, SC. Stung in the parking lot.' " Zoo grunted. "Bet that pissed Halo off."

" 'Submarine on Land, St. Mary's Georgia,' " Land added. " '*USS* George Bancroft.' "

"He attached a photo," Will noted. "A full-sized Navy sub on display, as if it's surfacing out of the grass. Pretty cool."

The men scanned the next twelve texts in silence. "I don't get it," said Will. "Halo's all over the map. Driving south, then east, then west."

Zoo rolled his shoulders, straightened. He was about to say something, but got sidetracked by a pair of twins. Redheads in skimpy sundresses and stiletto sandals. They were all legs. Swaying hips. And would double Zoo's pleasure, Landon thought.

Will cleared his throat, and Zoo returned his attention to the pitcher. "My sister-in-law used the Roadside America app when she traveled with her children from Texas to Maine to visit their grandparents. The stops broke up the monotony. I swear Halo is using the same app."

"But why?" Landon questioned. "I've never known him to play tourist. Not ever. He's fast-track. Getting to his destination as quickly as possible."

Zoo tapped the edge of Landon's smartphone with his finger. "Last night he slept in the Live Oak Villa Treehouse on St. Simon's Island, Georgia. This morning he crossed into Florida, making stops at Sarasota's Jungle Garden and Big Daddy Garlits Museum of Drag Racing in Ocala."

Landon's jaw worked. The museum might interest his friend, but he couldn't picture Halo sitting through a bird show with a bike-riding parrot. He sent one final text to his buddy. "*Get your ass here.*"

He was about to pocket his phone when Halo answered. "*My ass arrives in two hours. Barefoot Inn.*"

"Barefoot Inn?" Land puzzled. "The bed-and-breakfast reserved for the winners of the spring training contest."

"Still makes no sense," said Will. "Unless the person joining Halo planned to check in early. Jillian sent out itineraries. We're to meet our guests at the airport on Sunday. There's a welcome bonfire at twilight near the pier."

Zoo shrugged. "Whatever. He's a big boy. He'll get here."

A nudge on Landon's right, and a curvy brunette slipped between him and Will, and faced Zoo. An asymmetrical haircut flirted with her exotic features. She wore a belly shirt tucked beneath her boobs. Her wraparound skirt was slit over one thigh. Lady was bold in her attention. She traced a navy fingernail over *Top or Bottom?* on his T-shirt. Then licked her lips, and landed him with, "Both of us facing the TV."

Zoo threw back his head and laughed. He took her hand in his, said, "I'm Zoo."

"I know. I'm Nikki."

"Where to, sweetheart?"

"Wherever you're going."

"I have no immediate plans."

She hooked her arm through his. "I was headed to Goody Gumdrops, the penny candy store." She dipped two fingers in her cleavage. Produced a dollar. "I need some sugar. Root beer barrels, snow caps, and blow pops."

Blow pops made Zoo grin. Will, too. Their thoughts were on sex. Swirling tongues and sucking. Zoo jingled the change in his pants pocket. "I like pop rocks."

Her eyes shone. "I bet you do."

"We're gone." Zoo gave Landon and Will his back.

"That's the last we'll see of him tonight," said Will.

"Maybe, maybe not." Landon turned off his smartphone, pocketed it. "Guys' night out before spring training is tradition. Zoo may tap her early, but he'll catch up with us later."

"Twenty bucks says he's more into blow pops than his bros."

"You're on. But make it fifty. I'm sure he'll show."

"I'll take that bet, and raise you another fifty," Will said. "Bar where Zoo will walk through the door?"

"Lusty Oyster."

"A final hundred on what time."

Landon gave it some thought. "Around eleven. Give or take a few minutes."

"I'll give him until midnight, but it won't matter. We won't see Zoo again until the bonfire. He'd get fined if he doesn't make an appearance with his contest winner. It's a team event."

"Who did Zoo choose?" Land wondered.

Will told him. "Coach Holloway, as the man prefers to be called. He's a retired physical education teacher."

"How about you, dude?"

Will was solemn. Respectful. "Private Andrew Davidson. Army. Iraq. He was on patrol, enemy fire, and was severely wounded. His right arm was amputated. His baseball throwing arm. His sister sent in the entry. Praising her brother's love for his country and major league baseball. Andrew continues to play slow-pitch on a veteran team. The players have disabilities."

Landon approved. "Davidson was a good choice."

"Your winner?" Will asked.

"Eleanor Norris. She's ninety."

"In good health?"

"She uses a cane, but otherwise she still kicks ass, or so she says."

"She said 'kick ass'?"

"Lady is feisty," said Land. "Florida and baseball are on her bucket list. She can scratch off both next week."

Will rubbed the back of his neck. "Wonder who Halo chose?"

"Hopefully, someone appropriate."

"I'm guessing a female fan sent him an X-rated letter along with a nude photo. Halo is drawn to the visual."

Land gambled once again. "A fifty says he did right by the team and his winner is deserving."

"I'll match your fifty. I'm betting double-D's."

"We'll see."

Will turned back toward the beach. He shaded his eyes with his hand. "Oh, man. Woman in the white tank top and jogger pants at water's edge."

Landon tipped up the bill on his baseball cap, squinted against the sun. "Hard body. Smooth stride."

Will rolled his tongue inside his cheek. "I haven't jogged today."

"You don't jog any day."

"Good time to start."

"Go for it."

Will gave him a thumbs-up. The six-foot-six pitcher took off running. He didn't look like a jogger. He'd only recently arrived on the boardwalk, following a pitchers and catchers meeting at the stadium. There'd been early press coverage. Photo ops. He looked decent, in a cream-colored polo and tan chinos. Wingtips. He'd need to pace himself in order to catch the woman. She was sleek. Into performance. Perhaps a long-distance runner. Chances were good that she'd find Will passed out on the sand on her return.

Landon glanced at his watch. Hours to kill. What to do? His buddies were getting lucky. He was on his own, biding his time. He stood outside Molly Malone's Diner, at the curb of the Center Street crosswalk. The crosswalk connected two adjoining sides of the boardwalk. Saunders Shores stretched south. Barefoot William north. They differed greatly.

Barefoot William was as honky-tonk as the Shores was high-end. Couture, gourmet dining, and a five-star hotel claimed the southern boundaries. Waterfront mansions welcomed the rich and retired. Yachts the size of cruise ships lined the waterways. Private airstrips replaced commercial travel. The affluent were a community unto themselves. *Forbes* listed Saunders Shores as the wealthiest resort community in the country.

In comparison, the opposite side of the street shouted fun in the sun. Team Captain Rylan Cates's family owned Barefoot William, and his relatives operated the northern shops. Here, tourists never wore a watch. Beach attire was permitted in shops, diners, and bars. Casual was the name of the game. Free and easy worked best for Landon.

He debated his late afternoon options. Carnival rides and arcade amusements appealed greatly. He liked the carefree moments of feeling like a kid again. There were as many adults as children indulging in activities.

A century-old carousel whirled within a waterproof enclosure. Its walls of windows overlooked the Gulf. The merry-go-round cranked "Roll out the Barrel" as the hand-carved purple-and-white wooden horses went up and down and all around. The Ferris wheel turned slowly, while the swing ride whipped out and over the water. Late afternoon laughter rose from the bumper cars. An occasional shriek came from the rollercoaster.

He stretched his arms over his head, cracked his back. Then decided to take a walk. He'd taken only a few steps when a pedicab slowed beside him. The drivers of the three-wheeled rickshaws gave beachside tours, relaying historical and fun facts as they pedaled.

"Can I give you a ride?" a girl in her early twenties inquired. Her smile was flirty. She wore a khaki uniform: short-sleeve button-down and shorts, and high-top tennis shoes. Her legs were tanned and toned from miles of pedaling.

He passed. "Thanks, but I'm good."

She sighed heavily. Visibly disappointed. "Some other time, then."

"Definitely." That brought her grin back.

She pedaled off, and Landon sauntered the mile-long stretch. He people-watched and window browsed. He'd made a point to stop in Three Shirts to the Wind on his arrival in town. He liked T-shirts, and the shop had the best selection on the boardwalk. From plain cotton tees to brightly colored polos. Some had caricatures, while others had decorative designs. A few naughty slogans raised eyebrows. Most sayings were funny or silly. Overhead clotheslines stretched the width of the ceiling. Oversized clothes pins clipped beach hats, flip-flops, and towels to the rope. Window mannequins were dressed in the popular Beach Heat sportswear. Retired professional volleyball player Dune Cates kept his finger on the pulse of his designer line. Landon had purchased two Florida print shirts.

The Denim Dolphin catered to kids, offering toys and clothes.

The Jewelry Box offered costume jewelry. Collectible signature pieces. Rhinestones and precious metals. Gulf Coast glitz.

Waves sold ladies swimwear. There were a lot of women in the shop. A man could stand outside the window and enjoy the view all day. He moved on.

Toward the end of the boardwalk, a hot pink door stood out among the other shops. Old Tyme Portraits. The amateur photographer in him took a look in the window. He liked what he saw.

An arrangement of photographs showcased men and women standing behind life-size cardboard cutouts, their faces pictured above vintage swimwear, a flapper dress and zoot suit, a knight's armor and a medieval lady's gown. Interesting. He decided to go inside and look around. Perhaps have his picture taken as a 1920's gangster.

He pulled open the door, heard a commotion, and glanced over his shoulder. The Rogues were familiar faces on the boardwalk during spring training. He'd been recognized by a horde of fans and followed. He never minded shaking hands or signing autographs. It came with the territory. He took the crowd in stride. The guys craned their necks, curious, while the girls giggled nervously.

"Can I have my portrait taken with you?" a brunette in a Rogues jersey asked. She wore his number thirteen. "Care to be Adam to my Eve?"

Why not? He had the time. He held the door, and everyone filed in. He did a headcount. The shop was small; the crowd, fifty large. They pressed flesh. One woman leaned into his side. Another patted him on the ass.

The large cutouts were propped against the far wall, behind a raised platform. A woman stood off to the side, fooling with her camera. She had a nice backside, Land noticed. Slender in her white, oversized button-down shirt and black leggings. Her neon yellow flip-flops scuffed sand, tracked in off the beach.

She turned, scanned those gathered. Grinned. There was a small space between her two front teeth. Landon recognized her. Here was Eden Cates, his teammate Rylan's cousin, and one of the town's elite. She carried the ancestry, but there was little family resemblance. Her white-blond hair was short and frizzy. Crazy wild. Her eyes were a dark blue. Almost navy. Her cheekbones arced. Natural hollows beneath. Significant freckles. Her mouth tipped, full and pink. Her face had character.

They had been introduced the previous year at a board-walk fundraiser, but had only spoken briefly. He'd felt extremely awkward around her. Nearly tongue-tied. Strange for him. Definitely a poor first impression.

She'd taken his silence as lack of interest, and had blown him off. They'd gone their separate ways. He hadn't thought much about her. Until now. Perhaps she'd be more into him this time around. Or maybe not. Her nod in his direction was indifferent. She did a great job of pretending not to notice him further. He could be invisible, if she had a ghost cutout.

She raised her voice to be heard over the excitement. "I'm Eden, your photographer. Look around. I have thirty monochrome cutouts. I'm happy to assist, then shoot you."

Shoot you drew light laughter. Even Land smiled. The lady had great energy and a sense of humor. She engaged the crowd. Won them over.

"How much?" a bearded young man with a ponytail called to Eden.

"Twenty-five for the singles, forty for the doubles."

He gave her a thumbs-up. "Reasonable."

The crush around Landon eased, as his fans moved to the back of the store. Each one selected his or her favorite cutout. Many called to him with requests that he take a photo with them in the double-faced frames. He was happy to do so.

The girl who'd asked him to be Adam to her Eve came toward him now. She carried the lightweight cutout with a foldout stand and base. She nodded toward the dais. "Ready?" she asked him.

"Sure," he agreed. He took off his baseball cap, tossed it on a side table.

The cardboard cutouts were black, white, and shades of gray. Large-as-life and laminated. Landon went from

Adam to a medieval highlander, paired with the lady of the manor. "Nice legs, Braveheart," a woman called out. "What's under your kilt?" The shop erupted in laughter.

For photo after photo, Landon stuck his face through the cutouts. The cardboard scraped his forehead, cheeks, and chin. Eden Cates was a pro at organization. She directed the customers onto the platform, took their pictures, edited the images on Photoshop software, then produced a glossy print. A red plastic frame preserved the high-quality souvenirs, Land noted. Eden had the process down to a science. The line moved quickly.

He smiled when she told him to smile. Until his lips got tired and his mouth went dry. He continued with a wink. He couldn't help but stare at Eden. She was the eye behind the camera. She gestured with her hands. Gold nail polish tipped her fingers. Her hips gracefully rolled with each shift of her weight. She kicked off her flip-flops, went barefoot.

It was evident she enjoyed her work. She teased and talked with everyone but him. He may have been the center of attention, but he somehow felt ignored. That bothered him. A little.

An hour passed, and Land was patient. He stood as a cowboy to a dance hall girl. A caveman to a cavewoman. A pirate to his pretty captive. The Tin Man to Dorothy. The vintage swimwear was a favorite. He posed for eight photos. Once the crowd thinned, he planned to have his picture taken in the National Association old-fashioned baseball uniform with the bib shirt, button cuff full sleeve, and string tie knickers. Very nostalgic. The player held a bat at his shoulder, anticipating a pitch.

The session finally wound down. The customers paid for their portraits, then clustered around Land once again. He was asked to autograph each portrait, even the ones he hadn't taken part in. Eden found him a thin-tipped permanent marker. People patted him on the back, shook his hand, and gave him a hug. He was appreciated. It was time well spent.

"Best keepsake ever," was repeated over and over as the shop emptied. "See you at the ballpark, Landon. Have a good season, dude."

He closed the door after the last straggler. Public relations were all important. Fans liked memorabilia. The portraits were collectors' items. Better than key chains, bobble heads, and foam fingers.

He was proud of himself. He'd spread goodwill. Promoted himself and the team. The Rogues' community liaison would be pleased. Jillian liked when players mixed and mingled with ticketholders.

He glanced at Eden, and found her eyeing him across the room. They were the only two left in the store. He had an idea, and ran with it. Requesting, "Can you send copies of some of the double-faced portraits to Jillian Mac-Cates at the stadium? She could insert them in the Rogues' spring training newsletter."

"Your preference?"

"Not Adam and Eve," he was quick to say. "The pirate and cowboy would work."

"Sure. Will do. I'll get them to her before I close for the day."

"Appreciated."

"So . . ." She glanced toward the door, and let the word trail off. "Are we done here? Or did you have a further portrait in mind?"

He wasn't ready to leave. "I have a personal favorite," Landon told her. He retrieved the vintage ballplayer cutout, and approached the platform. He knew the history of the National Association of Professional Baseball Players. He thought to initiate Eden. "Eighteen-fifty-seven to eighteen-seventy, the NA governed early high-level but officially nonprofessional baseball in the United States. Teams were minor league."

"Eighteen-seventy-one, and the National Association was replaced by the National League," she added.

He blinked, unable to hide his surprise. The corners of her mouth twitched, but she didn't fully smile. "The majority of cutouts are period dated. I know the background behind the cardboard." She motioned to him. "On the platform, Jim O'Rourke."

His brow creased. "Why O'Rourke?"

"I have names for all my cutouts," she explained. "The man was renowned. He worked his parents' farm before he began his baseball career."

Land scratched his head. "He played for the Middletown Manfields, as I remember. An amateur ball club in Connecticut in 1872."

She nodded. "The team was short-lived, as you may know. When it folded, O'Rourke signed with the Boston Red Stockings. He had the first base hit in National League history."

"Orator Jim, as he was called, was quite a character," Land said. "He got his nickname from his glibness on the field, his intellect, and law degree."

She shared an additional fact. "One legend surrounding O'Rourke is that he would only sign with the Mansfields provided the team found someone to take over his chores on the farm."

"He was quite a guy. His career lasted past the age of fifty." Landon stepped onto the platform then, and awaited Eden's direction.

She studied him for a long moment before saying, "Angle the slugger left. Give me rough and rugged, Landon Kane. Narrow your eyes and stare down the pitcher."

He could do that. He stabilized the cardboard, stuck his head through the cutout, and glared.

"Darker, meaner, more intimidating."

What the hell? This was a fun portrait. He shifted his stance. He wasn't positioned to slam the ball down the pitcher's throat.

"Turn it on."

Turn what on? he wanted to ask. The power he felt at the plate? His vision of a home run? His frustration over a strike?

"Concentrate," she pushed him. "The score is tied. Bases loaded. The game rests on your shoulders."

He sucked air. He knew that feeling. The gut-need to save the day. To be the hero. It was as scary as it was satisfying if he succeeded in bringing a runner home.

He gave in, played along, locking his jaw until his teeth ached. He gave her his darkest squint. In that moment, he heard the roar of the crowd chanting his name. Pennants waved and foam fingers poked the air. His neck muscles tightened as he shouldered the bat. He imagined the perfect pitch. He swung on a cutter, connected with the sweet spot. Long and gone, the ball cleared the center field fence.

He returned to the moment, and his entire body relaxed. He backed away from the cutout, and allowed himself to smile. He realized then that Eden continued to snap his picture. Several, in fact. Consecutive *click-clicks* capturing more than his cardboard at-bat. He ran his hand through his hair. Hopped off the platform.

She lowered her camera on his approach, her expression unreadable. "You did Jim O'Rourke proud," she complimented him. She crossed to the computer. Processed his photos.

Landon Kane was the handsomest man Eden had ever seen. She could barely breathe around him. He had dark brown hair and light brown eyes and a face so sculpted, so fine looking, women hated to blink around him. They never wanted to look away.

She'd photographed many men in her shop. But Landon's wink alone sent female hearts to racing. Hers, too. Embarrassingly so. His slow smile was sexy, indecent, promising. Hinting at a possible date, giving a lady hope, even if he never asked her out. He kept women on edge. Waiting and wanting him. Badly. She was no exception. She'd taken a few extra shots of him as Landon the man. No reason. Just because.

He had everything going for him, she thought. Height, great body, charm. Athletic ability. His fans loved him. He treated them well, too. Genuine kindness went a long way.

Today he'd practiced patience, taking photographs and talking easily with all those gathered. He'd made each person feel special. A man that popular scared her. She'd dated jocks in college. They always sought attention. And bored easily. Landon played pro ball. He would always be in demand, and never satisfied with just one woman. That she believed.

"How'd my portrait turn out?" He came to stand behind her. "Did I look mean enough for you?" His breath blew warm at her ear.

His photo was spectacular, Eden realized, as she lifted it by her fingertips from the printer. The best portrait she'd ever taken. Contoured in black-and-white, and shadowed in gray, his features were all sharp angles and intense concentration. She held it up for his inspection. "Nice going, Landon. You made the cutout come alive."

He studied the print. "Alive, huh?"

Heat crept into her cheeks. He was exceptional. She should have expected no less. She went on to admit, "Most customers photograph flat as cardboard. Yours has life. Depth and substance."

"As compared to my usual fluff?"

"I never called you fluffy."

"I saw it in your eyes when I entered your shop. I know when someone's scrutinizing me."

Had she been so obvious? "Do people analyze you often?" she had to ask.

"Women mostly. They want to know what makes me tick. What catches my attention."

She huffed. "I'm not coming on to you."

"I realize that, babe. You raised your shield the moment I walked into your store. It was avoidance at first sight."

She grimaced. Her defenses had gone up. Her aversion to the man was based on their previous meeting. Which she doubted he remembered. Her cousin Shaye had introduced them at a boardwalk event at the end of spring training last year. Shaye presided over Barefoot William Enterprises and had her finger on the pulse of all activities.

A spring flower show offered fresh cut blooms and potted plants, and had drawn enormous interest. The boardwalk had been packed. Landon had had little to say. He'd fidgeted, and kept looking over her shoulder, as if seeking better company. A prettier woman. She'd saved herself embarrassment by walking away before he could ditch her. She hadn't looked back. Not even a glance. She'd thought him an ass.

For whatever reason, he was staring at her now, looking deep into her eyes. She felt as if he'd touched her. He made her squirm. She crossed her arms over her chest protectively.

He rolled his tongue inside his cheek, asked her, "Do you ever pose for portraits?"

"I did when the shop first opened." The memory made her smile. "I also photographed my entire extended family behind different cutouts. They were window dressing."

"Great advertisement." He seemed impressed. He then

scratched his chin, momentarily thoughtful. "I'd like to see you as Marilyn Monroe." His comment came out of the blue.

Marilyn Monroe? Was he crazy? Her throat went dry. The classic 1955 portrait featured the starlet in her iconic white halter dress. Her skirt billowed from the subway grating, exposing her shapely legs. The cutout was hot, sexy, and vibrant. So unlike her.

While Landon had a face that would never take a bad picture, she seldom took a good one. She'd blink at the last moment. Scrunch her nose. Pinch her lips. She preferred being behind the camera. Focusing on others.

She cleared her throat, said, "I'm the photographer, not the poser."

"I'll pay double the cost for your portrait," he persisted.

Fifty dollars? For her to portray Marilyn Monroe. She breathed deeply. She'd had a decent tourist season. The snowbirds packed the beach and boardwalk, but summer months could be slow. Every dollar counted. She gave in.

Landon slipped his wallet from a side pocket of his cargo shorts. A wallet fat with cash. He paid for his photo, then waved Ulysses S. Grant before her eyes. "For the Monroe portrait."

Fine. She rang up the sale and secured the money in the register. Procrastinated still. "No one's used my camera but me."

"First time for everything, sweetheart."

"My Nikon is old and can be testy at times."

"I can be testy, too." He held out his hand, wiggled his fingers. "Hand it over. Let's do this."

This made her uneasy. Her stomach squeezed.

She picked up her camera, gave him directions. Afterward, he gently lifted the Monroe frame onto the platform. He gestured for Eden to get behind it. She did so.

Albeit reluctantly. Her face fit easily into the cutout, but her frizzy hair escaped. One wild strand fell over her left eye; another tickled her upper lip. She tried to blow them aside.

"You're good," Land told her. "Looks natural."

Silence stretched between them as he hunkered down on one knee and focused the camera. "Low is my best angle."

"The portrait is cardboard—you can't look up her dress."

"She's already flashing her panties. I like." His voice was deep, sexy.

Eden blushed. There was no accounting for her red cheeks. Thank goodness the film was black-and-white.

"All set?" he asked.

She gave a short nod. She was as ready as she'd ever be.

"Channel Marilyn."

She rolled her eyes. "You're joking, right?"

"No more than you were when you told me to imagine hitting a home run."

Great. Just great.

"Give me hot in the city," he appealed. "Warm air rises. Almost steamy. Spread your legs over the subway grille. Feel that unexpected blast of air. Your skirt undulates, climbs your thighs. You're both innocence and seduction."

Eden got into the mood faster than she'd ever thought possible. She licked her lips and linked her present with Marilyn's past. She heard Landon snapping pictures as if from a great distance. The moment captured her. But then so did the man. She concentrated on the thickness of his hair, the width of his shoulders, the way his muscles flexed when he slowly pushed to his feet, shooting her from a different angle.

His movement distracted her. Time scattered. She was

no longer flirty and effervescent, but rather quite ordinary. A woman with frizzy hair and freckles. "Enough," she said, removing her face from the cutout and stepping back. Way back.

She returned Marilyn to her place against the wall between a Chicago gangster and a Colonial soldier. Landon crossed to the computer. Waited patiently for her. "Print the photos," he requested.

Photoshop did its job. She soon spread six portraits on a small worktable for evaluation. Landon stood by her side. His arm brushed hers. His thigh bumped her hip. Goose bumps rose. She briskly rubbed her forearms. They still tingled.

He shuffled through the photographs; took his sweet time making a decision. He finally held one up to the light. "You really brought it, Eden. You look hot. The steam from the subway turned you on."

It was true—she did look aroused. She died a slow death, yet couldn't deny her expression. She'd gone beyond Monroe's playfulness and sexy smile. Her own eyelids were heavy. Her gaze sultry. Her lips parted, the tip of her tongue visible. Moist.

She snatched the portrait from him, turned it facedown on the table. Anyone looking at the photo might not immediately recognize her. Those who knew her were aware she hated having her picture taken. Even in family photographs she stood in the back. Hiding. Showing only the top of her head or half her face. Posing for Land had been a whim. A stupid mistake. One she now regretted. "You're reading more into the photo than is there."

"Film doesn't lie." He flipped the picture back over. "I want this one. To go."

"Why?" She saw no point in the exchange.

"Why not?" Wasn't much of a reason.

Fine. Just fine. He was the customer. She'd been bought and paid for. She framed the portrait. Then clutched it to her chest. She'd revealed a side of herself she hadn't known existed. Her inner sexy. She hated to make it public.

Landon gave her no choice. "Give it up, babe." He moved on her then, reaching for the picture. She twitched, and he touched her without meaning to. His knuckles grazed the top of her left breast and two fingers tipped her nipple. She released the portrait so fast, it started to fall. Landon had amazing reflexes. He caught it at her waist. His thumb hooked on the bottom button on her white shirt. Right above her navel.

She jerked back, and jarred her hip on the corner of the worktable. She would bruise. A given with her fair skin. She tried to collect herself before he noticed his effect on her.

Too late.

His light brown eyes gleamed and his nostrils flared ever so sensually. One corner of his mouth hitched. No man should look so sexy. Or so amused at her expense.

She needed him to leave. Nodding toward the door, she moved him along. "Have a good day." She slipped both his and her portraits into a large, padded manila envelope. Passed it to him.

He took her hint. He snagged his baseball cap off her table, put it on backwards, then tucked the mailer beneath his arm. He moved toward the exit. "See you, Marilyn."

" 'Bye, O'Rourke."

He was gone. Eden stood alone in her shop. The room felt strange. Almost lonely. The company of her cardboard cutouts was no longer enough.

She caught sight of him through the front window as he returned to the boardwalk. He was once again surrounded by sunshine and his fans. Women shamelessly threw themselves at him.

He cast a final look at her shop, and their gazes locked through the glass. Her pulse gave an unexpected jump. She immediately turned away.

She valued peace, calm, and consistency in her life.

Landon was a man to be viewed from a distance.

Up close, he would devastate her, one heartbeat at a time.

Five

Halo Todd's heart beat erratically whenever he was near Alyn Jayne. He was attracted to her. There were things about her that he really liked. Also things he didn't. She was pretty, smart, and kind, yet she held him at arms' length. Distance sucked.

Time with Alyn mattered. It was difficult to single her out with her brother and mother in his Hummer. Whenever there was an opportunity for a moment alone, she made an excuse and evaded him. She was damn good at slipping away. He was tired of watching her sweet ass retreat. He refused to make a major move on her until she showed some interest. So far, nothing. He kept watching, waiting. Anticipating. Patience was not his virtue.

Six-thirty p.m., and they'd reached their destination. They'd arrived in Barefoot William without incident. The supper hour was upon them. Danny was already eyeballing restaurants and tossing out suggestions as to where they might eat. His stomach was set on a hamburger and French fries. Halo smiled to himself. The boy was a bottomless pit. Similar to Halo at that age.

Danny was perpetual motion. Energy personified. The kid went here, there, and everywhere whenever they'd stop to visit a landmark. Alyn continually reminded her brother to slow down. The boy listened half the time. He went full-out during the day. Then climbed into bed and slept like the dead. First light, and he was wide awake, dressed, and ready to go again.

Halo was not an early riser in off-season. More times than not, he partied into the morning hours. Then slept until noon. Or later. While he hadn't visited a bar during their travels, he'd stayed up and watched late-night TV. He'd had no cock-a-doodle-do in him. Double-espressos got one eye open.

Twilight now flickered on the beachside town, the night sneaking up fast as Halo parked his Hummer at the curb in front of Barefoot Inn, a local bed-and-breakfast. One block off the beach, the inn was ideal for vacationers. Along with the winners of the spring training contest.

Danny was first out of the vehicle. The eight-year-old had ridden shotgun much of the way. He'd pointed to every highway sign that advertised a side trip. His curiosity and exuberance were contagious. They'd taken detours, one after the other. So many, in fact, Halo had lost count. Alyn had given him an apologetic look more than once. He'd told her not to worry. He was flexible. Danny wanted to explore, to see and to do everything. The boy had a great time. That's all that mattered. Halo liked the kid.

Danny was now jumping about on the sidewalk. Halo exited, too, then opened the back door for Martha. He offered his hand, and she took it, climbing out slowly. "Creaky," she said of her knees. "I'll go inside and check on our reservation." She left them, limping slightly up the front walk.

Alyn stayed behind and dealt with Quigley. The pug had ridden strapped in a child's car carrier attached to the backseat for safety's sake. She released him now. Quigley was wiggly. She held and cuddled him against her chest, talking softly. The dog tilted his head, stilled, as if listening. Licked her chin.

They had stopped often at rest areas so Quigs could stretch his front legs. Danny wasn't known to sit still long either. They'd left Richmond early Tuesday morning. It was Saturday already. A drive that should've taken two days had become five. Halo took it in stride.

All in all, the trip had gone well. He and Danny had bonded at the Shadowhawk saloon. The Wild West movie set had come alive as they sipped root beer and ate beef jerky. Sleeping in the treehouse was Alyn's favorite. He could've made it a whole lot more pleasurable had they shared a room. There'd been no chance of that. The Jaynes took one suite, and he landed in the other. He'd been horny as hell and spent a restless night, tossing and turning, and taking two cold showers. Hand soap was not the answer.

He rolled his shoulders, worked out the kinks. Then headed to the back of the Hummer. Popping the cargo door, he removed the pug's wheelchair from amid the luggage. Alyn came to him, and they both bent down to seat Quigs.

"Danny," she called to her brother. "Grab Quigley's leash and take him for a short walk. Stay close on the sidewalk."

Danny did so. No questions asked. Halo watched as the boy adjusted his pace to the dog's shorter steps. Quigs stopped mid-block, and his ears twitched. More visibly than normal. The twitch turned into a spinal quiver, head to tail. His back left leg kicked out, shook, then went limp once again.

"Alyn! Look!" Danny shouted for her attention, his tone urgent.

"I-I saw, sweetie," she called back, a catch in her throat.

Halo had seen it, too. He stared as the pug recovered, unfazed. Quiggie barked, ready to move on. They continued to the corner. He side-eyed Alyn. "What just happened? Is your dog okay?" He was concerned.

A lone tear trailed down her cheek. Her voice was soft when she said, "He sparked."

"Sparked? He had feeling in his spine?"

She nodded. "For a split second his nerve endings connected."

"Like a shock?"

"Kind of. It just never lasts long."

Halo stayed positive. "One second is better than no second."

"I agree."

He turned toward her then, framing her face with his hands. He brushed away her tear with his thumb. "How often does it happen?"

"Six times now since the surgery," she said. "Each jolt gets a little stronger. A sign of improvement."

Halo couldn't predict the future, but he could give comfort. He gathered her close, tucked her against his chest. She didn't resist. "Better days ahead. I'm sure of it."

"You are, huh?" Hope rose with her question.

"For a disabled dog he's strong and gets around well in his cart. I believe he'll walk again," he affirmed. "It's just a matter of time."

She looked up at him then. Her voice was as small as her smile when she said, "Thank you for believing in his recovery."

"I'm on your side."

"People on my side come, go, and never stay too long."

"I'll stick by you." He'd keep his word.

"I can always use a friend."

Friend now. Lover later. There'd be no rushing this woman. He held her gently. Dropped a light kiss on her forehead. She was vulnerable, and he didn't want to take advantage of her. He struggled with himself when she went soft against him. Way too soft. His chest welcomed her breasts. He cradled her against his groin. Their thighs rubbed. His dick stirred. Poked her.

"*Really?*" she asked, pulling back.

What could he say? It happened, and would probably happen again. He was as uncomfortable as she looked. "I was offering comfort."

"With your penis?"

"No regulator switch."

She rolled her eyes. Her sigh was long-suffering. "You're not an understanding fiancée."

"As compared to your other fiancées?"

"I've never been engaged."

"How long do your relationships usually last?"

"Long enough."

"That's what I figured."

"You judging me, Alyn?"

"Not in the least. I'm the first to admit I don't read people well."

"How do you see me?" He instantly wanted to take back his question. He hated sounding needy. Men admired his athletic ability. Women loved his body. What did it matter what Alyn thought? Still, he awaited her answer.

She took far longer than he liked in responding, finally saying, "You have a kind heart." She was sincere. "You've been amazing with Danny. He's a happy camper. I will always be grateful."

"How grateful?" He pushed his luck.

"Not as grateful as you'd want me to be."

He grinned then. Alyn had put him in his place. He could live with that. He glanced down the sidewalk, noticed Danny and Quigley approaching. He needed to unpack the Hummer. He did so, pulling suitcase after suitcase from the cargo area.

Alyn stood off to his side, looking worried. "We packed a lot, didn't we?"

"You have enough luggage for a full summer at the beach."

"We're only here ten days." She tentatively touched his arm. "You took on a lot with us. We're more than you bargained for."

"Not necessarily."

"I saw your expression each time Danny wanted to detour off the interstate," she said. "When he asked you to backtrack fifty miles."

"You misinterpreted my look," he said to ease her mind. "The sights were worth seeing." He'd seen more of Roadside America than he'd ever thought to in this lifetime. It was over and done, and no longer mattered.

"Still," she continued, "you gave up a great deal. I saw your jaw work when we drove through Atlanta. Your expression was pained. You groaned deep in your throat. Were you to meet a woman?"

He shrugged. "Plans change."

"Was she someone special?" Lady was persistent.

Special for sex. "We'll connect another time."

"Hopefully soon. We won't be bothering you long."

"You're not in my way," he assured her. "Honest. Danny's my contest winner. He has two chaperones." In actuality, he liked having the Jaynes around. They were far more pleasant than his pilot had been when he'd broken their date.

Susan had had a few choice words for him. She'd grown shrill. He promised to make it up to her. There were several opportunities ahead. She was scheduled to fly into Tampa and Miami within the next month. The Rogues played both teams early in the season. They'd make up for lost time. He looked forward to seeing her. But not as much as he once had; not after meeting Alyn. That gave him pause. Caused him mild concern. He'd never met a woman who didn't like him for one reason or another. His looks, his popularity, his money, his rocking it in bed. Alyn wanted nothing from him. That was disconcerting.

"Hey, sis, we're back," Danny said on his return. "Quigley and I are hungry."

"We'll figure out supper shortly," she assured him. "Stay," she told her dog. The pug waited for her on the sidewalk. Crossing to the cargo deck, she retrieved a round fish bowl. A tiny goldfish swam around a plastic castle. She handed the bowl to her brother. "Be careful with Merlin. No sloshing."

"Should I return for Cadbury?" he asked about his rabbit.

"That would be helpful."

"Right back." Danny held the bowl in the curve of his good arm and took off, striding faster than he should up the narrow stone walkway. There was sloshing. Fortunately, Merlin stayed in the bowl.

Alyn momentarily turned her back on Halo. She reached inside the cargo area, stretching for the bunny's cage. He watched. It was a big carrier. Cadbury had plenty of room to move around. Cads was asleep when she eased the cage toward her. He woke up, gave a low hop of surprise. The travel cooler was within reach and, flipping the lid, she located a Ziploc with carrot sticks and lettuce leaves. She passed one of each through the narrow metal bars. The bunny's nose twitched.

She backed up, and tripped over an untied lace on her vintage leather ankle boots. Halo liked the old-fashioned style. Plenty sexy in a Victorian way. She bent to re-tie. Hands on his hips, Halo appreciated the slope of her shoulders, slender beneath a gauzy floral print blouse.

Skinny jeans encased the curve of her hips and roundness of her bottom. Very nice.

Danny returned in a flash. "Mommy's getting settled in our room. She put Merlin on the coffee table. He can watch everything that's going on."

Halo wasn't certain how aware the fish was of his surroundings, but Alyn seemed to know Merlin well. "He'll like being the center of attention."

Danny grinned. "I thought so, too." He lifted the rabbit cage without any trouble. "Thanks for feeding him."

"Go slow, sweetie," Alyn reminded him.

Danny walked slowly, for Danny. Minimally jostling the rabbit as he headed back inside.

"He's going to want supper soon," said Alyn. She looked questioningly at Halo. "I imagine you have plans. Can you recommend a restaurant within walking distance?"

He raised an eyebrow. "You trying to get rid of me?"

"I figured once we unloaded the luggage, you'd burn rubber in your escape."

"I have people to see and places to be later this evening," he admitted. "Let's get the boy fed, then I'm gone."

"You're sure?"

He tipped up her chin with one finger. An honest, intimate moment. "Let's get one thing straight now," he said. "I'll say this only once. I'm never where I don't want to be. Understood, babe?"

She released a breath. Nodded. "Got it."

Quigley took that moment to bark. A short, warning bark that alerted them to a new arrival. Landon Kane. The third baseman leaned against the hood of the Hummer, shadowed in the twilight. His arms were crossed over his chest, his thumbs hooked beneath his armpits. He looked on with interest and amusement. His expression smug.

Halo's senses were usually sharp. Yet he hadn't heard Land arrive. He'd been too into Alyn. How much of their conversation had his teammate heard? "We just rolled into town," he told his friend.

"Better late than never." Landon pushed off the vehicle, approached Halo. They exchanged a man hug and fist bumps. His gaze moved to Alyn and held on her. "Sweet delay, dude." His comment was meant as a compliment.

Alyn blushed. "It's not what you think," she told Landon.

"I'm thinking—"

"You'd be wrong," Halo stopped him. He felt protective of Alyn. He didn't need his best friend making assumptions. He caught Landon's eye, narrowed his own gaze. *Let it go*, he silently communicated.

For now, Land cut him some slack. "Landon Kane," he introduced himself.

"Alyn Jayne." She shook his hand.

Land glanced at the pug. "Who's the watchdog?"

"His name's Quigley."

"Nice chariot." Landon stepped up on the curb, then bent to scratch the dog's ears. He worked his fingers down his spine. The pug twitched. Smaller jolts than earlier, yet every spasm was significant. This time his right foot stiffened.

Landon's brow creased. "I didn't hurt him, did I?" he asked.

"Twitches are good," Alyn assured him. She leaned down and tucked Quiggie's paw back in the stirrup. She gave Land the condensed version of her dog's accident, surgery, and recovery. She finished with, "Halo's been patient with Quiggie. It was a long trip south."

Land kept a straight face when he said, "Halo has the patience of a saint. Plenty of restraint, too."

Landon had Halo's back. He let Alyn believe what she

would. Yet both men knew Halo was restless as hell. His attention span was short. Movement kept him sane. Control slipped through his grasp before he could close his fist. Alyn brought a new calm to his life. He'd managed the trip without losing it.

Landon gave Alyn the once-over. "Are you his contest winner?" he asked, obviously wondering where she fit into Halo's life.

"Not me, but my brother, Danny," she clarified. "He's eight. My mother and I are chaperones. I know little about baseball."

Land shot Halo a knowing grin. "A family affair."

A fact Halo couldn't deny. The Jaynes had slid into his life and somehow fit. Like human puzzle pieces. Now was not the time to explain the situation. He moved on.

"Grab a bag and make yourself useful." Halo's command was more an order than a request. There were six suitcases lined up on the curb.

"Do I look like a bellboy?"

"A career option when you're done with baseball."

Halo hefted three, Landon carried two, which left one for Alyn. The smallest and lightest of the six. Halo nodded for her to precede them up the narrow stone walkway. She took Quigley by the leash and stepped carefully, kicking several stones aside that might have slowed the wheels on his cart.

"She seems nice," Land commented, as he watched her walk away. "I'd like to know her better."

How much better? Halo wondered. He'd never taken offense when he and Land showed interest in the same woman. Alyn, however, was different. He had no claim on her. Still, he didn't want his best friend dating her. He didn't want the competition.

Landon brushed past him then, hitting Halo with a suitcase. High on his thigh. Close to his balls. No apology from Land. His teammate was too busy eyeing Alyn's cute butt.

Halo set his back teeth. Counted to ten. Then twenty. He growled his annoyance. Warned Landon off. Land chuckled. Goading and irritating. A total asshole.

Two could play the game, Halo decided. He quickly slowed his buddy down by stepping on the left heel of his Reebok. A brand he endorsed. Landon lurched, nearly dropped the luggage he carried as he walked out of his athletic shoe.

Land only laughed harder when Halo knocked by him. Catching him behind his knee. Landon set down his suitcases and adjusted his shoe, finding great humor in the moment.

Alyn Jayne glanced over her shoulder, and contemplated their actions. *What was with those two?* She noticed Landon kept smiling. Halo's scowl could've cut steel. They were at odds. For some unknown reason. Surely they weren't serious. Just men being boys. Their clash didn't involve or affect her. She ignored them. Let them hash it out.

She set her suitcase at the base of the stairs, then lifted Quigley in his wheelchair and carefully climbed the steps to the verandah. The dog and cart weighed little. She set him down gently. Went back for the case.

Dusk turned to darkness. The automatic outside lights came on. She found herself surrounded by tropical foliage and a wraparound porch. The sun-yellow two-story inn welcomed visitors. Halo joined her and held the door. She entered. Landon snuck in so close behind her, he might have been piggybacking. Halo glared him back a step.

She'd been pleased to meet Landon. He was male model, movie star handsome. He would have his choice of women. But then so would Halo. Halo had the same good looks, only sharper, edgier. More dangerous. He could pull off sexy as easily as he could kick ass. She'd seen both sides of him at the game show.

The men crossed to the reception desk, set down the suitcases. Quigley scrambled after Halo. One wheel on his cart squeaked. It needed to be oiled. Her dog had developed hero worship for the man, just like Danny. Alyn wasn't as charmed.

She followed more slowly, absorbing the atmosphere. Relaxed and calming. Wide windows reflected the rising moon on blond hardwood floors. Pale aqua furniture, an abundance of blooming plants, freshly cut flowers, and brass accents completed the décor.

A large chalkboard near check-in listed a continental breakfast, afternoon happy hour by the pool, and all local activities. A complimentary rack of tourism pamphlets directed guests to local and state attractions. Danny would be beside himself, wanting to see Disney World and Busch Gardens. Not this trip, but perhaps another. Florida wasn't going anywhere.

Halo motioned her toward reception, and introduced her to Sharon Cates, the owner of the inn. "Your mother has the keys. Second floor, and you have two rooms with an adjoining door," she told Alyn. "One room has a queen-size bed, the other a double and a single. Small bathrooms. Let me know if you need anything. More towels, extra blankets."

Alyn nodded. Her mom would insist that Danny, his goldfish, and bunny stay with her. That left Alyn with Quigley. The arrangements were perfect.

Halo looked from the pile of luggage to the pug. "Priorities, Quigs," he said. "Let's get you upstairs." The dog barked and spun in a circle around Halo's feet. Halo leaned down, undid the straps, and drew the pug to his chest. He held the diapered Quiggie like a baby. "I'll carry you now, but only until you can take the steps yourself."

Alyn watched the exchange. She swallowed hard. Her mother and brother treated Quigley as family. Halo, too. He cared. Her heart warmed. He scored points with her.

"That leaves me in charge of the luggage," Landon discerned.

"Make two trips," suggested Halo.

"I can help," Alyn offered. She gathered the suitcase she'd been carrying, the one packed with Quiggie's dog bed, diapers, toys, and food, then reached for another.

"Not on your life." Landon refused her help. "I work for beer. Halo's buying tonight."

The men had plans, she realized. Perhaps a guys' night out. She didn't want to hold them up. She left Landon to the luggage. Quigs would need his cart, so she brought it with her. She crossed the lobby and took the wide staircase to the second floor.

She located their rooms easily. She spotted her mother first, reclining on a dark brown wicker lounger, relaxed and smiling. Halo and Danny sat on the floor, playing with Quigley.

Her brother looked up, said, "Halo wiggles his fingers and Quiggie scoots, chasing his hand."

The man had big hands, Alyn noticed. Strong and long-fingered. Excited, playful, and panting, Quigs nipped at his fingertips. Not wanting to overstimulate the pug, Halo soon drew Quigley close. He began a slow massage along the dog's shoulders and down his back. Quiggie deflated, sighed. Alyn could only imagine how good that must feel.

Moments later, Landon announced from the door, "Bellhop." He was loaded with luggage. The suitcases he couldn't carry, he scooted in the door with his foot.

"Landon Kane!" Danny instantly recognized the third

baseman. He hopped up, grinning ear-to-ear. "I can't be-lieve you're here."

Land set down the cases, then ruffled the boy's hair. "Glad you could join us for spring training," he said.

"Ten whole days," Danny drew out, making it sound like a lifetime. "Has your winner arrived?"

"Not until tomorrow morning," Landon told him.

"Is he a kid like me?"

"No, she's an older woman."

"Mom's age or a grandma?"

"She's ninety."

"That's almost a hundred if you count by tens," Danny calculated.

"That it is," Land agreed.

Danny dropped back on the floor beside Halo. "Alyn, look, Quigs is asleep," he whispered.

The pug lay stretched on his belly, eyes closed, snoring softly, as Halo continued his gentle rubdown. Glancing up, he let his gaze meet hers. Her stomach went soft when he said, "Quigley's body is so relaxed, he feels like a bean bag."

Peaceful was good. The body healed in sleep.

Not wanting to hold the men up any longer than was necessary, she reached for a suitcase, only to have Landon intercept her. "Which ones?" he asked.

She pointed to two blue American Touristers.

"Door cuts through to your room, sis," her brother pointed out.

She went to take a look.

"Her bedroom," she heard Landon say to Halo. Suit-cases in hand, he followed her.

"On the bed," she said to Land.

"Me or the suitcases?" He winked at her.

"What do you think?"

"He wasn't thinking," came from Halo, entering right

behind them. He'd scooped up the pug without waking him. If anything, Quigs slept deeper, his snores even louder.

Alyn unpacked the dog's suitcase. His bed and toys went in one corner of the room. She motioned for Halo to settle Quigley on the plush velour oval. The pug slept on.

Danny came in a moment later. He crossed to Halo, took his hand. "I'm hungry," he said.

Halo had been their meal ticket the entire trip. He'd gone above and beyond, feeding them, paying for their hotels, purchasing tickets to the roadside amusements. No matter what the man said, Alyn didn't believe for a second their trip was completely free of cost for the winners.

She kept her voice light when she said, "They don't have much time. It may be just family tonight."

Danny's face fell. "Halo's family."

"Any chance you could adopt me, too?" came from Landon. "I'm up for supper."

Her brother perked up. "Wow, two older brothers."

Alyn agreed on one condition. "It's our turn to treat."

"I have a dollar and eighty-five cents in my peanut butter jar," Danny told them.

"I hope the jar is empty," said Landon.

Danny grinned. "You're silly. Mommy put it in the dishwasher. I eat lots of peanut butter sandwiches. Alyn always adds grape jelly."

"What's your stomach hungry for?" Land next asked.

"My heart's set on a hamburger."

Halo gave the boy's hand a tug. "Let's check with your mom and head out."

Martha yawned, passed on dinner. "I'm tired," she admitted, still camped on the chair. "There's fruit and bottles of iced tea in the mini-fridge. Perfect for me."

"You'll check on Quigley?" requested Alyn. "Feed him when he wakes up?"

Her mom nodded. "Leave the door open between our rooms so I can hear him."

Alyn cracked it. Danny opened his suitcase; hurriedly found his peanut butter jar beneath his folded shirts. He twisted off the top, poured the nickels and dimes onto his palm, and then passed the change to Alyn.

"Big spender," she said, accepting his donation.

Ready to leave, Danny hugged his mother. "Love you, Mommy."

Martha kissed him on the cheek. "You, too, son."

Gathering her paisley hobo bag, Alyn dropped Danny's money in a zippered inner slot, then slipped into the hallway. Landon came after her. He took her by the elbow as they descended the staircase. A considerate gesture, Alyn thought. His touch would excite most women. Just not her. No butterflies or accelerated heartbeat. No attraction whatsoever. She sidestepped once they reached the bottom. His hand fell away.

His smile was slow, knowing. "That's the way of it, huh?"

"Way of what?" He confused her.

He lowered his voice. "If you don't know now, you will soon enough."

A riddle? Soon might never come. She shrugged off what he knew and what she didn't have a clue about.

Danny saved her from commenting further. He bounded down the stairs beside Halo. "Fill 'Er Up or Molly's Diner. Where should we eat?" Apparently, Halo had described the dinner options.

"You tell me." She left the decision to him.

Danny scrunched his nose. "Fill 'Er Up is a repu—" He searched for the word.

"Repurposed gas station," Halo helped him out.

"The station is two blocks away. Walking distance. Molly's is on the boardwalk. Halo would have to drive.

He's been driving for five days. We'll go there another time."

He sounded so grown up, Alyn thought. His thoughtfulness left a lump in her throat. "Fine by me," she agreed.

The night was cool and comfortable for a walk. Blossoming hibiscus and gardenia wafted on the salt air. Danny talked nonstop. The men didn't seem to mind. Danny was so excited he bounced when he walked. He quoted a few statistics as well as personal facts about the players. The guys were impressed.

Fifteen minutes later, they arrived at Fill 'Er Up. The former gas station was on a corner. "It used to be a Texaco," Halo told her. The two aisles of gas pumps were rewired as outside lights now. The parking lot was packed.

Alyn looked around. The diner drew steady foot traffic from the beach, and was near a residential neighborhood. The owners had kept the character and tradition of three overhead garage doors, which were open to the night. Tile floors, aluminum fixtures, and square metal tables made up the casual décor.

Halo patted his stomach. "Best burgers in Barefoot William," he said as they entered. Danny rubbed his tummy, too.

Halo placed his hand on Alyn's back, eased her forward. The heat from his palm splayed up to her shoulders and down to her bottom. She warmed. Tingled. Felt a moment of loss when he let her go.

"Halo, Landon, over here," was shouted from the back.

"Will Ridgeway, your starting pitcher!" Danny craned his neck, recognizing the player immediately.

"Join me," Will invited. He sat alone, stretched out at a six-seater rectangular table. He was a tall, lean man with short dark hair and a crooked nose.

Danny's eyes widened. "Can we sit with him?"

"Sure, why not?" said Halo.

Danny took Alyn's hand, suddenly shy. For all his eight-year-old bravado, he needed her reassurance. Danny was sitting down to supper with three Rogues. His athletic heroes. She squeezed his fingers. He squeezed back.

The ballplayers were recognized by many fans. Customers stopped eating to smile and wave at Halo and Landon as they wound around the tables. Danny walked a little taller in their presence.

The long table was located near the kitchen. A swinging door separated the cooks from the diners. They breathed the scent of burgers, French fries, and onion rings each time a waitress passed with a tray of food.

Halo introduced Alyn and Danny to Will. Will stood, welcoming them. His gaze was gun-metal gray, sharp, inquisitive. His clothes were mismatched: a bright, red, parrot-print button-down and black-and-white checked board shorts. Leather sandals. He looked more tourist than ballplayer.

"Will needs a personal shopper," Halo kidded his friend.

"Hey, I wear what I like," the man defended.

Danny piped up, "We saw parrots at the Jungle Garden. They rode bicycles, walked a tightrope, and hopped through hoops."

"Cool," said Will. He then motioned them to take a seat. "I arrived just minutes before you. I haven't ordered yet."

Halo looked down at Danny. "Pick a spot, buddy."

"Between you and Alyn." Which separated her and Halo.

Landon seemed pleased. He held her chair. She sat, scooted in closer. He dropped down next to her.

Will took his place at the head of the table. Alyn felt his eyes on her, until Halo cleared his throat. Will side-eyed Danny next. Her brother sat low to the table, but didn't seem to mind. He was one big smile. As long as her brother was happy, she was happy. Halo was the only one who appeared unhappy. He glared down the table when Landon settled his arm along the back of her chair.

"How was your trip?" Will initiated. "Land shared texts from Halo. You made numerous stops."

Danny answered, "There were lots of roadside signs."

Halo nodded. "Lots." Landon and Will grinned.

"Halo let me pick the places I wanted to see most. Some signs led to a dead-end. Other places were no longer in business." He laughed. "One time we drove in a circle."

"Around and around," from Halo.

"What did you like best?" Will questioned.

A long silence from Danny, until Halo prodded, "The Western town?"

"Yeah, that was fun."

"The submarine?" asked Landon. "Halo sent us a photo."

Danny's brow creased. "I enjoyed that, too."

"I bet I know your favorite moment," said Alyn.

"You do?"

"Buzz, buzz," she hinted.

Danny understood. "Bee City."

"Town of the Beehives," Alyn added.

"There was a lot of buzzing going on," Halo said. "Over one million resident bees."

"Bee Town also had a petting zoo," Alyn told them.

"The ring-tailed lemurs were neat," Danny shared. "They pushed each other out of the way for Cheerio treats." He started to laugh, and could barely get the words out. "A llama spit on the man standing next to us at the fence."

"Not a pretty sight," Halo said. "In the llama's defense, the man was teasing him."

"'Dalai Llama' isn't exactly a taunt," Alyn said.

"Maybe it was the man's tone of voice," Will suggested.

"That, or the llama was having a bad day," said Landon.

Danny rocked forward on his chair, rested his elbows on the table. "The best part of my trip was in the parking lot," he finally admitted. "A wasp tried to sting me, and Halo swatted it away."

"Swatted it, and unfortunately got stung himself." The moment had stuck with Alyn, too. Danny was allergic to bee stings. He'd jumped around, afraid. Halo had stepped in front of him and waved his hand. The wasp turned its attention on Halo, got his palm instead.

Danny finished with, "Halo didn't blank his eye."

"Blink," Alyn gently corrected.

"That's our Halo," Will said. "He's tough."

"My sister removed the stinger with a fingernail clipper."

"Sounds like major surgery," said Landon.

"Alyn's hand shook."

It certainly had, she recalled. His palm had turned red and puffed up. The stinger needed to come out. She was concerned she'd hurt him. His calluses had prevented the barb from going too deep. It was a thirty-second operation.

Halo grinned at Danny. "I came out alive."

"I'm going to write about the bee in my travel journal."

Alyn elaborated. "Danny's missing two weeks of school. The daily diary is part of his homework assignment."

Landon made a choking sound. "Yuck, homework."

"Danny's a smart kid," came from Halo. "He's a good reader, and can count to one thousand. He showed me twice."

Alyn couldn't contain her smile. She swore Halo had gone cross-eyed after five hundred. Surprisingly, he hadn't tuned the boy out. When Danny got mixed up, Halo came to his rescue. "He's good with numbers," she praised.

"I could count for you now," Danny offered.

The three men visibly stiffened, but were too kind to dissuade him. It fell to Alyn to do so. "Some other time, sweetie. We're about to order."

Which was the truth. A second later, their waitress brought glasses of water and one-page laminated menus. "I'm Mindy," she said. She wore mechanic overalls over a white T-shirt. "Full Service is on special tonight, for anyone with a big appetite. A half-pound cheeseburger with the works. It comes with both French fries, onion rings, and macaroni salad."

"Order whatever you like," Alyn spoke up. "Supper's on Danny and me."

"I have a dollar and eighty-five cents," her brother proudly told the waitress.

Mindy didn't miss a beat. "You've got it covered then." She took their drink order.

Will started with, "Beer—"

Halo cut in with, "Root beer."

Will muttered, "Why not?"

Landon and Alyn went with the same.

The menu offered lots of possibilities. The men looked at Alyn. "Ladies first," nudged Landon.

She debated, finally went with, "Flat tire." A quarter-pound hamburger.

Danny eyed Halo. "I want what you're having."

"Full Service? A gut buster."

"Alyn says I eat my weight in food."

Halo smiled. "I did, too, when I was your age."

"Look how big you grew."

"And he's still growing." Landon chuckled. "He's going with a larger uniform this season."

"It's not my weight, it's the fit," Halo explained. "I like give at the shoulders and hips. No need to rip the seams."

Splitting seams. He looked at Alyn then, and their

thoughts linked. The memory of *Go Big or Go Home* was still vivid in her mind. Apparently, in Halo's, too. The rooster costume had constricted. His downward swing of the Strongman's mallet tore the zipper and seams. From his shoulders to butt crack. For all America to see.

The image of his broad shoulders, muscled back, and tight ass would never be forgotten. Her cheeks heated even now. Halo had the nerve to wink at her. Her blush deepened.

Landon noticed her color. "Am I missing something?" he asked.

"Same thing I'm missing," said Will.

"Private joke," said Halo.

Will grinned. "Private are the best kind."

"Intimate," from Land.

"What's 'intimate' mean?" asked Danny.

"Friendly," Halo defined.

The waitress cleared her throat, regaining their attention. The men ordered Full Service all around. It was decided whatever Danny didn't finish would be doggy-bagged for his mom.

The conversation turned to spring training. To the events ahead. "There's a big bonfire on the beach tomorrow night for the contest winners," noted Will.

"Monday is Media Day," said Landon. "We introduce our contest winners."

Danny bounced on his chair, unable to sit still. "Halo's going to give me a tour of the stadium. I get to see his locker, the field, dugouts, the batting cages, and—"

"Slow down, you're moving too fast." Alyn patted his shoulder. "There's lots to do. It may take more than one day."

Landon and Will looked puzzled. "I didn't get the memo on the full tour," Land said.

Halo scrubbed his knuckles along his whiskered jaw. "No official visitation. Just a few extras I'm doing for Danny."

"Lucky you," Landon told her brother. "I'll check with my contest winner, see if she's interested in the extras."

"Good idea," Will agreed.

Landon cut Halo a look. "You cleared this with Jillian, right? She likes updates."

Halo shrugged. "More or less."

"Less, I'm betting," Land muttered.

Halo waved Land off. "Dude, we're good. Jillie wants the best for our winners."

Alyn wondered if Halo was breaking rules for her brother. If Danny was getting special treatment. She hoped Halo hadn't crossed any lines. But expected he had.

Their waitress brought their drinks, served in tall glasses wrapped in thin, tire rubber beverage coolers. "The frosted glasses won't slip out of your hand," she told Danny.

Halo took his first sip and Danny matched him, drinking deeply, too. "A-ah," her brother said on a sigh.

The guys made small talk until dinner arrived. Danny sat wide-eyed, taking it all in. "Oh, wow!" He became even more excited when Mindy delivered their meal atop a Tank Force Tool Chest on castors.

Their burgers were served on hubcap-styled plates. The silverware was designed with wrench or screwdriver handles. Danny switched his screwdriver for Alyn's wrench. He liked it better. Oil cans pumped ketchup, mustard, and mayonnaise. Danny didn't like mustard, but he had to try each one. Halo spooned Danny's extra mustard onto his own burger.

All talking ceased as the men ate. Even Danny concentrated fully on his enormous cheeseburger. He ate a quarter of his food, then slowed down. Breathed.

"Surely, you're not full," Alyn teased him.

"My stomach's bigger than my eyes."

"Eyes bigger than your stomach." She turned his words around.

Danny took a few more bites of his burger, ate all his French fries, most of his onion rings, then shifted on his chair and leaned against Alyn. He yawned.

"Tired, slugger?" Halo asked him.

Danny straightened, only to tip back against Alyn. "If I was Quigley, I'd be dog-tired."

The men chuckled, and Alyn hugged him close. "It's been a long day." She glanced around the table. "I hate to hurry anyone—"

"We're done here." Halo finished off his root beer.

Mindy brought the bill, set it in the middle of the table. All three men reached for it, but Alyn was closest. Made the grab. Successfully.

"Mine," Landon insisted.

Will had his wallet out. "On me."

"All ours." She included Danny.

"Alyn, you sure?" Halo raised an eyebrow, questioned her.

Buying the meal was important to her. She wasn't working, and didn't have a lot of money. Still, tonight was worth every penny. Danny had had the time of his life. A priceless hour.

"We'll leave the tip," said Halo.

Before she could object, the men tossed money on the table. She swore they'd tipped as much as the bill.

Mindy cashed them out. She put the remainder of Danny's burger and side of macaroni salad in a brown paper bag. Passed it to Alyn. At the overhead garage door, she handed Danny a coupon for a free Full Service. "Next time, you'll eat the whole thing." He thanked her.

Will's SUV was parked in the lot. "Guys' night out. Where shall we meet?" he asked his buddies.

"Blue Coconut," Land decided. "In an hour."

"Gotcha. Later, Alyn, Danny. Thanks for dinner." He departed.

Her brother took her hand, dragged his feet on the walk back to Barefoot Inn. He was one sleepy boy.

"Piggyback ride?" Halo asked him at the corner.

He didn't have to ask twice. Danny circled behind him, hopped on his back. Wrapped his arms about Halo's shoulders. Halo made sure he was secure.

"Thank you," Alyn silently mouthed.

Halo nodded. Stepped out. Danny was asleep by mid-block.

"I'll take him upstairs," Halo told Landon when they reached the inn.

"I'll come with you."

"There's no need." Halo's tone brooked no argument.

Landon actually smiled. "I'm gone then. See you in thirty?"

"Give or take."

"Any longer, and I'll come back for you." He turned toward Alyn, and gave her a good-night hug. It was not a casual embrace, but a full-body press. She felt every inch of him.

"Give it a rest, Land," Halo said, warning him off.

Landon eased back, only to drop a light kiss on her forehead. " 'Bye, sweetheart." He stepped off the sidewalk and into the night.

Alyn followed Halo to the front door. She held it for him. They climbed the stairs to the second floor, where she knocked on her mother's bedroom door. Martha was quick to let them in.

Her mom's face softened when she saw Danny being carried. "My boy tired himself out today," she said. "Lay him on the bed. I'll deal with his pajamas later."

Alyn pulled down the blanket, plumped his pillow. Halo

lowered him on the mattress. Martha removed his tennis shoes, covered him with a sheet. Danny rolled onto his side. His eyes remained closed.

"A late night snack." Alyn handed her mother the doggy bag. "Half a burger and small container of macaroni salad." She glanced toward the bedroom door. "How's Quigley?"

"He's fine," her mom reassured her. "He woke up, ate, and went back to his dog bed. He's been quiet ever since."

Halo glanced at his watch, and Alyn nudged him toward the door. "I'll walk you out."

"Trying to get rid of me?" he asked, waving to Martha from the door.

"Do you really want Landon returning for you?"

"He would, too."

"He's a good friend."

"We're bullet brothers."

Alyn understood. They'd take a bullet for each other. Their bond was strong. She faced him in the hallway. "Have a good evening," sounded lame, but she didn't know what else to say.

"It's all about the team tonight. Tradition. Beers and bonding. Even the married players show up."

"Be careful."

His smile was slow, sexy. "You worried about me?"

"You're a big boy, Halo Todd. Don't do anything foolish."

"I'll hold that thought."

They stood staring at each other, neither moving. Time slowed. His gaze lowered to her mouth, a visual touch. The sensation was warm, seductive, and so strong she felt kissed. Her breathing deepened. Her breasts grew heavy. Her stomach warmed. Her knees went weak.

Halo slapped his palms against his thighs. "Don't look at me like that." His voice was gruff.

"Like what?"

"Like you want me to stay."

She did. She didn't. She was conflicted. "You're reading me wrong."

"Yeah, right." He didn't believe her for a second. "What are your plans for tonight?"

"TV, reading, taking Quigley for a walk when he wakes up."

His brow creased. "Sounds nice."

"Sounds quiet compared to yours."

"I would have invited you, but it's going to be loud, crazy. We act stupid. All before season starts."

"Season opener, and you get serious."

"Serious as I can be. I slip up sometimes."

"Danny thinks you're perfect."

"I'm not."

"I know."

"Ouch." Hand over his heart, he left her then. "Later, babe."

"Later."

Six

"Time to toast," said Will Ridgeway. The starting pitcher sat on a bar stool next to Halo. Landon and Zoo flanked them. Jake Packer stood to the side. Will held up his bottle of Heineken, his go-to brew for the night. He led off, "Look like a movie star, party like a rock star, fuck like a porn star."

Bottles clanked, and the men drank deeply. All but Halo.

Zoo went next. He raised a long neck Red Dog. "To being single, seeing double, and sleeping triple."

More drinking. Not Halo.

"May all your ups and downs be between the sheets," from Jake. Who chugged a Coors.

Chuckles, and consumption. Halo had yet to raise his beer.

Landon was next. He preferred Land Shark. "Here's to those who've seen us at our best and seen us at our worst and can't tell the difference."

Beers were polished off. Halo hadn't taken a sip.

The air went dead. The players stared at him. He was last to toast. He remembered a quote from Hemingway's Bar in Key West. "'Always do sober what you said you'd do drunk. That will teach you to keep your mouth shut,' my man Ernest."

Zoo's lip curled. "You yanking me?"

"Careful who you promise what to tonight."

Zoo got the message. "No more marriage proposals. That's a morning headache worse than a hangover." He cut Halo a look. "What's up with you, dude? Women have been shoving their tits in your face and flirting their asses off. You've ignored them. You sick or something?"

Or something seemed about right, Halo thought. Or someone. Alyn Jayne. She was in his head. Under his skin. He couldn't shake her. No matter how hard he tried. He'd been with her five days straight. He should be tired of her. He wasn't. He wanted more. The feeling scared the hell out of him. He'd never felt anything like it.

He cared more about what she was doing at that moment than about the girl trying to climb onto his lap. He turned slightly on his stool, nudged her toward Jake. She pouted full red lips.

"I'm starting out slow," Halo told his teammates. "I'll pick up speed."

Zoo snorted. "When have you ever paced yourself?"

Never, Halo realized. More often than not he was half in the bag by ten. It was after that now, and he continued to drink one beer to everyone else's three . . . or four, given the redness of Zoo's eyes.

"Beer here," Will called to the barkeeper.

Cold ones all around. Halo took a long pull on an Amstel. That pleased his buddies. They slapped him on the back, cheered him to kill the beast. He emptied the bottle. Then slammed it down on the bar. Zoo gave him a high five. Halo nursed the next one.

The players left him alone, then. For the moment, anyway. They were looking to hook up. The Blue Coconut was packed with women. All sizes. All shapes. All hot. All interested in ballplayers. Zoo had found two females to his liking. Both redheads. He liked threesomes. He split his attention, kissing one, then the other. Neither seemed to mind.

Halo rolled his shoulders, tried to relax. Found it difficult. Scanning the crowd, he caught sight of Rogues' captain Rylan Cates seated at a table near the back wall. Ry was talking to shortstop Brody Jones. They were the only married men on the team. The two hung out to show their unity. They were good for a couple hours, at the onset of the night. They would split when the coast cleared.

Halo had nodded to Ry on his arrival, but had yet to speak to him. Now was as good a time as any. Clutching his ice-cold beer, he pushed off his stool, and pressed flesh. The peanut bar was packed. Partiers continued to file in. No dress code. Women went skimpy. Board shorts on the bare-chested men. There was a lot of skin.

Baskets of shelled peanuts were offered to customers. Salty nuts that made everyone thirsty. Bar bills rose. The shells were shucked and tossed on the floor. They crunched underfoot. A corner jukebox played loudly. The oldies. "Whole Lotta Shakin' Goin' On" by Jerry Lee Lewis could barely be heard over the chatter and laughter. A life-size neon Elvis statue leaned against the vintage Wurlitzer. The skinny Elvis, not after he'd gained weight. Dartboards and pool tables drew customers to the back room.

The jukebox dropped a new record, and Creedance Clearwater Revival's "Bad Moon Rising" played. A chick with spiky blue hair who was drunk out of her skull fell into Halo. He steadied her with one hand. She wrapped her arms about him, went up on tiptoe, seeking a kiss.

"What the hell?" an angry male voice shouted in his ear. "Get your hands off Audrey."

Halo held up both hands, one with his beer, the other

open, palm out. "She knocked into me," he told the pissed off man. He wore a khaki work shirt with RON stitched over the pocket.

"I saw you grab her."

"You saw wrong, dude."

"You calling me a liar?" Ron's words were slurred.

"He's not, but we are," came from Landon. He stood on Halo's right. Zoo and Will now on his left. Game faces in place, they had Halo's back should the argument escalate.

Halo's accuser was not alone. Four men stuck by him, long-haired, narrowed-eyed, and built like bricks. Halo wasn't drunk enough to take pleasure in a fight. Still, Ron irritated the hell out of him.

The jerk's buddies came closer. The biggest, heaviest of the four poked Zoo in the chest. Halo had a bad feeling. Never poke a man who shrugged off life. Zoo was a six-foot-four death wish. He had a twice-broken nose, and looked more mixed martial arts fighter than ballplayer. His past was as dark as his expression. Bat-crap crazy ran in his blood.

Zoo's jaw worked now. He accepted the first jab from the man's middle finger with a sneer. *Do it again*, his expression challenged. The man took Zoo's dare. Socked him harder with his fist. Zoo grabbed his wrist, twisted, and the dude dropped. Like cement. He clutched his arm, crawled to his feet.

Time digested the incident. Breathing thinned. The crowd backed off. If a fight ensued, a misplaced punch could take out a bystander. Four ballplayers stood against five instigators. Anything could happen.

The woman who'd knocked into Halo had passed out on a nearby chair. Facedown on the table. She wasn't Halo's fight. He stared down her boyfriend. "Are we done here?" He kept his voice low, even. Giving the guy a chance to save face and back off.

"We're done if you're done."

Halo gave him a short nod. They parted ways.

"I'm blowing," said Will. "The Lusty Oyster's calling my name. What about you guys?"

"I'm gone. Let me grab the Reds," Zoo agreed, referring to his twins.

"I'm with you, too," said Landon. "I won our afternoon bets. You're in my debt, Will." He glanced at Halo. "You coming? Hank Jacoby just texted. He and Sam Matthews are on their way. They got a late start."

"They'll catch up." Of that Halo was certain. "I was headed to talk with Rylan before the confrontation. I'll sit for ten, then find you."

"Ry hired two stretch limos for the night. Chick chauffeurs. They'll get us to Boner's after the Oyster."

"Sounds good." A fist bump with Land, and Halo finished with, "Keep an eye on Zoo. He's had the taste of a fight. The littlest thing could set him off. No blood."

Land gave him a thumbs-up. Halo made it to Rylan's table without further mishap. "Take my chair," Brody offered. "It's past my bedtime." The big man from a small town in West Virginia finished off his beer, made his way to the door. He seemed relieved to leave.

Halo dropped down. He noticed Rylan's empty glass, and flagged down a barmaid. "Whiskey?" he asked.

Ry shook his head. "Coke."

"Make that a Coke and a club soda," Halo told the server. She left to fill their order.

Ry looked questioningly at him. "You're not drinking?"

"I had a beer earlier."

Rylan let it drop. "I saw your run-in," he continued. "I didn't recognize any of the guys. They're not from around here. I appreciate you not fighting. My cousin owns the bar. He'd hate to close for repairs. You guys never leave a table or chair standing. Only splinters and toothpicks remain. Damages are costly."

Halo shrugged. He'd initially wanted to flatten the son of a bitch, yet his conscience talked him down. He'd thought about Danny. The kid idolized him. Alyn was sweet. Gentle. How would he explain a black eye, bruised cheek, or broken jaw to them? No ballplayer wanted to start the season banged up. It wasn't worth it.

Ry shelled a peanut. "You've kept to yourself tonight."

"You've been watching me?"

"Someone has to." He popped the nut in his mouth, tossed the shell on the floor. "I heard you just pulled into town with your contest winner and two chaperones. A family affair."

A Landon broadcast. "My winner's eight. His mom's nice. His sister—"

"Is a total babe, according to Will."

His teammate would be right. Alyn was hot. And nice. It was her kindness and generosity that appealed to him most. She put others before herself. She kept track of Danny and took care of Quigley. She consulted and included her mother in all decisions.

He worried about people taking advantage of her. In Halo's mind, her previous boyfriend was a douche, and her business partner a criminal for wiping out her bank account. He would do his best not to let her down.

He rested his elbows on the table, admitted, "Alyn Jayne is a looker."

"Are you looking?"

"I've side-eyed her." A thousand times.

The barmaid brought their drinks; Halo paid for them.

"You tip bigger than anyone I know," said Ry.

Halo shrugged. "I make decent money."

"You're the—what?" Rylan scratched his head. "Third highest-paid right fielder in the league."

"Second," Halo corrected. He caught Ry's grin, and knew he'd been baited. Rylan knew exactly how much Halo earned compared to other players. Ry ranked first in center fielders. The Rogues were a highly competitive check-writing franchise. The organization paid their men well. The team paid the owners back with a solid season.

"It's a bonus year for you and Landon. High stakes," said Rylan. "Play hard, surpass last year's stats, and you'll bank a bundle."

It wasn't the money as much as proving to himself that he could focus and exceed expectations. It was do-or-die personal mission. One that started now. He needed to keep his act together, and get through the night without mishap.

"I hear you're in the best shape of your life."

Again from Landon. He shrugged. "I worked out some."

"You bought athletic training equipment, and hired a Pro-X handler. The company covers all bases of a sports-man's career. Fitness, nutrition, ambition. Three routines a day, each lasting ninety minutes."

Halo narrowed his gaze, stared at him. "Did you have a hidden camera at my warehouse?"

"I know Pro-X," Rylan confessed. "I used the company when I was traded from St. Louis to Richmond. I needed strength and body depth. They delivered."

Halo rolled his shoulders. "Their workouts were killer. I swore at my handler hourly. My muscles hurt so badly the first week, I invested in a small whirlpool tank. That helped some."

"The Pro-Xers are used to profanity," said Ry. "I had a few choice words myself."

"You, the dude who seldom gets mad, except at me?"

"You could tick off a priest."

"I have."

"You're getting your life in order."

Halo didn't get many compliments from Ry. "It's slow going."

"Fast doesn't stick. Keep at it. Steady wins."

He was working on it. But restlessness stirred his soul at the most inopportune moments. He could only contain it so long. Longevity was not his friend. Distraction his worst enemy.

Rylan rolled his iced glass between his palms. Thoughtful. "I wanted to personally extend my appreciation for your contribution to the Island Walk Project."

"What donation?" Halo played dumb.

"The six-figures you gave anonymously."

"Not me, dude."

"My sister says differently." Rylan was serious. "Shaye was blown away by your generosity. She's usually QT when it comes to private donations, but, in your case, she was out of her mind and had to tell someone. I just happened to be at the bank when she received your money transfer into her project account."

Rylan ate a few more peanuts, finished with, "Shaye's always envisioned a connecting foot bridge between Barefoot William and Shell Key. The island is small and barely a mile off shore. It's ideal for nature walks, shelling, and picnics. You can reach it by boat or Jet Ski, but not everyone has the means. The bridge will be a great addition. An ideal tourist attraction."

"I was glad to help. Keep this between us, okay? No one else needs to know."

"If that's what you want."

"Yeah, I do." Halo left it at that.

He stared across the thickening crowd. It was after eleven by the bar clock. Patrons continued to push through the door. It was standing room only around the dance floor. The noise made his ears ring.

Two sweet young things in tube tops and short-shorts navigated through the crowd to their table. Ben E. King's "Stand by Me" played on the jukebox, pressing couples together. Halo thought he recognized the girls from the previous season—they were townies, baseball groupies, and always in the bars. Their names both started with an "M." Misty, Missy, Marty, something like that. One now swayed to the music, while the other sang along. Badly. High-pitched and off key.

"Dance with me, Rylan," the taller of the two requested.

"Sorry, Mindy. I'm married now."

Not the answer she expected. "You consider dancing with another woman cheating on your wife?"

Halo had seen Mindy dance. She put the dirty in dirty dancing. Dry humping on the dance floor.

"It's a personal choice," said Ry, and left it at that.

"Your wife wouldn't know."

"I would."

Mindy stuck out her bottom lip, pouted. "Your loss."

No regrets for Rylan, Halo mused. There was no one like his wife, Beth. She was gorgeous, amazing, and fit right in with his household of dogs. That was no easy task.

The second girl came on to Halo. Her eyelids were heavy, and her words slightly slurred. She opened her arms, ready to embrace him. "Let's do it. Song's almost over."

A year ago, he would've been half-drunk himself. He'd have pulled her close, made out with her on the dance floor. Contemplated a quickie. Tonight, he feigned an excuse. "Groin pull, sorry."

The girl giggled. "Mindy's a massage therapist. She'll rub you."

Mindy nodded. "A massage you'd never forget."

Rylan had the balls to chuckle. He leaned back in his chair, amused by the exchange.

"Not tonight, but maybe tomorrow," said Halo, letting her down easy. The girls were getting persistent. He didn't want to make a scene. "No" seemed to piss women off. Made them more aggressive.

"The therapy office is closed on Sundays," said Mindy. "I have a two-fold portable massage table. I could come to you."

Halo nodded. "Good to know."

The girls left them then, weaving across the room on wobbly legs. It took them less than a minute to locate willing dancing partners. A second slow song drew twosomes together. Tightly. Kissing and roving hands came into play.

"Groin pull?" Rylan grinned.

"I ended last season with a pulled groin, and I had a sudden flare up," Halo said defensively.

Ry finished off his soda at the exact moment he received a text on his iPhone. He showed it to Halo. Halo laughed out loud. Ry's wife had sent a picture of their Great Dane Atlas standing before the front window, looking out at the night. His nose was pressed to the glass. The text read: *Waiting up for you.*

"Time to fly," said Rylan. He stood. "This is our year. World Series Trophy returns to Richmond. Let's make it happen."

Halo nodded his agreement. His own iPhone buzzed. A short text from Landon. *We're here, you're there.*

They'd have to wait a while longer. He had the sudden urge to drive by Barefoot Inn. The Jaynes were likely asleep, yet there was an off-chance Alyn might be walking Quigley. He could only hope the dog had wakened and needed to stretch his front legs.

It took him thirty minutes to make his way to the door. Women flirted with him and men offered to buy him a beer. He passed, going out of his way to be polite. He promised to buy a round for the house next time he was at the Blue Coconut. Freebies won them over. Hoots and cheers followed him into the parking lot.

Alyn Jayne stopped at the street corner, leaned over, and removed a pebble from her canvas shoe. The lamplight and half-moon softened the darkness. The scent of wet sand and salt air was strong. The sound of the surf soothing. She and Quigley walked alone, back and forth in front of the inn. Peaceful silence. Her pug was good company. She felt safe, but didn't wander far.

She scratched Quigs' ear, straightened, and was suddenly caught in the headlights of an oncoming, slow-moving vehicle. A big vehicle that rumbled, pulled over, and parked against the curb. A Hummer.

Her heart missed a beat when she recognized Halo Todd. Quigley barked excitedly, wiggling his body, and nearly tipping over his cart. She had no idea why Halo was driving by the inn at such a late hour, but she was genuinely glad to see him. She smiled when he reached them. "Guys' night out, and you're by yourself?" she questioned.

"I just left the Coconut and I'm, uh, taking the long way to the Oyster," he told her.

"Should you be driving?"

"No heavy drinking. Two beers. No more."

"You're here because?"

"Danny's my contest winner, and I feel responsible for your family. I came to check on you, and here you are. Walking around in the dark. You should have a flashlight. Whistle. Pepper spray."

Check on them? Hardly necessary. She put his concerns to rest. "Not so dark, Halo. There's automatic safety lighting at the entrance and stairs. Pole lights along the sidewalk. The moon."

That should've reassured him, but he didn't seem satisfied. He stared at her so intently, she felt exposed. She hadn't planned to bump into anyone on her night walk, and wished she'd taken more care. She hadn't worn a bra, and her small breasts bounced beneath the thin cotton top. Her terry cloth shorts sat low on her hips. Her navel was visible.

Halo appeared as uneasy as she was. Strange, to say the least. He never lacked conversation or confidence. Yet at that moment he appeared more little boy than adult male. She rather liked this side of him. More human than hero.

Quigley made a grumbling nose in his throat. He wanted his share of attention. Halo hunkered down beside her pug. "Quiggie Sparks, how's my boy?" He scratched the dog's chest.

His boy? Quigs liked the sound of that. His front paws pranced in place. "Quigley woke an hour ago." She brought Halo up to speed. "He scooted around the floor, feeling restless. A walk was the only answer."

"I understand restless," he said. "I'll walk with you."

"That's not necessary."

"It is for me." He'd made his choice. Enough said.

She wasn't certain how she felt. She'd witnessed first-hand the way women looked at him, all flirty and vying for his attention. The female manager of the villas on St. Simon's Island had shown them to their treehouse, then lingered and spoken privately with Halo. For a significant time. She'd slipped him a key card to a room other than his own. Had he used the key? Unknown.

Alyn's little toe was still sore from the tour guide at the drag racing museum stepping on her feet to reach him. Alyn had bitten her tongue, and not said a word. Halo had disapproved of the guide trampling her brother. The woman backed off.

The ladies in his life were defined as his past and present, but not his future. Alyn wanted more than a good time. She valued stability. Commitment. Forever. She'd been let down so many times in her life, she was perpetually wary. Trust did not come easy. Especially when it came to a man with a track record like Halo Todd's. He wasn't marriage material.

The spring training contest was a promotional event for the team. Halo was treating her family well. But at the end of the day, her time with him was temporary. She was no more than a chaperone. She'd be returning home in ten days. Her stomach sank at the thought. She tucked her feelings away, accepted what she couldn't change.

Halo took the dog leash from her, then held her hand. The transition was seamless. His grasp was strong, secure. They moved down the sidewalk. He shortened his steps, only to have Quiggie lengthen his own. The pug pulled with all his might, his front legs trotting. The wheels on his cart clipped along the sidewalk. One tire got stuck in a deep crack, and he worked himself free. Alyn praised him.

They reached the next corner, and were in full view of the beach. Moonlight sprinkled the white sugar sand. The ripples on the Gulf streamed like silver ribbons.

Alyn breathed in the moment. "It's so quiet. So beautiful."

"Want to cross the street?" he asked.

Her first thought was her dog. "Quigs can't navigate the sand."

"Got it covered," Halo said, dismissing her concern. He knelt down beside the pug, undid the straps, and then lifted him against his chest. Once secured, he scooped up the wheelchair with his free hand. "All set."

They made it across the road, and descended two wide wooden steps. She followed Halo to a stretch of compact sand. It was low tide, and the waves crawled in, crept out.

They stood side by side on the shoreline, taking in the night and each other.

Until Halo suggested, "We can sit if you want."

What was a little sand on the back of her legs, her butt? It would brush off. Quigley was a different story. Wet fur had a distinct smell. He'd need a bath if he got sandy.

Halo fixed the situation once again. He gently passed her Quiggie, then set down the cart. He undid his white button down, shrugged it off his shoulders. Big man, big shirt, he spread it on the sand. She now faced his big bare chest. Alyn stared, overly long. She couldn't help herself. Chiseled pecs. A brick-stacked abdomen. His male tiger line ran downward from his navel, dipping beneath his belt. The bulge behind his zipper was significant.

Quigley wriggled against her chest. She was holding him too tightly. She eased down on the shirt before her knees buckled. Buttons poked the back of her thigh, leaving small circular imprints. Halo lowered himself beside her. They sat so close, she was fully conscious of him. His body heat was warmer than the night. She set Quigley between them. The pug sniffed the air, attempting to inhale every new scent, all at one time.

Halo leaned back on his elbows and stretched out his long legs. Sand dusted his jeans. "Comfortable?" he asked her.

Jumpy, fidgety, might better describe her, she thought. She tried to relax. Wasn't successful. She wondered how many other women he'd brought to the beach. Did they end up at his spring training apartment? Sex until sunrise?

A sandy dampness sneaked through the cotton of his shirt, but she didn't complain. "I'm great," she said instead. "This is a first for me."

"Me, too," he admitted. "I've never brought a girl to the beach at"—he looked at his watch—"midnight."

"It's been a long day."

"Longer night. I'm thinking bed sooner than later."

She could picture him on a mattress. His hair mussed, his breathing heavy, a sheen to his skin. Naked, and primed for orgasm. Sure-fire satisfaction. Sated and languid.

Sex. She blushed at the thought, which was both frightening and exciting. She'd been overwhelmed by his kiss at the game show. Spontaneous and with tongue. A ten-second turn-on. An hour with the man and she would shatter. Might never recover. She was fractured enough.

"Your thoughts?" He rolled onto his side, still raised on one elbow. He scratched Quigley's ear. The dog yawned, already half asleep.

"Nothing's on my mind," she hedged. Nothing she could discuss with him, anyway.

He eyed her closely, then grinned knowingly. Maddeningly. "Dilated pupils, parted lips, pointed nipples. You're not at the beach, babe, you're in my bed."

Pointed nipples? That hit her the hardest. She lowered her gaze, saw what Halo saw. She couldn't claim it was cold outside. It had to be seventy degrees. Her sex-thought left visible imprints. She poked the thin cotton.

She groaned. Then flapped the hem, puffing it out and away from her breasts. Only to have it settle once again on her chest like a second skin. More pointing.

"Much better," said Halo, his grin far too wide and way too wicked.

She'd only made it worse. She ignored the outline of her breasts, and hoped Halo would, too. He did not. His gaze lingered long and hot. Penetrating. Her stomach fluttered. She pressed her inner thighs together, as discreetly as possible. Inched her bottom away from him.

Halo reached across Quigley, curved his wide hand over

her knee. Squeezed. "I brought you here to breathe, Alyn. To get to know you better. Not to have you tighten up and move away from me."

She exhaled so fast, she blew raspberries. Halo chuckled. He was slow to release her. Two of his fingers lingered on her thigh, lightly stroking. "You have very soft skin."

This said by a man with the hardest body of anyone she'd ever met. She was glad she'd shaved her legs during her shower. Applied lotion. "Now you know something about me that you didn't realize before."

"That I do." His hand slid away, settled back on Quigs. He massaged the dog to sleep. "I like your brother, Danny. He talked a lot about your father on the trip south. He really misses him."

"We all do." She sighed. "It's heartbreaking for my mother to spend time in the greenhouse, once my dad's sanctuary. She sees him everywhere. She'll return again, when she's ready. My father died so suddenly. There were no good-byes."

"Same with my old man." His words came slowly, choppily. The sharpness of his cheekbones was made more prominent by the muscle ticking in his jaw. Alyn listened as he spoke of their relationship. The arguments that caused more grief than good. The older man's eventual heart attack. The fact his mother blamed him.

She took it all in, uncertain of what to say when he'd finished. "I'm sorry. I wish things had been different for you," she managed. "My dad was my champion. Every time I got shoved down, he gave me a hand up. He never let me lose sight of my goals. Opening a vintage store topped my bucket list."

"You'll have your shop, and you'll be successful," Halo said optimistically. "A professional ballplayer only has so many good years. I'd thought about returning to the lumberyard when I retired. Working beside my dad wouldn't have been half bad. But I never got the chance. Instead I bought the warehouse."

"What does a man do with a warehouse?"

"He lives there."

"Oh . . ." She tried to picture his home, but saw no more than a big, vacant building.

"I have a forklift."

"That should impress your dates."

"It doesn't."

"Danny would be out of his mind."

"I'll have to show it to him sometime."

Sometime. Alyn wondered when that might be. Once he returned to Richmond after pre-season? A year from now? She wouldn't mention anything to her brother. She didn't want to get his hopes up. "He'd like that," was all she said.

"So," he broached. "Do you permanently live with your mom?"

"I had my own apartment before my dad died." She dug one hand in the sand, let the white grains filter through her fingers. Sighed. "Bad things often occur in threes, in my case, fours. I lost my father, my business partner stole from our joint business account, I got dumped by my boyfriend, and Quigley got hit by a car. Danny's yet to forgive himself."

"He will, once Quigs walks again."

"I'm hoping so."

A tiny shell stuck between her fingers, broken down the middle with uneven edges. It reminded her of herself. She went on to reflect. "Life flattened me for a short time, but I'm standing again. My previous partner and I never had a permanent retail location. We advertised and sold refurbished pieces from two rental units. The space was costly, and my bank account dwindled. I closed one unit, and moved half the furniture home. It's crowded, but my mom hasn't complained."

"You have plastic on your couches."

"To protect them. Danny spills soda and drips ice cream."

"You've enough lamps to light Richmond."

"The brighter the better."

"All those mirrors."

"I caught you looking at yourself."

"I was checking you out. I liked what I saw."

"I'm not much to look at." Stated as fact; she wasn't fishing for a compliment.

"You're more than you know, babe."

Nice of him to say, but she didn't believe it. She was the woman of the moment, sitting beside him on the beach. It was extremely late. She tossed the shell aside and stared out at the Gulf. The water was dark, dappled by moonlight. Quigley snored softly between them. Her pug looked so comfortable, she hated to move him.

Small talk. Halo next asked, "Have you lived in Richmond all your life?"

She nodded. "Born and raised."

"Me, too. Odd we never ran into each other over the years."

"It's a big city."

"I've found you now."

"No, I found you," she corrected him. "On the sidewalk outside Jacy's Java."

He chuckled low. His dimples, deep. "I went in for a double espresso, and came out to a chicken."

"We never did see the show air."

"I have connections, and can get a copy of the tape if you really want to watch it."

She wondered if he'd call Alex or Natalie the model.

Natalie would offer more than the tape. "Thanks, but no thanks. It's not worth reliving."

"I agree." Halo sat up then. He kept one leg straight and bent the other, resting his elbow on his knee. "What do you do when you're not a chicken?" he asked, genuinely interested. "When you're not collecting antiques?"

"Spare time is spent with my family," she told him. "Growing up, I assisted my dad in the greenhouse. He had a green thumb, but most everything I touched turned brown. Still, he welcomed my help. I like movies, double-features. Buckets of popcorn. Big jigsaw puzzles. Reading. Quigley's become a top priority. He pretty much goes wherever I do." She cut him a glance. "How about you?"

"Action keeps me sane," he said. "I'm flammable as hell, and sports burn energy. If I'm not playing baseball, I'm shooting hoops. Jogging. Working out. I'm not good at sitting still."

"You're sitting with me now."

"Your calm rubbed off on me."

"Not me, the beach. It's restful and relaxing. Although you should be with your teammates."

"I talked with most of the guys at the Blue Coconut early on. I'll check on them before last call at Boner's."

The players didn't wait for Halo to check on them, they began texting him. His iPhone rang with four consecutive posts. Long and detailed. He ran one hand down his face, relaying to her, "Will was playing darts, and didn't wait for Jake to retrieve his round from the board. Will darted our first baseman in the ass. Jake retaliated, threw one back. Nailed Will in the thigh."

"That had to hurt."

Halo frowned. "They've had a lot to drink by now, so aren't feeling any pain. Hank Jacoby invited one of the female limo drivers to breakfast. She dropped the players at

Boner's, then drove him to Scramblers, an all-night diner. They've yet to return. The team's one limo short. Sam Matthews passed out in a booth. The chick he picked up got pissed, and took a permanent marker to his cheeks. Shit. Sam now has cat whiskers. Will's calling him pussy face."

That didn't sound good.

His brow creased with concern. "Son of a bitch," he muttered. "The guys lost Landon outside the Oyster." He closed his eyes for half a second. Opened them. "I need to find him."

"Go, then," she encouraged. In one continuous motion, she collected Quigs and stood. Her pug was all warmth and snuggles. They brought comfort to each other.

Halo scooped up his shirt, shook it out, and slipped it on. Buttoned up. Then grabbed the dog's wheelchair. "I would've liked to sit a while longer," he said as they trooped across the sugar sand. He sounded as if he meant it.

"The beach isn't going anywhere."

They walked in silence. Each holding his and her own thoughts. Alyn was leaning toward sleep and Halo needed to track down his best friend.

They soon reached the inn. He walked her up the sidewalk, assisted her onto the porch. "See you upstairs?" he asked.

"We're good from here."

He handed her the cart. Stood at her side. Both her hands were occupied when he made his move, careful not to disturb her dog. But she wouldn't have pushed him away, even if her hands were free.

The warmth of his palm settled on her shoulder as his fingers brushed back her hair. Leaning in, he kissed her neck softly, slowly. All warm breath and scratch of stubble.

Her eyelids grew heavy.

Pure sensation. Prickles, tingles, a rash of goose bumps.

An undisguised shiver. *More*, she silently sighed, but got less.

Halo eased back. "Sleep sweet." And he was gone. Before she even opened her eyes.

Arousal shared her bed.

Seven

Last call at the Lusty Oyster, and Landon Kane stood outside the bar. Hands in his pockets. Face to the sky. Breathing deeply. He was in need of fresh air. He had a major buzz going, and hoped to clear his head. Even a little. Two of his teammates were stumble drunk. His own eyes were blurry. He blinked to bring the street into focus.

The morning hour would take him to Boner's. A bar beyond the city limits that tipped the scale on cheap booze and loose morals. He decided to loop in, loop out. Sleep was suddenly more important than another six-pack.

He crossed his arms over his chest, wrinkling his blue button-down. Then scuffed his short boots on the sidewalk. Where was their limousine? he wondered, scanning the street. One vehicle had already left. A second should be parked in the general vicinity. He just couldn't locate it. Shit.

The bar door swung wide, and stayed open as after-hour singles became couples. Despite being paired up, women still winked, grinned, and openly flirted with him as they walked by. A brunette took his hand, raised her eyebrows, willing to dump the guy she was with for him. Land shook his head. It wasn't going to happen. There would be no woman in his life tonight.

Or so he thought, until a black Porsche stopped at the

red light on the corner. It was an eye-catcher. Everyone on the sidewalk stared. Including him.

Land knew his classics; he was a collector. The 1965 coupe 911 was undeniably one of his favorites. Moonlight shimmered on its polished surface. Reflected off the windshield. The sunroof was open, and Jon Bon Jovi's "Livin' on a Prayer" rose on the night air.

He looked closer, checked out the driver. Damn if he didn't know her. It was Eden Cates, with her wild hair and quirky glasses. He wondered why she was out at this hour. Alone. Driving a hot car on a main party strip.

The traffic light turned green, and she crossed through the intersection, cruising slowly, toward him. Her window rolled down, and she lowered the radio. She blocked traffic. Her glasses sat low on her nose, and she stared at him over the rainbow rims. "O'Rourke, is that you?"

He couldn't help but grin. She'd called him by his cardboard cutout. "It's me, Marilyn," he responded in kind, unreasonably glad to see her. He stepped into the street, and approached her vehicle. "I missed my ride to Boner's." He held out his thumb, as if hitchhiking. "Going my way?"

"Not to Boner's."

"Where then?"

"Home."

Her place, why not? "Works for me." Anywhere was better than standing on the street corner. "Offer me a cup of coffee and I'll be your best friend."

"I already have a best friend."

"Just coffee then?"

How much thought had to go into his question? Yet she took her sweet time responding. Behind them now, a man in a mini-van lay on his horn. Eden needed to move. "Okay, fine," she finally agreed. "Hop in."

He was inside before she could change her mind. He dropped on the seat, placed his feet on the floor mat. He inhaled the scent of aging leather and appreciated the original wood of the dash and rimmed steering wheel. He hand-rolled down his window, rested his elbow on the edge. "Nice ride. Yours?" he asked her.

She drove barefoot, he noticed. A gold ankle bracelet flashed when she pushed in the clutch and shifted gears. Her black dress slid above her knee when she released it. Her thighs were toned, lightly tanned. Easy on his eyes.

She rounded the block before answering, "My cousin Zane restores vintage cars in his spare time."

"Zane, the hurricane hunter?" Rylan spoke of his brother often. Zane was with the Air Force Reserve 53rd Weather Reconnaissance Squadron, based at Keesler Air Force Base in Biloxi, Mississippi.

She nodded. "He worked on Geddes for a year. The car was a rusted, dented frame pulled from the junkyard. She's all original parts. A true beauty now."

Eden had christened her car. Somehow that didn't surprise him. It took him a moment to place the name. *Anne Geddes.* He was disbelieving when he asked, "You named your Porsche after a baby photographer?" Her sports car was high-end luxury. He owned one himself. A later model. Geddes was not a fitting name. Or so he thought. "The woman takes pictures of babies in flowerpots and chocolate Easter eggs. Wrapped in lettuce."

Her chin went up and her words were clipped. "I admire her talent. She takes emotional photos that go beyond their individual elements."

Great. He'd ticked her off. He made amends. "My sister has an Anne Geddes calendar." Twelve months of vegetable infants hung next to the refrigerator. "I got choked up over the baby peas in a pod."

"No, you didn't."

She would be right. "Photography's subjective," he said.

"I like action shots. Especially in sports. A runner taking a hurdle. A swimmer off the starting block. A basketball player making a jump shot. A hockey player shooting the puck. A race car burnout. A perfect click of the camera stops time."

She glanced his way. "Sounds intense. Do you shoot?"

"I've taken a few photos, now and again." Quite often, actually. Becoming a professional ballplayer had topped his list of ambitions as a kid. Sports photography came in a close second. Preserving athletes and events on film fascinated him. Their expressions, musculature, told a story. An underdog's struggle to become success. A star's tragic moment of defeat. The ultimate win.

Landon drifted with the night. He relaxed deeper in the seat as they cruised the main beach road. The sunroof opened to a partial moon. Numerous stars. The occasional streetlight. He was a day person who found nighttime challenging. His teammates came alive after midnight. Land functioned best on eight hours of sleep.

He turned slightly, asked Eden, "Why are you out so late?"

"I was at a wedding shower for one of my girlfriends. Time got away from us."

"Partying?"

"Not in the way you were tonight."

"I'm not drunk."

"You've never spoken more than a few words to me on your own. I think Land Shark's talking for you."

Whoa. "You know my brand of beer?"

"You and Halo Todd were drinking Land Shark at Rylan's backyard picnic last year."

Lady had one hell of a memory or perhaps she'd been more into him than he'd initially imagined. "You were watching me?" he asked.

"I was seated on a lawn chair near the metal ice bucket. You and Halo Todd were discussing fast cars and super-heroes. You hit the watering hole hard."

They'd drunk their fair share of beer. He'd noticed her, too, from the corner of his eye. Wild ponytail, big sunglasses, and a continual smile. Sipping pink lemonade. He remembered her graphic T-shirt designed with small puzzle pieces. His teammate Jake Packer had stood before her overly long, staring at her chest, trying to fit the parts together. Jake never had figured it out. Landon immediately recognized the image as the Eiffel Tower. The observation deck rounded her right nipple.

He hadn't spoken a single word to her at the picnic. Their second meeting at the boardwalk flower show hadn't gone much better. She put him on edge. He didn't like being at a disadvantage.

He yawned, rested his eyes, and she tapped the brake. Jarring him. "No passing out," she said.

"Not even close." He was wide-eyed now. He concentrated on the street signs. He knew the basic layout of the town. But didn't recognize Sandpiper Boulevard or Starfish Way. She turned off the main road, heading east, away from the beach. Driving rural. The two-lane road was paved, but bumpy. Palm and cypress trees flanked the sides. Low-hanging branches made a grab for the Porsche. She eluded them.

"Where to?" They'd been on the back road for fifteen minutes now.

"You'll see."

He soon did. Another five, and the woods parted to a small clearing, stalked by vegetation. The Porsche tripped a security system, and flood lights pushed back the darkness at the front of the property. She pulled in, and parked. Killed the engine. Hopped out. Motioned for him to follow her.

He sat tight. For the moment, anyway. He stuck his head out the window, looked around. There was no sign of a house or trailer. Not even a tent. Only the beginning of a stone walkway. Eden had already disappeared down the path.

Where had she gone? Alone in the woods didn't sit well with him. She might be Rylan's cousin, but Landon barely knew her. He hadn't taken her for psycho, but she was quirky. Did she like to scare people? This was the perfect setup for her to jump out of the bushes or sneak up behind him. He was big and strong, and basically fearless. Still, he didn't like being fooled or played. Not when he could avoid it.

He got out of the Porsche, stretched. Then followed the trail of stones, listening for sounds. Crickets. Frogs. A creepy bird. The change in his pocket jingled. Quarters to feed the jukebox at Blue Coconut. Maybe he should drop a few coins to find his way back. He let two dollars' worth slip.

The path curved, and dim spotlights brought a tall, latticework arch into view, one woven with vines. When he ducked under, dead leaves crunched beneath his shoes. A small wooden cottage with a steeply-pitched roof was dead ahead. A heavy, scrolled metal sign hung to the left of the entrance: WEDDING CHAPEL.

What the—? It took a minute for his destination to soak in. Why would she bring him here? he wondered. Weird as hell.

The door creaked, and Eden appeared. "Coffee's made," she told him. The scent of dark roast crooked a finger and drew him inside. "Welcome to my home." She stepped back, let him enter.

"You live in a wedding chapel?" His surprise was evident.

"People no longer get married here," she explained,

"not for a long time anyway. William Cates founded Bare-foot William in 1906. He met his wife in southwest Florida, and had the chapel built for their ceremony. Many Cateses and future townspeople followed in his footsteps. Eventually, the town outgrew the tiny church, and a larger one was built."

He appreciated the history. She continued with, "So-phie Cates, Dune's wife, is the local historian and museum curator. We came across the chapel a few years ago when we were documenting old buildings. Weathered and di-lapidated, the church had long since witnessed its last wed-ding and heard its last sermon. Still"—she gave a soft sigh—"I fell in love with the place. I asked Shaye if I could renovate it as a home. She agreed, but only after I took countless photos for posterity. My cousin Aidan's a con-tractor. He did the work, leaving as many original boards and beams as possible."

Land took it all in. The chapel wrapped him in days gone by. Impressive high ceilings and soaring white walls were balanced by worn, wood floors. Stained-glass win-dows surrounded the small raised sanctuary. Wall sconces shed light. An ancient upright piano pressed against one wall.

The old and the new. Pretty cool. He followed Eden down a narrow center aisle between several rows of refur-bished pews. She ran her hand over the smooth wood. "We were able to save six."

Just beyond, a modern black leather sofa and glass oval coffee table angled toward an entertainment center and computer pull-out desk. A compact combination.

Then there were the framed photographs. Hundreds of them. Floor to ceiling, they covered every inch of wall space. Eden saw his eyes widen and said, "I shoot more than cutout portraits. I've also restored old pictures of

William Cates and early family members. The growth of the town, past to present day."

Landon moved closer to one wall. He didn't recognize anyone in the black-and-white photos. They dated back to the Model-T and railroads. To a time when the board-walk had only three stores and industry centered on com-mercial fishing.

Moving farther along the wall, he came across a picture of Rylan as a boy, playing tee-ball. Then Shaye and her grandfather Frank on the pier. Aidan building a tree house showed his childhood skills as a contractor. The photo-graphs brought a warmth to the chapel. Told the story of lives intertwined, and the way the Cateses had prospered.

He scratched his jaw; there was someone missing here. He cut Eden a look. "Who takes your picture?" he asked her.

"I don't photograph well."

"You looked good as Marilyn Monroe."

"My hair was in my eyes and I was behind a cardboard cutout."

"I liked it."

Her brow creased. Color rose in her cheeks. His words seemed to confuse her. "Beer goggles."

"I'm not drunk, Eden," he told her straight. "I've never used booze as an excuse for my words or actions."

Their eyes met, and she drew a deep breath. "Me, ei-ther."

"You don't drink at all, do you?" He had her figured out.

"I enjoy a glass of champagne on special occasions."

"There's lots of joy and happiness within these walls. You have an unusual home," he admired as they crossed the sanctuary and entered the kitchen. A square, two-person space at best.

"This used to be the chaplain's office," she informed him. "Aidan constructed a small kitchen."

Miniscule, actually. He noted the slim-line refrigerator and compact two-burner stove. There was very little counter space. Barely room for the toaster, electric can opener, and Mr. Coffee. No microwave, trash compactor, or dishwasher. The closet door was cracked, and he caught sight of a stackable washer-dryer.

The peaked window over the sink was dotted with pastel Mason jars and vintage glass. She'd planted herbs in tiny galvanized pots. None of her cupboards had doors. Everything was visible at a glance. She kept things neat. She poured his coffee into a ceramic photo mug. Passed it to him. Land studied the action shot. It showcased Rylan scaling the center field wall in order to catch a fly ball.

"I remember that game." Ry's heroics were legendary. "We played Tampa Bay in late July. It was a hundred-ten degrees on the field, and the heat beat us down. We felt fried. Bottom of the ninth, and Rogues led by one. Rays took their bat, landed two men on base. Two outs followed. Then their third baseman drilled a fastball to center. It appeared over the wall to those of us in the dugout. Rylan jumped blind against the sun's glare. So high, we swore he had jet packs in his shoes. He caught the ball. Saved our win."

"I was at the game," she said. "I was in Tampa looking at new camera equipment. Ry got me a ticket. I screamed so loud, I was hoarse the next day." She filled her mug with coffee. A mug with a photograph of Atlas, Ry's Great Dane. The big dog had a large branch in his mouth. "Atlas helped a tree removal service take out a cypress hit by lightning," she explained. "Cream or sugar?" she next asked.

"Black's fine."

She added a few drops of low-fat milk to her own.

"Stand or sit?" she questioned.

"I'm fine standing." She didn't have a table or chairs. There was no need to return to the living room and get comfortable. He wouldn't be here that long. He did have a question for her though, "Where do you eat?"

"I have TV trays."

Interesting life style, he thought. He liked different. She was definitely unique. He kept their conversation light. "Rogues have several events coming up. Bonfire tomorrow night."

"I'll be taking pictures."

"I'm looking forward to the charity Dog Jog next weekend. Proceeds benefit the no-kill animal shelter."

"I'm participating."

"So is the team. Not all of us have dogs, so we'll choose from the shelter. Hopefully, once they're presented in the race, they'll get adopted."

"Rylan mentioned entering Atlas."

"The Dane could win a horse race."

Eden smiled. "Ry will be fair. He'll hold him back, give everyone a chance."

"Dog or cat person?" Land was curious.

The corners of her mouth turned down. "I had one of each. Old age took them. Animals never live long enough."

"I agree. My parents have a geriatric black Lab, Leopold. Leo gets around, but there are times he sleeps the day away."

He sipped his coffee, remembered, "I can't forget Media Day on Monday. We introduce our contest winners to the press. Reporters want us to predict our upcoming season. Then a few personal questions."

"Personal . . ." The corners of her mouth twitched. "I have a couple."

He shrugged. "Float your boat, sweetheart. Ask away."

She immediately questioned his intellect. "What was the last novel, picture, or comic book you've read?"

She took him for a dumb jock. "*The Martian,* by Andy Weir," he said. "A dust storm, an astronaut left for dead who actually lives—great science fiction."

Her eyes rounded. "It was a *New York Times* bestseller."

"I'm not allowed to read bestsellers?"

"That's not what I meant," she assured him. "I'm surprised, that's all. I've read it, too. I'm a fan of survival."

"For the record, the only comics I read are Sunday funnies."

"I like Dilbert."

"Doonesbury."

She topped off their coffee mugs before asking, "Is your world more free-wheeling or frustrating?"

He pinched the bridge of his nose between his thumb and forefinger. "Frustrating tonight," was damn sure. "Rylan supplied us with two limousines, for safety's sake. I caught the limo from Blue Coconut to Lusty Oyster. Then a girl grabbed me at the door as I was leaving the Oyster and wouldn't let go. Woman had a grip. She swore we dated last spring and wanted to start up where we left off. I remember the ladies I've been with, and she wasn't one of them. By the time I cut her loose, the limo was gone."

"I can't believe the guys forgot you."

"I can. They were having too good a time and weren't keeping count of who was with them, who was not." He grinned at her then. "I'm glad you came along."

"Someone would've offered you a ride."

"But not to a wedding chapel."

"It's quiet out here. Perfect for one."

"What about a second person?"

She looked amused. "You asking to move in?"

"Not today," was his elusive response. He let it hang. "Give me some notice so I can make room for you."

She thought he was teasing. Maybe he was, maybe he wasn't. He honestly didn't know. He left the door open. For some unknown reason.

She drank her coffee; eyed him over the rim of the mug. Went on to ask, "What fascinates you most?"

No hesitation. "The universe."

"Vast, Landon."

"A simple sunrise."

Artistically, she understood. "The promise of a new day, all painted in red, orange, pink, and gold. There's no place like the beach at dawn. The colors reflect on the water, and you get a dual-image photograph."

"I'll head to the boardwalk one morning."

"The boardwalk stirs early. Brews Brothers has a strong, dark, wake-up blend. Bakehouse makes the best dough-nuts. They have a fresh fruit-filled breakfast pastry that's amazing. Strawberry's the best. I buy them by the bakery box."

"Motivation to get up."

"Locals know to arrive early."

She offered him a drop more coffee, but he waved her off. He was clearheaded now. He was having a decent time. Which he'd only admit to himself. Perhaps he'd stay a few more minutes. No longer.

She fidgeted a little with a drawer near the sink that was slightly ajar, opening and reclosing it. Surely she wasn't nervous around him. At least no more than he was with her. She kept his pulse up. Left his stomach tight. In a good way.

She glanced at him from the corner of her eye. "Last time you were inspired?"

He didn't have to think long. "I'm inspired by people who pull their lives together after injury or illness. I do hospital visits on non-game days. Last fall, an orthopedist at Richmond Memorial asked me to stop by the rehabilitation center and meet a boy named Noah, an eighteen-year-old high school wrestler with both collegiate and Olympic potential. Until he went on his senior trip to Cabo San Lucas."

"A Mexican playground for graduates."

"Been there. Done it all. It can get wild. According to his doctor, Noah partied, but he was also responsible. One afternoon he and a couple friends rented WaveRunners at the marina. Noah sat second on the watercraft. His driver was cautious. However his buddies on the second Jet Ski raced around, raising hell, taking chances. An accidental sharp turn, and the two collided. Hard. Noah's watercraft flipped; came down on him. He nearly died."

Eden put her palm over her heart. "Oh . . . no."

"Noah's father is CEO at the hospital. He's well-connected. He chartered a plane with medical staff and flew his son back to the States in record time. Concussion, dislocated shoulders, broken arm, ribs, and both legs. After several major surgeries, he started to mend. He's slowly regained his memory. His speech is improving."

Her eyes welled and she swallowed hard. "Thank goodness."

"The day I dropped by the center, Noah recognized me. He follows the Rogues. He was about to take his first steps, using short parallel bars. The physical therapist positioned me at the opposite end. I encouraged Noah to go the distance. I gave him incentive."

"A bribe?" Eden was curious.

"More or less. I bargained my Rogues baseball cap and jersey if he got halfway through the bars. Then tossed in six home-game tickets if he made it to me."

She held her breath. "He did, didn't he?"

"A super struggle that took him nearly an hour, but he

got there. With clenched jaw and white knuckles. Some swearing." He finished off his coffee, set the mug in the sink. "We went to lunch in the cafeteria that day, celebrating. I pushed his wheelchair, and he wore my cap and jersey. One of the therapists lent me a medical scrub top. Noah ate two cheeseburgers and fries. I've returned twice to catch his progress. He uses a cane, but can walk on his own now. We stay in touch. He once wanted to become part of the World Wrestling Federation. Doubtful now. He starts college soon. He's smart, and eyeing a business major."

"I'm so glad he recovered. I had a close friend in a similar situation. A water skiing accident. He didn't fare as well. His funeral was last week." She sighed, her expression sad, right before she hugged him spontaneously. Coffee splashed from her mug onto his shirt. A minor stain. His story touched her. His had a happy ending. Hers had not.

He widened his stance, and she stepped even closer. She fit him. He held her gently; stroked her hair, her back. Until she calmed. He had the strange urge to comfort her. To kiss the top of her head, her brow, the tip of her nose. While his intent was honest, he instinctively knew those kisses would lead to something more. They'd just started a dialogue. He hoped to keep it going. Slow worked best for him.

For her, too, apparently. He curved his hand about her neck, tipped up her chin with his thumb, and felt her skin warm against his palm. She was embarrassed by her show of emotion. "You okay?" he asked. Wiping away her tears with his shirt sleeve.

"Dreams and bodies broken." Her words were watery. "The world can be harsh." She eased back, noticed the splatter. "Sorry about that."

"Coffee stains come out. No big deal."

She stifled a yawn, covering her mouth with the back of her hand.

"You tired of me?"

"It's not you. I'm sleep deprived."

"I'm keeping you up." He glanced at his watch, couldn't believe it was four a.m. "What time do you get up?"

"Five."

"An hour's sleep isn't much."

"I manage on very little."

He reached for his smartphone, and immediately noticed there were a dozen texts from Halo. All asking where he was and who he was with. He sent a quick message. *Headed home,* and left it at that.

"Name of a cab company I can call?" he asked her.

"Where are you staying?"

"Driftwood Inn." He'd moved his clothes and important items into the team's hotel near the stadium. The inn was comfortable, with all amenities. Meals, housekeeping, laundry, spa, anything the men required. Landon appreciated the masseuse the most. He'd scheduled a standing appointment every afternoon following practice. Wind-down time.

"I can take you," she offered.

"And miss your hour's sleep? No way," he teased her. "I don't want you dropping me off and driving back alone."

"I drive alone a lot."

"You need a mannequin or Teddy bear in the passenger seat so it looks like someone's with you. Much safer."

"I'll keep that in mind." She scrunched her nose, said, "Try Shoreline Taxi, owned and operated by my cousin Brent."

"Cateses are everywhere."

"It is our town."

Landon made the call. He was told a cab was in the vicinity and to be outside the wedding chapel in five minutes. "Will my coming out of your cottage have people talking?" he asked.

"Who's up at this hour to gossip?"

"What about the taxi driver?"

"He'll want to talk baseball, not about me."

He turned to leave, and she was right behind him. Following him down the aisle and to the door. He glanced over his shoulder, then said, "I have a question for you. When were you last wrong?"

"Tonight. About you." The words seemed difficult for her to say. "You're different than I expected."

"Is that good or bad?"

"I'll let you know at the bonfire," was all she would give him. "Don't stand too close to the flames."

He didn't need his marshmallows roasted.

"I see you made it home all right last night," Eden said to Landon as they stood a good distance from the bonfire that was burning north of the pier. This was no small campfire. More a significant signal fire that could be seen miles out in the Gulf. Firemen and a truck monitored the blaze.

"Halo met me in the parking lot," Landon relayed. "He'd been out looking, and couldn't find me. He read me the riot act. Worse than a father."

"It's good to have a friend who cares about you."

"You're right about that."

"Where's your contest winner?" she asked.

"Eleanor Norris needed to use the ladies room. Shaye walked her to the boardwalk facilities." He ran one hand down his face. "For ninety, she sure is chatty. She informed me of all her ailments and medications and gave me emergency contact numbers should something happen to her."

"Did she travel alone?"

"She came with her walking cane, Herman. Named after her late husband. She talks to the cane, as if it was a person."

"I talk to my Porsche."

"Does Geddes talk back?"

She shook her head. "No."

"The cane speaks only to Eleanor and she responds."

"So you can't hear it?"

"Not yet, but maybe by the end of the week."

"Good luck with that."

"Thanks."

Eden took a moment and looked around, absorbing the atmosphere. She made mental notes on lighting and angles. The types of shots she wanted to take. The bonfire was as private an activity as could occur on a public beach. Yellow tape circled the area. Her cousin Rylan had introduced her to everyone, even those she already knew. He was considerate. Wanting her to feel comfortable at the event. She'd exhaled. Relaxed.

The Rogues starting lineup was out in force. All except Sam Matthews. Apparently the cat whiskers drawn on his face with permanent marker at Boner's were still visible, even after a hard scrubbing. He refused to draw attention to himself. His winner didn't mind. The sixty year old elementary school crossing guard from small town Wytheville, Virginia, took Sam's absence in stride, and hung out with pitcher Will Ridgeway and the disabled veteran.

The attending ballplayers were personable and accommodating to their contest winners. Everybody seemed to be having a good time. Smiles and laughter. Lots of interaction.

The flames danced against the twilight, casting fiery color on the people, across the sand, and into the Gulf. "Your community liaison asked me to take some pictures," she said to Land. "I need to mingle."

"Jillian likes to mark the moment. Stop back when you're done," he requested. "We need to continue our conversation from last night."

The fact he wanted to talk with her further made her smile. "Will do, but it could be a while."

"I'm not going anywhere."

Camera bag hooked over her shoulder, Nikon in hand, she walked away from the best-looking man at the bonfire. His freshly creased Florida print shirt and board shorts did him justice. He was pure beach heat.

Over the next hour, she strolled around the fire, capturing the event. She avoided the posers, Zoo in particular, preferring honest, unguarded shots when people weren't looking.

She moved toward the turquoise lifeguard stand, focusing on Halo Todd and the Jaynes. They gathered beneath the structure, at the cement base. Halo rested one hand on the young boy's shoulder, brushed arms with his sister, and conversed at length with their mother.

He hunkered down every so often to pet Alyn's disabled pug in his handicap cart. No dogs were allowed on the beach. But diapered Quigley wasn't an issue. Quigs barked whenever Halo scratched his ears.

Eden knew Halo only by reputation. The man was hard-edged handsome, and impatient to a fault. Rumors said his relationships were quick and easy. His women, replaceable.

What a difference a year made. The right fielder had acted crazy and immature the previous season. Had thought only of himself. He was calm at the moment. Not the outrageous jerk who'd once made Rylan cringe.

Halo concentrated on the boy, yet his gaze strayed to Alyn. Repeatedly. The camera lens didn't lie. Eden photographed their souls. Halo showed more than a casual regard. *Family man* crossed her mind, as she shot several frames. She believed Halo's interest in the pretty brunette was genuine.

Only time would tell how long it would last. Perhaps Alyn would bring out the best in him. Eden could only hope so. Even from a distance, she sensed Alyn's vulnerability. Her body language spoke volumes, in the way she dipped her head, half-smiled, and didn't fully commit to the conversation. It was obvious she had been burned by someone or some situation. Surely Halo was smart enough not to let her down. Not to break her heart.

Eden went on to photograph the catering cart, rolled onto the sand by several husky guys. The opportunity to roast hot dogs and toast marshmallows had arrived. The person in charge passed out long, forked metal skewers. Those wanting to eat gathered near the lower flames.

An hour passed, and she slowly worked her way toward Landon. His back was to her. She watched Eleanor tuck her arm through his, wink, and say, "If only I was sixty years younger."

To which Land replied, "Or I was sixty years older."

The older woman sighed. "You're kind, Landon."

"And truthful. You're still a looker."

Her wrinkles faded into her smile. "How do you like my new T-shirt?" she asked. "I used the restroom at Three Shirts to the Wind, and saw the tee on my way out." She'd pulled on the red shirt over her white collared blouse. "My new mantra," she said of the gold script lettering: I WILL NEVER BE OLD ENOUGH TO KNOW BETTER.

"Definitely you," said Landon.

"Herman liked it. He encouraged me to buy it." Her cane. The shirt was bright, youthful. Eleanor was pleased by her purchase. That's all that mattered.

Eden focused on the two of them, and took a profile photo. An interesting composition. Darkness backed them, while a mirage of flame crept toward them. It was surreal.

The click of the camera caught Land's attention. And drew his grin. "You're back."

"I've made my rounds." She was glad to return to him.

He seemed happy to see her, too. He gave her a slow wink, and his smile tipped up, sexy and appreciative.

Eleanor looked her over. "I met you earlier. You're a gypsy."

Not quite the look Eden was going for, but close to it, she guessed. Free and flirty was the image she'd had in mind when she'd wrapped her hair in a gray-and-silver paisley bandana. A gauzy pink blouse tucked into a pastel, ankle-length, tiered skirt. She carried her orange flip-flops. A coat of raspberry polish on her toenails.

Eleanor eyed her still. "You snapped my picture as I came down the boardwalk stairs, holding on to Landon's arm. Landon was great support. Both he and Herman."

"Would you like a copy?" Eden asked. "I print duplicates."

"Yes, I would." Eleanor extended her hand, touched Eden on the arm. "I like you, dear. You're most kind." She looked toward the caterer's cart. "What's it take to get a weenie?" she requested. "Do I have to roast my own?"

"I'll roast you one," Land offered. "Hot dog buns are available at the cart. What would you like? Ketchup, mustard?"

"The works," Eleanor replied. "I took an antacid earlier today. So lots of relish and pile on the onions." She nudged Eden with her cane. "You go with him. Make sure he gets it right. I'm going to wander over and meet that handicapped dog. Cute little pug. I hope he doesn't bite."

"Quigley is gentle," Landon assured her. "The back half of his body is paralyzed, and he has an occasional twitch. Don't let that scare you."

"Poor little guy. I'll try not to frighten him with my own aches, pains, pops, and twitches. Old age is challenging," she said. "I still get around. Thanks to Herman." She shuffled through the sand toward the lifeguard stand.

"She's a neat lady," Eden said as they headed toward the big metal cart. "Spunky."

"Eleanor's adventurous," said Land. "She's traveling with a friend to Peru and China next year. They want to climb Machu Picchu and walk the Great Wall, which could take some time."

"How old is her friend?"

"Ninety-five."

"Good for them," Eden admired. "I hope I never slow down."

"You have too many pictures to take to ever retire."

"I capture life on film," she slowly said. "I need to get out and live it more."

"Where would you start?"

"I've lived in Barefoot William all my life. There's no place like it." She loved her home, but she also dreamed. "I'd love to photograph Europe. From the cities to the countryside. Soak in the culture and history."

"Richmond has history. Old mansions and Civil War battlefields. Cemeteries," he noted. "Museums and monuments."

"I want to travel outside the States."

"Why? When there's so much to see here."

Her heart was set on going abroad. "Where are you from, Landon?"

"Milwaukee."

"Cheese," she murmured. "I always associate cheese with Wisconsin."

"We're more than dairy land," he said. "Wisconsin Dells, Lake Geneva, Green Bay, an incredible place."

"I believe you," she said, then had to add, "every time I make a grilled cheese, I'll think of you."

"You eat the sandwich often?"

"Several times a week."

"I'll be on your mind a lot."

Yes, he would.

They reached the caterer's cart, and stood in line for their hot dogs and long, metal roasting skewers. Eden scanned the boardwalk and shops while they waited. Loud voices and merriment rose on the night air. A huge crowd hovered at the railing, catching the activity of the bonfire below. The Rogues dominated the town during spring training. Wherever they were, people wanted to be. Once the event ended, those watching would swarm the ballplayers.

Nighttime entertainers emerged, visible beneath the neon signs and pole lights. Slow-moving stilt walkers towered over the crowd. Unicyclists maneuvered in tight circles. Pedicab service stalled. The rickshaws were swallowed in the crush.

"Six inch or foot-long?" Landon asked, nudging her arm.

The line had progressively moved forward, and they were next to order. She was hungry, but wasn't certain she could manage the larger of the two. "Six," she decided.

Landon gave the caterer their order. "One six and two foot-long."

Eden couldn't help but grin. "You're getting Eleanor a big one?"

"And you're going to take her picture when she eats it."

Eden liked his idea. "A Kodak moment. A photo worth framing."

The food server skewered their hot dogs. They crossed back to the bonfire to roast them. Once cooked, they would return to the cart for buns and condiments.

They stood on the edge of the flames, had their own techniques for roasting. Eden had campfire days behind her, and she cooked her hot dog evenly.

Even though Landon turned his skewers, the meal caught fire. He shook the skewers to put out the flame. "Crispy but not completely burnt," he muttered.

"Eleanor will appreciate whatever you bring her," Eden assured him. "You're covering it with the works."

Land blew out a breath. "You're right. She'll barely be able to taste the hot dog with mounds of relish and onions."

They soon walked back to the cart. "You can toast the marshmallows," he suggested. "Eleanor likes them golden brown."

She took his mention of the marshmallows as an invitation to stick around. She would hang out for a while. Take a few more pictures.

Juggling paper plates, napkins, and sodas, they located Eleanor. She saw them coming, and met them halfway. The older woman's eyes popped when Landon passed her the food. "A foot-long! I haven't had one since 1937," she reminisced. "Virginia State Fair, I was twelve."

"Did you eat the whole thing back then?" asked Land.

"Hot dog *and* a basket of onion rings." She sighed. "I'll be lucky to get through a third of it now."

It became a balancing act to hold the sodas and plates, and eat all at the same time. Land was considerate. "There are beach chairs, if you'd rather sit."

"I sit so much of the day, it's good to stand tonight." Eleanor dug in.

"Hold my plate?" Eden asked Landon. She side-eyed Eleanor. "Photo op."

Eden took a series of six pictures. They were priceless. Her favorite was Landon taking a napkin to Eleanor's cheek when she smeared mustard. The older woman surprised them both, and even herself, when she polished off the foot-long. She grinned. "I can't believe I ate the whole thing."

Landon had accomplished the same feat. He was a big guy, Eden thought, and could've gone for seconds. He didn't. Instead he winked at Eleanor and asked, "Did you save room for marshmallows?"

"Maybe one, but only after I walk around a bit and my food settles. Don't wait for me to enjoy your own." She handed Landon her empty plate, then took a final sip of her soda. Land took the empty can from her. She then looked around, came to a decision. "I've chatted with Danny, Halo's contest winner. I've not spent any time with the war vetcran. I need to express my gratitude to him for serving our country." She was gone. Which left Eden and Landon alone.

"I love her spirit," said Eden.

"I immediately knew when I read her letter that she was my front-runner."

"A man fast to judgment."

"Not often. I always weigh my options. Decide what's best for me. For the long run."

"I tend to be cautious, too."

"Even with me?"

"Especially with you."

"You mentioned last night I was different than you expected. How so?"

She finished off her hot dog before responding. What should have been one bite, became three.

Landon eyed her, amused. "You're stalling."

She delayed further by taking slow sips of her soda. She stretched out the last swallow as long as she could.

"Good to the last drop," said Landon.

She'd drained the can, and her throat was again dry. It was difficult to speak. "I didn't like you when we first met," she forced out. "You blew me off."

His brow creased. "Time and place?"

"Last season. Flower show on the boardwalk."

His gaze narrowed and his jaw worked. Momentarily confused. "That's not how I remember it," he talked it out. "I saw you seconds before your cousin Shaye introduced us. You were hyped, happy, and dancing down the boardwalk. To the music in your head. No partner, just you."

Sheryl Crowe's "Soak Up the Sun" was her go-to beach song.

"You had a big pink flower in your hair—"

"A gerbera daisy," she remembered.

"You wore dark blue wraparound Ray-Bans. I couldn't see your eyes. I had no idea if you were looking at me or at someone else on the boardwalk. I kept glancing over my shoulder to see who'd caught your attention. You barely said two words, so I looked away."

She'd been staring at him. Intently. Her heart racing. The man was gorgeous. Blindingly so. When she hadn't held his attention, she'd danced herself away. Two-stepping and twirling to the mental beat of "No Time Left" by The Guess Who. He hadn't been on her list of re-peat performances. Not for a year anyway. Here they stood now. Discussing a misunderstanding on both their parts. It felt good to air it out.

"So . . ." he released on a long breath. Scrubbed his knuckles along his jaw. "Are you interested in knowing me now?"

"I'll let you know after you toast me a marshmallow."

"You saw what I did to the foot-longs."

"You're in luck, Landon. I happen to like them burnt."

Eight

"How's your tummy today?" Halo Todd asked Danny when the boy and his sister stepped from the shuttle bus. Transportation was provided for the contest winners. They were picked up at Barefoot Inn and driven to the stadium. Halo awaited them in the parking lot. "You ate a foot-long hot dog, a ton of marshmallows, and drank two sodas last night."

Danny pulled a face. "Not a ton. Fifteen."

"That was ten too many," said Alyn. Halo watched as she gently rubbed her brother's back, right between his shoulder blades. An affectionate gesture. She looked pretty in a white tank top and black shorts. Red ballerina flats. She wore her long hair in a fancy braid down her back. "Thank goodness Mom had Alka-Seltzer," she added.

"Made me burp."

"He was starving again this morning," Alyn said.

Danny held his hands wide apart. "I ate a stack of pancakes," he exaggerated. "What about you, Halo?"

"Steak and eggs."

"I've never had steak for breakfast."

"One morning I'll treat you," said Halo.

Danny bounced on his tennis-shoed toes. "Can Alyn and Mommy come with us?"

"They're invited, too." He raised an eyebrow then. "Where's Martha?" She hadn't gotten off the shuttle.

Alyn relayed, "Mom's knee was bothering her this morning. She has arthritis. She sent me with Danny, and stayed behind. She'll sit in the shade by the pool, keep an eye on our pets. I exercised Quigley before we left. He'll be fine for a few hours."

"Twitches?" Halo hoped so.

"No, but he kicked out his back leg on our walk. That was a first. Could be no more than an involuntary muscle spasm, but still—"

"A kick is a kick."

"We'll take it."

"I'll give you a tour of the facility, if you like." He noticed the other winners and players were headed toward the clubhouse. Ninety-year-old Eleanor was in the lead. No one dared pass her on the sidewalk. If someone did, she stuck out Herman to slow them down. No one wanted to get whacked in the shins by a cane. Especially one that talked to her.

Danny was all energy and excitement. "What's first?" he asked.

Halo was patient with him. He outlined their day. "I'll show you the locker and workout rooms, the field, and batting cages. Afterward, I need to change into my uniform for Media Day."

"You get reported?"

"Reporters interview the starting lineup," Halo corrected. "It's an hour of questions and answers. We sit on tall stools outside in Rogues Plaza. You and your sister will be seated on bleachers. You'll be introduced as well, as my contest winner."

"Will I get my picture taken?"

"I'm sure you will. Someone from the media might even ask you a question."

His eyes widened. "What if I don't know the answer?"

"It's not like school, sweetie," Alyn assured him. "No math or science. Halo will whisper a response if you get stuck."

"You will?"

"I always come up with something." His prediction of winning the World Series had fallen short the previous season. National League Division Series, and he'd been humbled by the Rogues' loss to the Arizona Diamondbacks. The press hounded him afterward. Telling him to polish his crystal ball and look deeper next year.

"What are we waiting for?" Danny reached for Halo's hand. Then Alyn's. He stood between them. Tugged. Ready to start their day.

They left the parking lot and entered the gated facility. A tall chain-link fence wrapped the grounds. Fans were already gathering for Media Day. The collapsible bleachers could only hold so many, and people arrived early to get a seat. Standing room only was limited.

A group of young women followed them in, calling to and flirting with Halo. "How's my favorite player?" "Looking good, Halo, babe." "Catch you tonight at the Coconut." "After party at my place," came his way.

Halo waved back. He couldn't ignore the women. He'd partied with them. He'd had sex with the curvy blonde. Over the past week, his priorities had shifted. He focused on Danny and Alyn now.

Danny looked up at him. "What's an 'after party'?"

"I'm curious, too." The corners of Alyn's mouth tipped up.

Halo went with, "A smaller party that continues after the main party ends."

Danny puzzled. "Like a double-birthday party? Two cakes?"

"More or less," said Halo.

The boy grinned then. "I want an after party for my next birthday, sis. More friends. Lots more presents."

"I'll mention it to Mom," said Alyn.

A convertible sports car honked from the access road on the opposite side of the fence. Slowing, a girl with wavy hair and red lips seated shotgun shouted at Halo, "Missed you last night at Boner's. Wild night. Check out Sammy boy. He looks like Grumpy Cat."

Sam Matthews. Cat whiskers. Lesson learned. Never hook up with a girl wielding an indelible Sharpie. Disaster struck. His date was creative, albeit drunken crazy. Forcing Sam to skip the bonfire. Halo wondered if he was still whiskered. If so, at least his catcher's mask would hide the black lines.

"I drew on my arm once," said Danny.

"He made his own tattoo," added Alyn. "A baseball."

"How'd you remove the marker?" Halo hoped she had a solution. For Sam's sake, anyway. One he could relay to him, if needed.

"It took several tries, actually," she said. "We experimented with nail polish remover, baking soda toothpaste, rubbing alcohol, baby wipes." She smiled, finished with, "WD-40 finally did the trick. It's greasy. Be sure to wash it off."

"There should be WD-40 in the workout room," said Halo.

A female jogger passed them on the far side of the chain-link. "Halo, baby!" Big boobs, small halter top. Lady was bouncing. Danny was staring. "Love you, stud. Call me." She moved on.

"You going to call her?" Danny asked him.

"I can't remember her name." He was honest with the boy.

"She knew you."

"The Rogues have a lot of fans," he explained. "People know my name, but I don't always know theirs."

"Do you like being popular?"

It had both advantages and disadvantages. "It's nice to have friends."

"Do you have a girlfriend?" The boy was full of questions.

"I like your sister," was said without thinking.

Alyn started, but Danny wasn't fazed. "I like Frannie Nathan," he said. "She's in my class. She shared her groin—"

"Granola," Alyn corrected him.

"During snack time. The sunflower seeds were best. Her mom's a veggie—"

"Vegetarian." Again from Alyn. "Their family eats healthy."

"Healthy is good," said Halo. "But sometimes I like junk food, just to round things out."

Danny grinned. "I round out a lot."

Halo smiled back, before moving them on. "Let's take the fan walkway," he suggested. "It's worth seeing."

The long, winding sidewalk around the perimeter of the stadium had been Jillian's idea during construction two years prior. Fans had been allowed to leave their footprints for future generations. There were hundreds of prints. All different sizes and shapes, from boots to flip-flops. One set was barefoot. Danny matched his own footprints to nearly every pair.

It took them some time to reach Rogues Plaza, located near the front of the facility. The plaza was wide and tree-lined, set up with benches and collapsible bleachers. It was there that team members had left their marks. Large cement squares showcased cleated footprints, along with the players' names.

Danny immediately went to Halo's prints. Stood inside

them. "Wow, you have big feet," he said. He gave his shoe size. "I'm a four."

"Thirteen," Halo returned.

Danny spun around, faced backwards in the print. The toes of his sneakers met Halo's heels. Still not a good fit. "I need to grow more," he said. "Taller, too."

Halo patted his shoulder with his free hand. "You will, dude." He then nodded toward the main entrance. "To the locker room. Ready?"

"Set, go!" Danny took off ahead of them. He entered the building before Halo and Alyn got beyond the players' footprints.

"He won't get lost, will he?" Alyn was concerned.

"Security will slow him down. They won't allow him beyond the lobby without supervision."

He held back a moment, glancing at Alyn. "Good morning." He hadn't officially welcomed her to the park. He did so now. "I'm glad you're here today." He meant it.

Her light green eyes were bright; her expression, re-laxed. "I'm happy to be included."

"I wanted you with me." He was serious.

She didn't take him seriously. "You have so many women wanting you. What's one more?"

"Because that one means more than the others."

Still, she put him off. "Danny needs a chaperone."

"I need a girlfriend."

She blinked, taken aback. "A girlfriend? Whatever for? You don't seem the one-woman type. Can you even spell monogamy?"

He spelled o-n-e-w-o-m-a-n instead.

She rolled her eyes. "You're impossible."

What he was about to offer her was possible. Doable. If she'd agree. The idea had formed last night, following the bonfire, and after the contest winners were shuttled back to the inn. He, Landon, Will, and Zoo had opted for a beer at Parrot Pete's, a bar new to them. A green parrot perched on a swing in a long, narrow cage that hung above the bar. He was a foul-mouthed bird. *Screw you* was said loud and often. Along with *Kiss my ass.* Zoo offered to buy the parrot. The owner declined.

The bar had a steady stream of customers, but wasn't packed. The guys selected a table in one corner. They talked serious baseball, outlining their season ahead. Strategy was all-important.

What the men couldn't avoid was the tease. Frequent and feminine. Halo's past caught up with him. He'd freestyled over the years. Making himself available and easy. Hot babes wearing next to nothing stopped by their table, looking to hook up. It became disruptive. Monotonous. Annoying.

Landon had finally turned his back on the room, as had Halo. Even Will and Zoo stayed tuned to their conversation, which was unusual for them. They were easily distracted. The night was young, and the ladies' interruptions got old fast.

An hour passed, then a second. Fans sent pitchers of beer to their table. Halo and Land drank minimally. Zoo and Will felt no pain. They soon welcomed the attentions of the ladies.

Sex was the last thing on Halo's mind. He'd just left Alyn. Her presence lingered, even after the groupies gathered. They leaned against him, stroked his shoulders. Ran their fingers through his hair. Whispered in his ear. Explicit invitations to party.

There'd been so many women. He'd lost sight of the bar and the exit door. Most men would be out of their minds with the female attention. The more women, the better. A harem fantasy. Halo wasn't even tempted. He'd grown bored. Gotten up to leave, despite the sexual requests.

Somewhere in the last week, morality had kicked him

in the nuts. Sex for sex's sake no longer appealed. He sucked air, frustrated and horny. Blue balls were not his color.

In the light of day, he faced Alyn with the truth. Sharing what he believed would solve their problems and satisfy them both. He began with, "I don't want any distractions this season. Rylan wants us to go the distance. We all do. We can make it happen. I need my mind fully on the game. Not sidelined by—"

"Pouty lips, big breasts, and long legs?"

"Something like that."

"A lot like that. You're a big boy, Halo. Be strong. Beat them off with a stick." Lady could be sarcastic. Not pretty.

He shifted his stance, said, "I've options. A girlfriend would help hold off those who hang on."

"Women who want you will stalk you, girlfriend or not."

"Work with me, Alyn."

"In what capacity?" She appeared leery.

"Hang with me, babe."

"You've got to be joking."

"Serious as a sermon."

"You're delusional."

"Think about it."

"No."

"Take your time."

"My decision's made."

She wasn't budging. Danny eventually called to him from the front entrance. "Halo, you coming? The guard took me to the workout room. I lifted a barbell. Rolled the medicine ball. I ate an orange off the food cart." He held up his hands. "Sticky."

"Be right there," Halo said. "We'll get your hands washed." He curved his arm about Alyn's shoulders, snugged her close. "Nice fit, don't you think?"

She elbowed him in the side. Hard. "Stop that."

He released her, tried another tactic. "I have a business proposition for you."

That got her attention. Her eyes widened, and her breath caught. "Business?"

"You need a backer for your antique business. I could be your silent partner. My capital in exchange for being a couple." A short pause. "So, what do you say?"

"You need an answer right this minute?"

"In a second or two."

"I hate to be rushed."

He wasn't good at waiting. "Our deal is simple. I've spelled it out. Once you agree—"

"*If* I agree."

"I'll reserve the shop on the second floor of the brick building in downtown Richmond. You'll be living your dream."

She sighed, a sign she was giving in. That's how Halo saw it, anyway. "How long is a season?" she questioned.

"World Series takes us to ten months."

"Almost a year." She met his gaze. "We need terms."

Conditions to their deal. He'd never played within boundaries. He wasn't certain he even could. "Hit me," he said.

"I will pay you back every cent you loan me, once I get up and running and show a profit."

She could keep the money as far as he was concerned. He wouldn't miss it. But she was honorable. So he nodded. Agreeing.

She licked her lips. He wished he was licking them, too. "No sex."

Low blow. And painful. "Ah, babe." His balls were getting bluer by the second. "Some public affection, then, otherwise no one will believe we're a couple."

"Kisses, no tongue."

She was no fun. "Touching?"

"You can put your arm around me. Hold my hand."

He was pretty certain he could charm his way to feeling her up. Maybe she'd stroke him down. The thought left him hard.

She noticed the bulge behind his zipper, and her eyes rounded. *"Really?"* she asked.

"It's who I am."

She pursed her lips, thought ahead. "I'll need to explain our deal to Danny and my mom. So they don't read more into our arrangement than is actually there."

"I'll talk to your brother man-to-man."

"He's eight." She clutched her hands at her sides. Unsure. "No matter how we explain 'us,'"—she made quotation marks with her fingers—"he'll see you as family. You'll let him down when you leave."

"Maybe I won't leave."

"I could leave you."

"Harsh, Alyn. Take my money, then dump me."

"Such is life."

"So . . . you're in."

"I'm . . . in."

They'd go the distance, he was certain. He'd already sketched the outcome of their relationship in his mind. One he could live with. He was happy with the ending.

They hadn't discussed when to make their announcement. Halo figured soon. Very soon. Their verbal agreement bound them now. Neither would go back on his or her word. He took her hand, and she laced her fingers with his. Her palm was small in his. Soft. Tentative.

Danny was tapping his toe by the time they reached him. He didn't question their holding hands. Instead, he reached for Halo's free one. The boy's hand stuck to his. Juicy.

The locker room was empty by the time they arrived. The contest winners and players had come and gone and moved to the field. "Let's wash your hands before we do anything else," Halo suggested. He led Danny toward the restroom, only to glance over his shoulder and wink at Alyn. She blushed. Prettily.

Danny scrubbed, avoided getting his cast wet. He then paper-toweled his hands dry. He dunked the used towels in the trash can like a basketball player. Then turned to Halo and said, "You're always looking at my sister."

The boy was observant. Halo was honest. "She's easy on the eyes. I like her."

"I like her, too."

"I might ask her on a date, if that's okay with you."

"You stuff her now."

"Do stuff with her now," Halo interpreted, trying not to smile.

"Mommy and Daddy went to movies. Alyn would babysit me. They needed to grow up sometimes."

It took Halo a second to figure out, "Some grown-up time." Adults needed to stay connected. Danny's parents had scheduled date nights. He found that very cool.

Danny grinned then. "They would kiss in the kitchen when they thought I was playing in the yard. In the greenhouse, too. But I saw."

"They loved each other."

"Daddy left us."

Death was never easy on a family. "I wish I'd met your father."

"Mommy says I look just like Daddy when he was a boy."

"I looked a lot like my dad, too." He'd learned a hard lesson after his father's passing. He reflected, "It's important to be kind to people we care about." He and his old man had never expressed regret over their arguments. Their silence. They'd never shaken hands. Never agreed to disagree. It was too late now.

"Be nice to my sister. Mommy said she's frag-able."

"Fragile." Halo would do his best never to hurt her. "Are we good, dude?" He held his hand out to Danny. They fist bumped, then shook. "No matter what happens down the road, you and I will go the distance. I promise."

"Quigley, too?"

"Quiggie Sparks makes three."

"We're the Muskets."

"Three Musketeers."

"Guys? Is everything okay?" Alyn called from the main locker room. "How long does it take to wash hands?"

"Guy talk," Halo told her when they returned. He rested his hand on Danny's shoulder, guided him to the row of lockers. The starting lineup filled the row against the south wall. "Mine," he pointed to the second one. There were thirty preseason games. Three batting practice uniforms, five boxes of athletic shoes, a collection of sunglasses and terry-cloth wrist bands stood ready. He would change into one of his uniforms shortly, when the team met with the media.

"I like your locker," said Danny.

"Yeah, so do I."

Clubhouse manager Walter Atwater made the spring training locker assignments. Atwater had placed Halo by Rylan. Which was fine by Halo. Walt believed the veteran's work ethic and stability would rub off on him. An empty locker separated him from the team captain. The space was meant for Ry, yet Halo would pitch his wallet and keys on the top shelf. Oftentimes hang an extra set of clothes. The coveted real estate put him adjacent to the lounge and food cart with easy access to the showers. He could settle on a La-Z-Boy, put up his feet after nine innings, and enjoy a snack or catered meal. It was all good.

Halo glanced at Alyn. She sat in the background, on a gray-enameled bench. He smiled at her, and she smiled back. He liked looking at her. He wanted to share his career. To give her an understanding of who he was. Deep inside, beyond his public image. He turned to Danny. "Where to next? Field, batting cages?"

The boy closed his eyes, and imagined, "I've just hit a home run and I'm rounding the bases."

"Let's go, slugger. No sliding home," he reminded.

Halo refused to let Alyn lag behind. She was allowing him and Danny to bond, but he needed to strengthen their personal connection, too. Danny swung out the door, shot down the short tunnel, his feet flying. He would round the bases, which gave Halo a private moment with his sister.

A dim bulb lit the hallway. Casting them in shadow. He let Alyn catch up, then caught her to him. "Are we having fun yet?" he whispered near her ear.

"Danny's having the time of his life."

"How about you?"

"I'm taking it all in."

"Take me in." He gave her no warning. He kissed her. Claimed her. In an instant. He lifted her full against him, effortlessly. She stood on tiptoe. Her parted lips let his tongue slip in, and move hotly over her own. Possessive, passionate. She savored his masculine taste; the heat of his body wrapped her in his scent. All male.

Their chemistry was undeniable, strong and potent. Overpowering. So sexual, she couldn't keep her hands off him. She explored the corded strength of his shoulders; her nails scored his back. His muscles flexed, rippled, beneath her fingers. Her composure wavered. The wall pressed her back. Halo, her front. His chest was as wide and hard as cement block.

There was no sweet exchange with this man. He kissed with his entire body. He pleasured her. Appreciated her. Raw, restive, capturing, he drew her out of herself and into him. She went, willingly. He stroked her back, the high curve of her bottom. He squeezed her hips. Cupping her butt, he kept her flush against him. His breathing deepened. He was hard for her. The zipper on his jeans distended. Largely so.

Sensation pooled in her belly. She was lost to the moment. Lost in the man. He was addictive. Restless, he shifted against her. Impatient, she arched, pressed her hips tighter against him. She wanted to wrap her legs about his waist. She would have, had the side door not opened, and sunlight splashed the hallway. They were visible to a little boy's eyes.

Halo groaned, low, deep, as if in pain. Frustration etched his handsome face. He released her, stepped back. Her thighs locked before her knees buckled. She was that turned on. Danny ran inside, stopped short. Dirt smudged his face, and he was panting. Alyn was as out of breath as her brother. She concentrated on her breathing. Which was difficult.

Public affection. How much had Danny seen? If anything. She was embarrassed by their display in the hall. She'd kindled with Halo's first kiss. Her control escaped her. She fanned herself now. The fire still burned. Her breasts felt heavy. Her belly, soft. Her panties were wet.

"Did you run the bases?" Halo found his voice first.

"Three times," Danny said proudly. "I thought you were watching me, but I crossed home alone."

Alyn's heart squeezed. She should've been there for her brother. Clapping and cheering him on. She apologized, saying the first thing that popped into her head. "Sorry, sweetie. Halo's shoelace came untied, and he stopped to fix it."

Danny lowered his gaze. "Halo's wearing loafers, sis."

Her cheeks heated. Halo had the balls to laugh. He lightly cuffed Danny on the shoulder, admitted, "I stole a kiss."

"You can steal more if you want." Danny gave them permission.

"No more," she assured him. "We're done here."

"For now," said Halo. "Let's go, guy."

Danny banged out the door. Excited, and nearly tripping over his feet. Alyn and Halo followed more slowly. He took her hand with the ease of a long-time boyfriend. They'd only been a couple for an hour. Yet everything seemed easy, comfortable. Meant to be, although she knew it wasn't long-term. She would take him one day at a time. That was all she could afford. Becoming too involved, too fast, would complicate her life forever. She couldn't afford for that to happen.

On the field, Halo chased Danny around the bases. Danny was beside himself from the attention. He jumped with both feet on home plate, raised his arms high, then turned and hugged Halo.

"This is a great ballpark," said Danny. He pointed toward the batting cages on the far side of the bullpen. "Can I swing, just once, please, Halo, please."

Alyn's heart slowed. She didn't want her brother to get hurt. "Your cast," she reminded him.

Halo figured out a way to ease her mind and make Danny happy. "The ball machine can be regulated, but there's no slow pitch. I'd need to stand behind you, and go hand-over-hand on the bat. Will that work for you?"

She watched it all unfold from outside the fence that surrounded the batting cages. Halo loaded the ball machine, and set the speed of the pitches. Alyn thought they still came fast, but her brother wanted faster. Halo was light-handed on the bat. Still, he protected Danny's cast when her brother stepped into a pitch. They connected on ten of twelve balls. Danny was elated.

Halo gave Danny a fist bump. "Superstar," he praised.

"Now what?" her brother wanted to know. Still hyped, and ready to go.

Halo glanced at his watch. "You and Alyn need to go back to Rogues Plaza," he directed. "Locate Jillian, our community liaison. You met her at the bonfire. There's designated seating for the contest winners and media. You'll have a good view of all that goes on."

He gave Danny a final pat on the shoulder, then kissed Alyn full on the lips. Her whole body sighed. "Later, babe." He left them then; jogged back toward the locker room.

The man looked as good going as he did coming, she thought. He filled out his black T-shirt and packed his jeans. His body shouted agility and strength. He'd left a permanent imprint on her from the hallway.

Danny took her hand as they walked toward the front of the facility. He looked up to her. "Halo likes you."

She missed a step. Stumbled. "How would you know that?"

"He told me."

"When, sweetie?"

"When I was washing my hands."

They'd had a private conversation amid the soap, water, and scrubbing. "Anything else you want to tell me?" she prodded, but didn't press him. She respected their guy time.

Danny gave it some thought. "He and his daddy looked alike."

"And . . ."

"Him, Quigs, and me are Three Musket-ears."

He gave a little hop, and she knew he'd relayed all that he remembered, all that was important to him. She let it rest. They soon rounded the corner of the stadium, and became part of a large crowd. Alyn couldn't believe the number of people already gathered, along with those who stood in line at the gate.

Jillian saw them before they saw her. She waved them down. "So glad you're here," she greeted. "Halo has texted me a dozen times in ten minutes, making sure you have the best seats available. The man can be persistent."

"Wherever we're assigned, we'll be fine," Alyn assured her. She didn't have to be front and center. The top row of the bleachers worked for her.

"I've left two rows open for the contest winners," Jillian informed them. She pointed to the lower left, to the empty spaces. "Fans will try to sneak down to be closer to the players. So grab a space now. The guys should be here shortly. They'll field media questions. Then chat with the crowd. It's a fun hour."

Alyn and Danny settled beside Eleanor Norris. The ninety-year-old wore a wide-brimmed straw hat, a long-sleeve blouse, white gloves, and slacks. "Sun will never touch my skin," she told them. She had a lovely complexion.

Twenty minutes, and the starting lineup emerged. Tall, strong, swaggering. They looked hot in their uniforms. Alyn admired each one. They lived and breathed baseball.

Halo stood out to her. He had a restless edginess. He wore his baseball cap backwards, his game face was set. He looked serious as he took his seat on a tall stool in the center of the plaza. He and Landon flanked team captain Rylan Cates. She located Sam Matthews, far right. His face appeared red and slightly raw, as if scrubbed, with only a hint of squiggly black at the corner of his mouth. Most of the marker had disappeared.

Halo scanned the crowd. Looking for her. Finding her. He stared overly long. Her pulse jumped. She fidgeted. His slow grin aroused her. She grew warmer than the sunshine. Danny saw him looking their way, and waved. Halo nodded back.

She glanced about. The press was well represented, from what she could tell. A gathering of national and local television stations, newspapers, and sports magazines. Introductions of the players soon followed. Jillian detailed each man's career, beginning with veteran Rylan Cates, and moving down the line.

Ry was the hometown boy. The extended Cates family was in attendance. He received a solid round of applause. Halo and Landon came next. They received standing ovations. Alyn had never seen anything like it. Fans went crazy for them. They were good-looking and single. Desirable and admired. And known for playing as hard off the field as on. She wondered if Halo could be faithful. Or if his DNA was wired for multiple partners.

Halo and Landon went on to salute the crowd, but didn't do anything that drew attention from the other players. They were unified. One for all.

Five reporters took turns asking questions. One asked if the team was prepared for the upcoming season. Rylan responded, "We're primed."

Which team was their biggest challenge? Halo answered, "Each team we face on any given game day."

Were the players looking forward to Opening Day? Landon kept it simple. "It starts our season."

The reporters ran through their list of questions. Depth of the bullpen. Any minor injuries. Predictions. Toward the end of the session, one reporter asked if veteran Rylan Cates was a father figure to the team.

Halo fielded it. "We call him 'Dad.'"

The crowd clapped, liking his response. From what Alyn could tell, Rylan was a few years older than his teammates. Maturity was on his side. Every team needed a leader.

Jillian joined the guys once again. She appreciated everyone's enthusiasm and participation during the spring training contest. She then requested that the players introduce their winners, and read a short paragraph from the letter they'd received.

Alyn's breath caught. Her stomach sank. Halo hadn't read Danny's letter. He'd admitted as much to her in the living room of her home. Her brother would be disappointed. And she had no way to save the day.

The men took over the microphone and, one by one, called their winners forward. Jillian passed each player the appropriate letter. There was both humor and seriousness conveyed over the next half hour. Landon told the crowd Eleanor enjoyed baseball. She and her husband hadn't missed a game when he'd been alive. Eleanor took the mic from him, and stated she was ninety years old. She'd lived a good life and could cross spring training off her bucket list. She tapped her cane, adding that she and Herman were happy now.

Not everyone understood "Herman," but Alyn did. She smiled. The woman and her cane would continue on their journey. Wherever it would take them.

There was continuous applause and a few tears shed during the introductions. The army veteran brought the fans to their feet. Cheers honored his military service.

Rylan's winner surprised everyone present. It was a Doberman named Lassiter, led out by his owner. The letter stated that Lassiter loved to chase and catch baseballs. They were his favorite toy. Somehow, while playing in the park, he'd caught a ball, and it got lodged in his throat. He nearly died. Thanks to successful emergency surgery, the dobie had survived. Rylan held up the letter. Signed with a paw print.

The fans went crazy. Good wishes for Lassiter rose on the air. It was a joyous moment. Halo was the final Rogue to call up his winner. Danny jumped off the bleachers and was headed to Halo before the ballplayer finished saying his name.

Alyn clutched her hands in her lap, so tightly her knuckles turned white. Surely Halo wouldn't embarrass her brother. What could he say that would come even close to what Danny had written?

The right fielder locked eyes with her across the plaza. He knew that she believed he'd failed Danny. His look said he was about to prove her wrong. He placed his big hand over the boy's shoulder, went on to withdraw an envelope tucked into the back waistband of his uniform pants. Halo took out the letter, and began to highlight the contents. "Danny Jayne has been a baseball fan all his life." Pause. "He's eight." The crowd responded with arm pumps and *woot-woots*. "His father took him to his first baseball game, and he has happy memories of the time they spent together. My bobble head is on his bedroom dresser." Smiles from the crowd.

Halo paused, allowing his next words to sink in. "Danny's father passed away, following the end of last season. His mother promised he could still attend our games. She would take him. Still, it wouldn't be the same. Guys watch baseball better than girls." Chuckles and a few sniffles.

Alyn pressed her palm over her heart. She bit down on her bottom lip to still the trembling. She listened as Halo said, "This week is guy time. Danny's here, chaperoned by his mother and sister. We will celebrate America's pastime in memory of his dad." Hearts opened, and applause welcomed Danny to spring training.

"A question for you, Danny," came from one of the reporters. "How happy are you to be here?"

His smile spoke for him. Ear-to-ear, and eyes shining.

The reporter nodded. "Good answer." A photographer took his picture.

Her brother gave Halo a huge hug, then ran back to Alyn. Sitting still was not an option, so he stood before her. Rocking heel-toe and bobbing. Fortunately, he was short, and didn't draw any complaints.

She felt Halo's eyes on her, and met his gaze. He raised one eyebrow questioningly, almost smugly, and she nodded in turn. She had no idea how he'd pulled off the letter, until he side-eyed Jillian. She then understood. Assistance from the community liaison had saved the day. She was grateful. Beyond words.

Jillian retrieved the microphone, allowed the Rogues one final comment. "Anything personal you'd like to share with your fans?" she asked them.

Pitcher Will Ridgeway announced he'd recently purchased a house in Barefoot William. This would be his off-season residence. The townies loudly embraced his move.

Landon told those gathered that he was setting up a sports camp in Richmond. Hopefully, a second one in Barefoot William the next year. Major League players would hold clinics. Professional teams loved to scout young talent.

Zoo drew mass approval with, "I'll be visiting the hospital while I'm in town. Times and dates will be posted on the Rogues' website. You're welcome to join me. One condition, dress as a superhero. I'm Captain America."

Rylan's news centered on his Great Dane. Atlas had fathered a litter of puppies. He was a local canine legend. Fans barked.

Halo came up next. The last to share news. Alyn had no idea what he might say. The man was unpredictable at best. She listened intently along with all those present. "I recognize so many of you," he began. "My party squad. The wild and reckless. We've shared pitchers of beer. Swapped stories. You're like family."

Hoots and hollers. Whistles. "Yeah, baby," and "You go, man," echoed behind Alyn. From both men and women.

"Life can throw you a curveball when you least expect it." He spoke slowly, distinctly. "My curveball, a woman. We found each other when neither of us was looking. Times change. Often for the better. You have to take advantage of those moments that feel right. *Really* right," he emphasized. "I have. I'm recently engaged."

He shocked the plaza to silence.

Jaws dropped.

Eyes went wide.

Female hearts broke.

Men had lost a sexual hero.

Alyn wanted to kill him.

Nine

Engaged? Alyn thumped the side of her head. Needing to clear her ears. Had she heard him correctly? Apparently so, given his teammates' stares. Confused and disbelieving. They thought he'd lost his mind. No one could wrap their head around Halo's announcement. Least of all her.

What had he just done? They'd agreed to hold off on the announcement until she'd spoken to Danny and her mother, and explained the *real* reason behind their public relationship. Which wasn't genuine commitment. It was all business. To get aggressive women off Halo's back and to allow her to open her vintage shop. Theirs was far from an actual love affair. And she'd never agreed to an engagement. Idiot man.

She shrank down on the bleacher, trying to make herself small. Invisible, if it were possible. Standing before her, Danny took it all in. His nose scrunched. He didn't fully understand. There was no little-boy bounce to him now.

Questions flew all around her. The ballplayers hit Halo hardest. The microphone was on, and their concerns aired live.

"*Who's the woman?*"

"*Where did you meet?*"

"How long have you been seeing her?"

"What the fuck?"

"Dude, you crazy?"

Halo took it all in stride. Not a flinch. Not a change in his expression. "She's my mystery woman for the moment," he said with ease. "I've taken her by surprise by going public. She'll come forward when she's ready."

Twisting toward her, Danny put his hands on her shoulders, leaned close. Whispered, "Are you Halo's mystery?"

Her brother was one smart cookie. "If I am?"

"I'd keep your secret."

She touched her fingers to her lips. "Sshh. I'll fill you in later."

He crossed his heart. "I'll wait to be filled."

People were looking around now. Craning their necks. Speculating on whether Halo's fiancée was seated in the stands. "Is she here?" one of the reporters asked.

"How long have you been engaged?" rose from the back of the media group.

"Have you set a wedding date?" from the feature editor of the local newspaper.

Halo responded with, "This isn't twenty questions."

"You can't broadcast an engagement and not give details," said a radio announcer.

"You're getting personal, and I'm giving my lady space," Halo said. "She's a private person."

"Will we meet her during spring training?" Once again from the feature editor.

Halo nodded slowly. "Chances are good you will." He raised his hand, palm out. "Enough said. Back to the team. No predictions from me this year. We'll let our bats and fielding speak for us."

The community liaison rescued the microphone. Jillian looked at Halo, deciding how best to handle his engagement news so it wouldn't overshadow the team.

"We appreciate every player's update," she said. "Let's give the Rogues a big round of applause." Clapping resounded. "Come November, bring the World Series Trophy back to Richmond."

Agreement came in hoots and hollers. Arm pumps. Jumping on the bleachers. The energy was tangible. The starting roster signed autographs for an hour afterward. Female fans pouted and stroked Halo's arm, as disbelieving as Alyn that he'd become a one-woman man. Even if he could spell it.

He was a long way from settling down, she thought. If ever. Restless, testosterone driven, his bad boy hid just beneath the surface. Waiting for the right moment to come out and play. Hard. Fast. Fierce.

She wondered how long he could sustain the façade of commitment without falling to temptation. The women who approached him were all beautiful. Beach babes and athletic groupies, all toned, tanned, willing, and available. His loyalty would be tested hourly. She'd give him a month, at best, maybe less, before the novelty of being a couple wore off. She'd be amazed if he made it through spring training without cheating on her. Despite the fact they weren't really together.

The players soon returned to the locker room. The plaza slowly cleared. Ninety-year-old Eleanor nudged Alyn with her elbow. "Are we supposed to sit and wait for our player or should we take the commuter bus back to Barefoot Inn?" she asked.

Alyn stood up, stretched. "I'm going back to the inn," she decided. Halo hadn't made afternoon plans with Danny or her. She didn't want to crowd him. Halo deserved his own free time.

Eleanor walked with them as they left the plaza. Danny's disappointment showed. He dragged his feet. "I won't see Halo until tomorrow," he muttered.

"Tuesday will be a big day for you," Alyn pointed out, attempting to brighten his mood. "The team holds its first practice. The contest winners have full-access passes and seats behind the home dugout. You'll see every move Halo makes."

"Tomorrow's not today," said Danny.

Alyn had an idea. "Once we get back to the inn, we'll check on Mom, take Quigley for a stroll, and then head to the boardwalk. There's carnival rides and an arcade. I need to buy a small cooler and sunscreen. Sunglasses and a hat. We'll do it all. How's that sound?"

He sighed. "It would be more fun with Halo."

"You're stuck with me, sweetheart. I can be fun."

He took her hand then, as they crossed the parking lot. He perked up a little. "Can I have ice cream, nachos, popcorn, and a snow cone?"

"Not all at once."

"Can I get a Barefoot William T-shirt?"

She'd work the shirt into her budget. "A great beach souvenir."

"Can we build a sand castle?"

"If not today, tomorrow." Danny wanted to do everything. Straightaway. They had plenty of time to spread things out. She had no experience in sand creation, but would give it her best shot.

He looked at her then. Cheered up. "Thanks, sis."

They'd reached the bus. Politeness turned Alyn toward Eleanor. She asked, "Would you like to join us on our afternoon outing?"

Eleanor lifted her cane. "What do you think, Herman?" She listened, nodded, smiled.

Danny was drawn to the exchange. "What did Herman say?"

"That a walk down the boardwalk and pier reminds

him of our time at Atlantic City. It's just what the doctor ordered."

"What doctor?" asked Danny.

"It's an expression," Eleanor explained. "An afternoon with the two of you is perfect for me."

"Perfect for us, too," said Alyn.

"Do you have a swimsuit?" asked Danny.

"I wouldn't take a pretty picture."

"Who's taking your picture?"

Eleanor patted Danny on the head. "No one, son. I'm not thirty anymore. I don't want to scare the other sun-bathers."

"Alyn's thirty."

"And beautiful."

"Halo thinks so, too," popped out.

Danny caught Eleanor's interest. "He does, does he?"

"It's a secret."

"Ah, so that's the way of it," the older woman said. "The mystery continues."

"It's not what you think, Eleanor." Alyn needed to stop any and all speculation.

"Let's just see." She and Herman climbed on the bus.

The remaining contest winners straggled onto the commuter. The conversation on the way back to the inn centered on baseball. The players. Media Day. And Halo Todd's engagement.

Alyn kept a close eye on Danny, not wanting him to comment on Halo. Her brother sat quietly. Eleanor's shrewd side-glances gave nothing away, yet she knew more than she was saying.

Back at the inn, Eleanor headed to her room to change clothes. She would meet them in the lobby in thirty minutes. Alyn and Danny sought their mother, locating her in the sun room, just off the main entrance. Here Martha sat alone, relaxed on a wicker lounger. An iced tea and stack of magazines rested on a table nearby. Lemony sunshine filled the room. A ceiling fan spun slowly overhead, gently stirring the air.

Alyn watched, listened, grinned as her brother hugged their mother, and then went over every detail of the stadium and Media Day at record speed. He took only one breath, and his words ran together. He wrapped up their entire morning in five minutes flat.

He finished with, "We're going to the beach. El'nor and Herman, too. Come with us, Mommy?"

Martha nodded, agreed. "I've scanned the city brochure, and there are lots of neat shops on the boardwalk. The Rogues Store sells memorabilia." She ruffled Danny's hair. "You can choose something special, if you like."

Danny hopped from one foot to the other, excited. "A jersey with Halo's number on the back."

"Twenty-eight will look good on you."

Halo Todd. Alyn recognized the deep male voice, and felt her body go soft. She turned slightly, and found him leaning negligently against the doorframe, arms crossed over his chest. He wore the same clothes he had earlier, black T-shirt and jeans. Loafers. His gaze was locked on her. His expression unreadable. His smile tipped when Danny ran to him. He drew the boy close for a hug. A natural interaction.

Danny was beside himself. "You found us," he said.

"When you didn't wait for me, I came for you."

Hands on his hips, Danny eyed Alyn. "We should've stayed. I would've waited all day."

"But your sister didn't."

"She said you might have other plans."

"My plans are with you, while you're in town," Halo said firmly. His gaze shifted from Danny, touched on

Martha, when he said, "I have something to share with you privately, while we're all together."

Privately. Alyn knew what was coming and held her breath.

Martha touched her hand to her heart. "I hope it's not serious."

"Nothing that will affect us long-term," Alyn was quick to assure her.

Martha clasped her hands on her lap. "Tell me."

Halo crossed to Alyn, drew her to his side. Heat and sensation enveloped her. He held nothing back. "Alyn and I are engaged."

Martha was so stunned, she couldn't speak.

Danny looked smug. "I knew it before you, Mommy."

Comprehension came slowly to Martha. Her eyes rounded; her lips pursed. Always practical, Martha pointed out, "You've only known each other a short time."

"The engagement is strictly a business arrangement," Alyn said. "One that benefits us both."

Martha shook her head, bewildered. "I don't understand."

"Let me explain." Halo filled in the blanks. Slowly. Precisely. Describing their deal as beneficial to them both. He ended with, "A fiancée discourages groupies. My mind will be fully on the game."

"I'll have my antique shop," said Alyn. "And a very silent partner."

"You'll never hear a word from me," Halo affirmed.

Alyn rolled her eyes. She didn't believe him for a second. He was opinionated. Outspoken. Known to jump the gun.

"Sis is Halo's mystery lady," Danny repeated what he'd heard at the ballpark. "She's in hiding."

Martha looked at Alyn, questioningly.

"Halo didn't introduce me to the press," she informed her mother. "I've yet to be named."

"She's 'sguised," said Danny.

"Disguised." Alyn helped him with the word.

"We'll be discovered eventually," said Halo. "Beforehand, we need to get fully acquainted. I don't want to be blindsided and botch questions when asked how we met. Her favorite color?"

Danny piped up. "Purple."

"Her birthdate?"

"January twelfth," her brother said.

"How long we've dated?"

Danny counted on his fingers. "Eight days."

"Amount of time we've been engaged?"

"One day."

"Our wedding date?"

Danny scrunched his nose. "No wedding, but I won't tell anyone."

Alyn caught the flicker of disappointment in her brother's eyes. She sighed. Danny was seeking a happy ending. Romance would not be the end result in this case. She would involve him in her shop instead. Take marriage off his mind.

In the next day or two, she and Halo had a lot to learn about each other. Even if they were on the same page, the man tended to wing it. Scarily so. She recalled the game show, and how he went unscripted. He said things that seemed right at the moment, but caused a ripple effect. He penned her in, with no way out.

Martha's forehead creased. Worry curved deep lines at the corners of her mouth. She twisted her hands in her lap, questioned, "No love?" She was visibly shaken.

"Support and respect," Halo supplied.

"Friendship, and a chance to live my dream," Alyn said.

"Dreams should include a man." An old-fashioned notion from her mother, but one she believed.

"The man will come someday," Alyn assured her. "Shy Lily is now."

"So there's nothing between you and Halo? Nothing at all?"

"Who knows?" Halo gave Martha hope. He finger-tipped Alyn's chin, so she looked up at him. "A lot can change in ten months."

Alyn had no such expectations. She was attracted to Halo. He was one gorgeous male. Her feelings amplified around him. Looking at him now made her heart quicken. Her stomach quiver. His smile alone turned her on. He could take her to bed with a flash of deep dimples. His body made her weak in the knees.

Daily, her mind gave her heart a reality check. Halo Todd's presence in her life was short-lived. Still, her heart was unconvinced. Maybe there was more to them than met the eye. Just maybe.

Martha looked at her fondly, if not a little sadly. "You deserve happiness, Alyn. Wherever and however you find it."

Halo skimmed his hand down Alyn's arm, raising goose bumps. He took her hand, held it loosely. Surprised her with, "I've already reserved your shop."

"You have? When?" The news was heart-stopping.

"On my drive from the stadium to the inn," he said. "I called a realtor friend. I didn't want the space rented out from under you. You're set for a year. Then we renegotiate."

We. Halo was all action, Alyn realized. When he wanted something, he went after it. Got it. She was grateful in this instance. Even if he had selective memory. Recalling only what suited him. She'd only agreed to be his girlfriend for ten months. He'd made her his fiancée and just added two more months to their deal. Apprehension prickled the back of her neck. He was getting ahead of himself. And way ahead of her.

Martha was expectant. "Which location?" she asked. "We looked at several."

"Downtown," said Alyn. "The empty store on the second floor of the historical landmark building."

Martha remembered. "It was quite expensive."

"Halo will support me until I turn a profit," Alyn said. "Then I'll pay him back."

"Be sure, Alyn," her mother requested. "I don't want you—"

"Disappointed?" Halo filled in. "Dumped?" He was blunt. "I won't hurt her, Martha. No breaking her heart. You have my word."

Danny gazed up at Halo, his eyes filled with hero-worship and trust. "I believe you, bro."

Bro? Halo's influence continued to rub off on Danny. Alyn trusted Halo, perhaps more than she should. He was kind to her family, including Quigley. "It's workable," Alyn told her mom. "Our word is binding. We've sealed the deal."

Martha gave in. "While I don't wholeheartedly approve, you're a big girl, Alyn, and can make your own decisions. I'm on your side, whatever you do. If Halo provides you with a means to an end, and you're his arm candy for a few months, so be it."

Arm candy? Where had her mom gotten such an expression? That's when she noticed a copy of *Lady's Life* on the coffee table. The glossy magazine featured "Statuette of a Trophy Wife" and "Arm Candy: Female Bling." Articles recently read by her mom, and written from a superficial perspective. A beautiful woman on a man's arm was all for show. Her value: no more than a pair of cuff links.

Cuff links didn't come close to capturing a man's heart. Alyn wondered if any one woman could keep her finger on Halo's pulse. His heart beat for so many.

In her case, she would stand by him, discouraging fangirls and groupies, so he could concentrate on the upcoming season. She was average looking. Few women would see her as a threat. She'd go with it, despite her misgivings.

"When do you and my daughter plan to go public?" Martha asked Halo.

"The announcement will come when friends, fans, and the media put us together. Not before. Let them figure it out," said Halo.

Martha breathed easier. "So as of right now, no one knows you're a couple?"

"Only me." Eleanor Norris reappeared, wearing a Rogues baseball cap, a peach seersucker jacket and matching slacks, and an I-knew-it smile. "I have no plans to tell anyone," she assured them.

Eleanor settled on a wicker armchair with a bright orange cushion. Sunlight from the window cast soft highlights in her gray hair. Her expression relaxed. She looked more eighty than ninety. She tapped the end of her cane on the hardwood floor. "I'll sit right here while you get ready for our outing."

"Where are you headed?" asked Halo.

"Beach and boardwalk," Alyn told him. "You're invited to join us."

He gave her a look that said, *You're my woman, I don't need an invitation.* It made her breath catch. "What about Quiggie Sparks?" he asked.

Alyn appreciated his concern for the pug. "I'm going to take him for a walk, then he'll come with us."

Halo frowned. "No dogs on the boardwalk, babe. Even one in a handicap cart."

"He won't be walking."

Never in his life had Halo imagined he'd be walking the Barefoot William boardwalk carrying a twenty pound pug in a front carrier backpack. Made of a water-resistant nylon fabric, the pooch pouch was soft and durable, with mesh sides for well-ventilated rides.

Halo shook his head when he caught his reflection in a store window. Dog days of spring. People stared and smiled. Stopped him, wanting to give Quigs some love. The pug responded with soft barks and doggie kisses. Halo received a few pats on the arm, too.

As they proceeded, Halo wanted nothing more than to casually hold Alyn's hand. To ease her close. To feel her sweet woman's body brush his. Instead, he cupped her dog's butt, supporting Quigley against his chest. The pug was having leg spasms. His back legs shot out unexpectedly. He'd recently kicked a lady in the chest. She'd stood too close while scratching his ears.

A muscle tremor was a tremor. Alyn's breath caught with each contraction. She would then lean over Quigley, praise him, and give a hug. The top of her head tickled Halo's chin. She wore her hair in a long braid. The breeze had tugged a few strands free. They flirted with his jaw, his cheek. Shiny and apple-scented.

Alyn Jayne was sexy without meaning to be sexy, Halo noted. She had no idea how hot she looked in her turquoise sundress with a narrow, gold necklace strap. He knew, and appreciated her. Nearly every man they passed gave Alyn the eye. Or sent her a smile. He wasn't crazy about the attention given his fiancée. No one knew she belonged to him. Not yet, anyway. In the men's minds she was a free agent. That would soon change.

Danny bounced along at Halo's side. Pointing out every store and sight on the boardwalk. Wanting to go here and there, and uncertain what to do first. The afternoon was all about the boy. Once something caught his full attention, they would stop. Take part. Until then, they kept pace with the other tourists. Browsed the storefronts.

Martha and Eleanor chatted up a storm. They had a lot in common, despite their age difference. Both were born in Richmond. Astonishingly, they'd grown up mere miles apart. Each had two children of their own. Eleanor beamed over six grandchildren and three great-grands. The ladies were both widowed. Eleanor's husband, Herman, had been a florist. Martha's husband, a landscaper. The women made plans to get together when they returned home.

Even during the afternoon, the party atmosphere on the boardwalk was endless and unbroken. It was the *season*, the snowbirds were in town. There was an eclectic blend of singles and families; grandparents and toddlers. Barefoot William had character. A life of its own. The air stirred with perpetual motion. The daytime was as exciting and explosive as the neon and torchlights of night.

Danny soon spun around, punched the air. "The carousel," he shouted as they neared the hand-carved purple-and-white horses with the amber eyes and gold saddles. "Ride with me, Halo," he pleaded. "Grab the brass ring."

"I'll take Quigley," Alyn said. "It's time for him to change positions anyway. There are benches shaded by beach umbrellas at the entrance to the pier. I'll sit, and let him stretch out."

"I don't mind watching him, honey," her mother offered. She fanned her face. "I'm parched. There's a metal cart selling lemon ice next to the ticket booth." She glanced at Eleanor, and the older woman nodded. "Two, please."

Halo had his wallet out, and five dollars extracted before Martha could unzip her fanny pack. He handed the money to Danny; nodded toward the vendor. Danny made the purchases, returning with the right amount of change and no spilling. Not one little drop. He was proud of himself. He'd remembered spoons and napkins.

"Can I go talk to the fishermen?" Danny asked. A group stood farther down the pier, casting their lines.

"Don't get too close to the railings," Martha warned.

The boy agreed and was gone, his feet flying. Halo kept an eye on Danny as he shot past Hook It, Cook It. The two shops were some of the oldest on the pier—Hook It sold bait and tackle, and Cook It stood next door, a small chef's kitchen where fishermen could have their daily catch cleaned and filleted for a small fee, then baked or fried for lunch or dinner. A salad, hush puppies, and fries came on the side. The tourists found it a novelty to eat their meals fresh from the Gulf.

Danny had listened to his mother, stopping and standing off to the side, out of the way. He watched, fascinated, as the fishermen's lines stretched with each hit, and they reeled in their catch.

Halo shifted his stance, casting his weight on his left hip. He found it difficult to stand still while Alyn removed the backpack. Her hands slid beneath the safety harness attachment, working upward along his ribcage as she unhooked the carrier clasps and loosened the drawstring. One of her fingernails flicked his nipple. The flick went south, straight to his groin. He stirred, talked himself down, while she lifted the padded straps over his head, freeing him. She then scooped the pug to her own chest. Quigs gave her so many kisses Halo lost count.

He watched her settle Quigley on his belly, cushioned by the flexible carrier. The pug wiggled his shoulders, stretched out his front legs. Alyn adjusted his back legs for maximum comfort. She stood, sighed, preoccupied. Unguarded, she leaned against Halo. She was a natural fit at

his side. Curving his arm about her waist, he settled the
flat of his hand on her hip.

The sun was in his eyes when Shaye Cates-Saunders approached. He squinted, took her in. A woman with curly
blond hair, strong opinions, she was the driving force behind Barefoot William Enterprises. Warm and welcoming,
she immediately went down on her blue-jeaned knees beside Quiggie. She was a hands-on animal lover.

"I heard there was a dog on the boardwalk, and I came
to see for myself," she told them.

The Cateses were a grapevine of news, Halo knew.
What one person saw or heard was known to them all in
a matter of seconds. "We're aware of the no-dog regulation," he said to Shaye. "His paws haven't touched the
boardwalk or pier."

Shaye grinned at him. "I heard you were backpacking
him."

"So we're cool? No fine?" he asked. A sign at the onset
of the pier socked dog owners with one hundred dollars
out of pocket for breaking the rule. He didn't want Alyn
to shoulder the expense. He'd write the check if a citation
was issued.

Shaye looked from him to Alyn, and shook her head.
"The pug is diapered. No accidents. We're good." She
pushed up, then, added, "I was tracking you for a reason.
To bring you this decal, so all's legit." She reached into the
side pocket of her jeans, removed a miniature blue-and-
white handicapped parking sticker. "Hook it on Quigley's
wheelchair," she suggested. "I have no problem with him
on the boardwalk. I hope he's back on all four paws soon."

Alyn exhaled, and sank farther into him. Relief softened
her features. She hated to leave Quigs at the inn for any
length of time. The pug could now go wherever they
went.

"Thanks, Shaye," he said.

Shaye eyed him then, closely. "I was at Media Day. Am I to believe you're engaged? For real?"

He gave her a short nod. "For real."

Her gaze shifted to Alyn. "To anyone I might know? To someone with a pug?"

"She guessed!" Danny returned, his mouth full from his visit with the fisherman. He'd apparently stopped at Cook It, and received a hush puppy. Eaten in one bite, or so it appeared. His cheeks bulged like a chipmunk's.

"No guessing," Shaye returned. "It's obvious, to me, anyway. Let things evolve. I wish you well."

"Thanks." Halo had always liked Shaye. She was one savvy woman.

Beside him, Danny swallowed hard, burst out with, "Let's ride the merry-go-round." He took Alyn's hand. "I want a horse next to Halo. He's got long arms. He can grab the brass ring."

"Let's do it," said Halo. "I'll buy the tickets."

"No need," Shaye said. She produced an all-day, all-event pass from her back pocket. Handed it to Halo. "On me. Enjoy."

She was being inordinately nice to him because he'd donated to her Island Walk Project. He lowered his voice, said, "You don't have to do this, you know."

Shaye whispered back, "Neither did you, but you did. I'm going to name a nature trail after you. Halo Run."

He rather liked that. "Sounds all sunshine and serious exercise."

"And scenic. The trail will cut through the middle of the island, showcasing natural vegetation and foliage." She nudged him on his way. "You'd better go now. Your fiancée and her brother are waiting. Danny's close to diving beneath the safety chains. Go catch the ring."

Halo produced the pass to ride the carousel. Twice. It

took him two tries to snag the brass ring. The ring scored them ten free tickets. To return on a later date.

They debated what to do next. Halo was too big for the rollercoaster and weighed too much for the Wave Swingers. Still, Danny pleaded to go. He was eight, which was the minimum age for riders. He dragged Alyn with him. His sister was reluctant.

The chairs were suspended from the rotating top of a red carousel; they tilted for additional variation of motion. Riders hung on tight as the chairs lifted and began to turn. The spinning accelerated.

Halo heard Danny's whoop and Alyn's shriek. The boy waved at him with every pass. His sister's face was as pale as a cloud when the ride slowed, stopped. Halo was at her side when she slid off the chair, and into his arms. He liked holding her. Danny wanted to go again, but Alyn convinced him there was a lot to see and do. The swing ride would be there tomorrow.

A breeze cut in and out along the pier. Clouds gathered, providing cover against the heat of the day. They moved on to the bumper cars. The ride was deserted. Twenty cars were grouped along one wall, in numerical order. All were metallic black with racing stripes down the middle and silver numbers on the back. Thick rubber bumpers wrapped the frames.

Danny chose number one. Alyn went with three. Halo took sixteen. They settled into their cars and strapped on their seat belts. One size bumper car did not fit all. Halo struggled to sit. His knees banged the steering wheel. His elbows poked out the sides. He was uncomfortable as hell.

"Start your engines," the operator shouted.

Small electronic cards drew power from the floor and ceiling. The cars vibrated. The metal floor gave a smooth ride.

Halo was at an immediate disadvantage. He couldn't

fully straighten out his foot to accelerate. The slight press of his toe was the extent of his power. He watched as Danny sped around the perimeter. Steering like a pro. Alyn was pedal to the metal. They soon got together and tag-teamed Halo.

"The sign at the entrance said NO HARD BUMPING," Halo growled as Danny bumped him from the back, and Alyn rammed him head-on. Hard enough he went all bobble-head.

He managed to sideswipe them both. Only to have them gang up on him once again. Somehow they managed to angle in, bump, and spin his car around. Full circle. Brother and sister were getting the better of him. Halo let them. Their laughter rose above the noise of the cars. They high-fived each time they passed. They were having fun. The rides and games allowed grown-ups to be kids. He felt twelve, but quite big for his age.

The operator eventually shut off the power, and the cars stilled. They unbuckled and climbed out, meeting at the entrance. A crowd had gathered, and a line formed. Halo was recognized. He shook hands and signed autographs. Talked baseball. He introduced Danny as his contest winner. He looked around for Alyn; located her against the pier railing. She openly watched him with his fans, accepting his popularity.

The operator called for the next round of riders, and the line edged forward. Halo nudged Danny toward his sister. Then took her hand. She laced her fingers with his. There were curious stares and a few craned necks, which he ignored. Alyn might wish to remain his mystery woman, but he wanted her acknowledged. Wasn't that the purpose of having a fiancée? Having her with him? Visible and available.

Danny bopped along beside them. Checking out every kiosk. Wide-eyed, he watched as a vendor hurled a boomerang out and over the Gulf, then it came back. He loved the colorful kites that lifted on the breeze.

He peered into the amusement arcade as they passed. "What's next?" he asked Alyn. "Whack-A-Mole? Pinball?"

"Let's check on Mom, Eleanor, and Quiggie," she suggested.

Late afternoon, and the crowd had thinned considerably. Enough so that Quigley easily caught sight of them. He was beside himself to reach Alyn. He barked, whined, and began to scoot. He was awkward, but fast, and got past Martha. The older woman panicked.

Alyn raised her hand, eased her mother's fear. "Let him come to us," she said. Twenty feet separated them.

On the worn wooden boards of the pier, a very determined Quigley rolled his body side-to-side, generating enough energy to partially rise on one knee. He shook out his leg, as if trying to wake his paw. To stir feeling. Wobble, limp, wobble, his gait was lopsided, but steady.

Nearly to them, he quivered, breathed heavily, and tilted left. Alyn rushed to him then. She dropped down and cuddled the pug close. She massaged his stronger leg. Tears came with her praise. "Look at you, big guy. Trying to walk. Soon, Quigs, soon. You'll be running to us."

Halo stood beside her. He curved one hand over her shoulder, squeezed his own reassurance. "He's getting sturdier."

Martha was all choked up, and Danny, too. Eleanor joined them, talking to her cane. "The little fellow scuttled, Herman. A sign he's healing."

Halo had a good feeling, too. Quiggie Sparks deserved a reward. He left them, returning to the dog carrier near the bench. There, he located a small bowl, a bottle of water, and two biscuits in the zippered pocket.

Alyn delivered Quigs just as he filled the bowl. The pug

chomped his Milk Bones. He had the occasional leg spasm, and his spine rippled once. Settling down, he rested his chin on his front paws, yawned. Content.

Martha returned to the bench. "Quigley will be fine now that he's seen you, Alyn. He worries when you're gone too long."

"I worry about him, too."

Halo gave Danny the choice of what to do next. "Your call, dude."

Danny sighed. Rubbed his stomach. He glanced from the amusement arcade to the rollercoaster; from the food carts to the beach. He weighed the decision carefully. There was so much to do. More than one day could hold.

His stomach growled, and Martha made his decision for him. "Your tank's running low, son. How about a basket of chili-cheese nachos? We could all use a snack."

Danny was all for eating. Eleanor, too. She offered to treat them. Halo refused to let her pay. "Got it covered, Ellie," he said. Eleanor blushed, seemingly pleased at his shortening of her name.

Martha gave Halo the eye, suggested, "Why don't you and Alyn ride the Ferris wheel while we eat. Danny likes action rides like the chair swing over the Gulf, but he doesn't like heights. Alyn could climb a mountain."

Martha the matchmaker. Halo liked her idea. "I'm good with that. We'd have privacy to talk."

Alyn nodded slowly, somewhat unsure, but agreeable.

It took Halo and Danny little time to locate the vendor who served nachos. The next metal cart over sold soft drinks. Halo bought an assortment. Once the snack was delivered, Halo pressed his palm to Alyn's spine, and steered her toward the Ferris wheel. They arrived as the ride was being loaded. One passenger car remained. They slid onto the suspended aluminum seat.

Halo flashed the all-day pass. "We'd like a long ride," he told the man. "We'll signal when we're ready to get off."

"Sure thing. Not a problem." The operator lowered the bar across their laps.

Another tight fit, Halo thought, but in this case, snug felt good. It beat the hell out of the bumper car. Alyn sat flush against him. Their shoulders brushed, and their hips and legs bumped. He took her hand as the ride jerked slightly, then swept upward. The wheel lifted them high. The view was magnificent; the entire boardwalk and pier stretched out before them. They sat in silence for three turns of the wheel.

Until he said, "You've gone quiet on me, babe."

She gave him a small smile. "I was thinking how much my life has changed in a week."

"For the better?"

"For the uncertain. We've a lot of variables between us."

"Name one."

"Can we pull off being engaged?"

"So far so good."

"Four people know we're a couple—Eleanor, my mom, Danny, and Shaye Cates-Saunders."

He leaned forward. "You want me to stand up and shout it from the Ferris wheel?"

"Don't you dare shake the seat."

He settled back, grinned at her. "Let's talk. A crash course in Halo 101. Ask me anything."

"Where did we meet? Don't go all rooster on me, and say a Rogues baseball game. We wore costumes at the game show. No one knows we were contestants."

"Let's keep the show between us. Our secret." He ran his thumb along the side of her hand. Gentle, intimate, deepening the contact with his woman. "People see me as someone who'd never settle down. I've raised hell, drunk myself under the table, been with"—pause—"more than one woman." He kept the number low, although given Alyn's expression, she knew he'd had his fair share of ladies. They'd been available. He'd indulged.

She worried her bottom lip, mulled over possible scenarios. "You're good with Quigley. We met in Richmond, while I was walking him, before his accident. Afterward, you stuck with me during his recovery."

"You paint me in a good light."

"You'd rather I paint you black and bad-ass?"

"That's how most see me."

"I don't."

He was damn glad she was giving him a chance. "I'm fine with the Quiggie angle. I like your dog. So where were you walking him? Park or sidewalk?" He needed visuals. Specifics.

"Centennial Park," she decided. "Near my neighborhood."

"What was I doing at the park?" He hadn't been at a park since he was a kid. Not since he'd bounced his end of the teeter-totter hard on the ground, and sent his best friend flying. His buddy had bruised his tailbone on the landing. And later punched Halo in the nose. Made it bleed. Not an even trade-off.

"There's a recreational center on the grounds. Do you ever participate in youth activities?"

"On occasion. Workable." In the off-season lots of ballplayers made impromptu stops to hang with the kids and meet their fans. To toss a baseball.

"You were immediately interested in me, but took it slow."

He shook his head. "We had instant chemistry. Made love that night."

She laughed in his face. Almost hysterically. "Never happened."

"Two dates, then."

"No one's going to ask when we slept together."

Sex made for a better story. "We've dated for what? A couple months."

"Followed by a long, platonic engagement."

He released a frustrated breath. "Platonic stays with us. No need to share my blue balls."

She ducked her head, blushed. "It has to be that way, Halo. Sex complicates relationships. We're complicated enough."

The Ferris wheel slowed, stopped to let several groups off. Halo saw Danny wave, and he waved back. The boy sat on the bench beside his mother, leaning against her side, his head on her shoulder. Recharging.

"Danny's a neat kid," he told Alyn.

"He's so happy to be here. No one would fault you for choosing him as your contest winner despite the connection of our engagement. We recently lost our dad. He wrote a sympathetic letter. You gave him the gift of spring training."

"Danny was a shoe-in." No one would dare argue with his choice. His decision was his own. Period. He had additional questions for her. "How do we share a free Saturday afternoon? Movie, shopping mall, sporting event?"

She eyed him. "I can't picture you antiquing."

He couldn't either. Neither would his buddies. Too girlie.

"How about if we volunteer at a senior citizens retirement village," she suggested. "Play games. Bingo to horseshoes."

"I like old people." Frank Cates, Rylan's grandfather, was one cool dude at eighty-eight.

"What about fun, Alyn? Since we're not having sex—"
Yet, he assured himself. He hadn't given up on sleeping
with her. "What sets you free?"

"I like to rollerblade. Read. Take long walks."

"I've never rollerbladed. I prefer to see the movie before I read the book. I jog instead of walk."

"We have so much in common."

Alyn's sarcasm made him smile. The Ferris wheel again
turned. Halo shifted on the seat, sliding his arm about her
shoulders. He kissed her temple, her cheek, then blew in
her ear, bit her earlobe. Lightly. She lurched forward.

Lady's ears were sensitive. Good to know. He braced his
free arm across her chest. "Careful, babe, no nosedive."

She tried to scoot away from him, but he squeezed her
even closer. "Your best and worst trait?" he asked her.

"I believe in people, covers both."

He understood. She saw the best in people, took them
at their word, yet they continually let her down. Still, she
kept believing. Some would say that was good; others
would call her foolish. Halo had no intention of hurting
her feelings.

"My best and worst traits walk a fine line," he told her.
"I push myself. I'm aggressive, competitive, and like to
win."

"Strong traits for an athlete," she said admiringly.

"I've made life a competition," he admitted. "I thrive
on rivalry. Sometimes I find myself holding my breath,
unable to exhale."

"Holding your breath will only turn your face as blue as
your balls."

No truer statement was ever spoken. She was teasing
him, and he liked it. He realized in that moment that Alyn
brought a calm to his life that he'd never experienced with
another woman. She allowed him to breathe. She didn't
expect him to show up nightly at bars, to buy drinks and

get drunk. To be the center of attention. To get rowdy. To spin out of control. She anchored him. He liked being grounded. It was new to him. But felt right.

She pointed to a couple near the entrance to the Ferris wheel. The ride had stopped, and they stepped forward. Both carried boxes of popcorn and soft drinks. They appeared nervous. "First date?" Alyn wondered.

She'd no sooner spoken, than the man tripped. He fell forward, into the woman, and they both went down. Their popcorn got tossed and their drinks spilled. The operator was quick to help them up, then to sweep away the mess. The couple brushed popcorn off each other's clothes, and their smiles curved. The woman actually laughed.

"Shit happens," said Halo. "No harm, no need to be self-conscious. Snacks can be replaced."

Alyn nudged him with her elbow. "Your most embarrassing moment?"

He ran one hand down his face. "Besides wearing the rooster costume?"

"There has to be something worse."

There was. Halo didn't embarrass easily. However there was that time when he was fourteen. "I dated a girl in high school who had braces. And really big boobs. Her father was a minister. Really strict dude. No hand holding. No kissing. He'd read a Bible verse before each date. I faced an interrogation when I brought Mary Theresa home."

"All those rules, and you stayed with her?"

"Bided my time. Big boobs, Alyn," he emphasized. "That's all a sophomore sees when he stares at a girl."

"Blinded by breasts. You dated young."

"I was old for my age. We had group dates until I finally got her alone. Storeroom at the church, during Sunday service. We were surrounded by stacks of hymnals and sacramental wine."

"Hallelujah."

He grunted. "Not quite. We kissed, and I managed to feel her up. Major fumble, and my wrist looped in the elastic of her bra strap. Twisted. I was snared."

Alyn giggled. A commiserating giggle for a horny teenage boy trapped in an awkward situation. "What happened next?"

"We were still getting it on, kissing, when I jerked my hand, only to have her strap tighten. The elastic nearly cut off the circulation in my hand. Mary Theresa was startled, bit down on my tongue. A wire popped on her braces, and stuck in my lip, like a fish hook."

"You're making this up."

He touched his finger to the corner of his mouth. "I still have the scar." No more than a pinprick, yet still visible, if someone looked closely. Alyn did.

"A very bad moment," Halo continued. "We're banging around in the dark, my hand up her shirt, wire locking our lips, when her dad flips the light switch. Seems we made enough noise during silent prayer to draw him from the pulpit."

"Last date?"

"Satan escorted me from the church, or so her dad said. Bloody-lipped and sinful." He shouldered her. "Your turn now."

"I've nothing to compare to your story."

"Give me something, anything."

"You're going to keep after me until I do?"

"Damn straight."

"Fine." Her sigh was heavy. "Several years ago, I was on the board of advisors for the Richmond Fine Arts League," she said. "Literacy, art, drama."

"Sounds snobby."

"It wasn't. The board supported community participation in all aspects of the arts. Small theater groups, book clubs, music, art shows. It was fall, and a drama ensemble produced *Fuchsia Duct Tape*, a renowned murder mystery by Fuqua Ducstan."

"Never heard of him."

"He's as famous to Broadway as you are to baseball," she noted. "The play was performed in the Griffin-Hill amphitheater."

"I know the place. It's close to our stadium. They host a lot of rock concerts."

"I met Ducstan at a cocktail party."

"I didn't take you for social."

"Not as social as you," she stated. "I get out on occasion. This was a special event. Fuqua and I hit it off. He requested that I introduce him the night of the play. In front of hundreds of people."

"Sounds like an honor," said Halo.

"Sorta was, sorta wasn't. I later found out everyone else on the board had declined the honor."

"Why?"

"Try saying Fuqua Ducstan's *Fuchsia Duct Tape*."

He did. Slow, then fast. "It's a tongue-twister."

"Worse when you're nervous."

"So what did you butcher?"

"I stood on the stage in a long black dress, beneath dimming lights, and presented him as 'fuck a duck' before God, a packed amphitheater, and the players."

Halo couldn't help himself, he laughed. A gut-busting laugh. "Oh, babe, priceless."

Alyn hung her head. "There were a few snorts, several coughs into the hand, but mostly silence. A stiff-necked audience." She scrunched her nose. "I resigned from the board, and was embarrassed for days."

"Not so bad."

"Not so good, either."

"We've both shown our asses."

"You more than me in that rooster suit."

"I've been told I have a great butt."

"You . . . do." Her voice was as soft as the breeze.

He glanced at his watch. They'd ridden the Ferris wheel for twenty minutes now. Danny would be getting restless. The sun had shifted, and the beach umbrella no longer protected Martha and Eleanor. He didn't want them sunburned. It was time to collect Quigley and move on. Still, he gave himself an extra minute. He'd yet to kiss his girl. No one rode the Ferris wheel without sneaking a kiss. It was tradition. He'd noticed, with the last turn, that the couple who'd spilled their popcorn had locked lips. Nice.

Unknowingly, the operator stopped the ride once they'd reached the very top. People got off, others got on. His time was now. Halo rolled his hip, and his thigh pinned hers. She tilted her head, met his gaze. There was both reservation and need in her eyes. Damn if he didn't hesitate. "I want to kiss you." He was asking, not taking. A first for him.

"You have one turn of the wheel."

He smoothed his mouth over hers. Smiled against her lips. "I'm taking two."

Ten

"Isn't that your teammate Halo kissing some woman at the top of the Ferris wheel?" Eden Cates asked Landon Kane as they approached the entrance to the pier.

She drew her glasses down her nose, and squinted skyward. Land tipped back his baseball cap, caught his own glimpse of the couple seated in the uppermost passenger car. He was fairly certain the man was Halo. The woman was shadowed by his wide shoulders. He bet the babe was his fiancée. He'd gamble it was Alyn Jayne.

He was right, he realized, moments later. Ten yards ahead, seated on a bench, were Martha and Danny, along with his contest winner Eleanor Norris. Quigley was stretched at their feet. Eleanor noticed him within a second of his seeing her. She flagged him down.

"Landon and the pretty photographer." She sounded glad to see them. "What brings you to the pier?"

"You," he told her.

"And Eden." Eleanor called it like she saw it. "I want to stop into Old Tyme Portraits before I leave town. Get my picture taken in a vintage swimsuit. That's the style we wore, back in my day."

"I'm sure you wore it well."

Eleanor tapped Land with her cane. "Still sweet-talking me, boy. I like it."

"How are you doing?" he asked the older woman. "Is there anything you need?"

"Sitting pretty, me and Herman. Here with the Jaynes."

Danny popped off the bench, came to shake Landon's hand. "I ate chili-cheese nachos," he said. "Two baskets. They're all gone. I didn't save you any."

"We're good," Landon assured him. "You didn't know we were coming. Dinner comes later for us. Eden's here to shoot a sunset wedding." He glanced at his watch. It was closing in on four o'clock. It was February, and the sun dropped at six. They had some time to kill.

He hunkered down to pet Quigley, and Danny knelt, too. Land scratched the pug under the chin. The dog wiggled. "How's your day going?" he asked the boy.

Danny gave him a quick, but thorough rundown of the day's activities, finishing with, "Halo and my sister are doing circles."

Kissing circles, thought Landon, smiling to himself, as the Ferris wheel turned. His best friend was claiming his fiancée publically. He was a witness.

Eden came to stand beside him. Danny returned to his mother. "Are you surprised?" She kept her voice low. Her camera was strapped around her neck, and she lifted it now, focusing on the riders. She snapped three consecutive shots. "I'm not."

"Why not?" he questioned.

She shrugged. "Photographer's eye, perhaps. The pictures I developed from the bonfire defined them as a couple. Halo's gaze was hotter than the flames. Alyn eyed him with interest."

"You're reading a lot into the pictures."

"It can't be missed. They reflect a future together. It's there for anyone to see."

Landon rose. Towered over her. His back was to Eleanor and the Jaynes. "We're talking Halo here," he reminded her.

"He's a person, not just a reputation."

"Like you know him."

"You don't have to know someone well to read their features. Alyn and Halo are committed, whether you believe me or not."

He'd have to see the photos to trust her instincts. Or see them face-to-face, as he was about to now. He saw Halo signal the Ferris wheel operator, and the ride came to an end. Halo climbed out of the car, then offered Alyn his hand. She took it, all natural and easy, as if they'd been holding hands for years.

They'd known each other *eight days.* Landon had difficulty reconciling that fact with the intimacy between them. Or maybe he chose not to. He'd seen initial sparks between them, the night they first arrived in town. How close Alyn stood to Halo. How protective he was of her. The way they glanced and caught each other's eye. Halo would stare until she blushed. Then grin broadly.

Attraction was one thing. Acting on it, another. Halo was raw, rough—all indulgence and gratification. He wasn't known for his longevity with the ladies. He lived for the moment. Alyn looked to the future. She was sweet and shy. With a subtle strength. A woman of substance and permanence. So unlike anyone Halo had ever dated. He hoped neither would get hurt.

Land kept his eye on them as they approached. They were too busy looking at each other to notice him. "Entwined," Eden whispered over his shoulder. He still had his doubts.

Danny spotted Halo and his sister, and took off running. Drawing their focus off each other and onto him. Alyn gave her brother a big hug. Halo fist bumped him. A sense of family surrounded them.

Eden spoke once more. "Give Halo the benefit of the doubt. The bigger the man, the harder he falls for the right woman."

Landon would support his best friend, no matter the outcome. He only wished Halo had confided his engagement prior to Media Day. He'd been as blindsided as the next guy.

"Dude," Halo said when he reached Landon. He nodded to Eden. Then tucked Alyn under his arm, fit her to his side.

They looked comfortable together, which helped Land to relax. "Your mystery woman." It was more statement than question. He thumped Halo on the back. "Congratulations are in order."

"Surprised?" Halo asked.

Land shrugged. "Not as much as you might think. When the time's right, it's right." He leaned toward Alyn, dropped a kiss on her cheek. "Halo's a lucky guy."

Alyn eyed Eden. "You're fortunate, too."

He had to agree. Eden was insightful. Unique. Her own woman. She'd moved outside the group. Landon took that moment to leave, as well. But not before he asked, "Eleanor, would you like to have dinner with us?"

She passed. "Full on nachos."

He trailed Eden down the wide set of steps that led from the pier to the beach. She held an inexplicable appeal. Today round Benjamin Franklin–style wire-rims replaced her rainbow glass frames. The day was humid, and her hair was full-blown frizz. She'd spent time in the sun since he'd last seen her. Her freckles stood out on her sunburned cheeks. She gravitated toward oversized button-downs and leggings. He figured she found them comfortable. Especially for work.

She waited for him on the sand. Smiling up at him as he came down. She had an honest face. The gap in her teeth made her look vulnerable. She was quick to kick off her flip-flops. Hung them over her fingertips. Dug her toes in the sand.

He came down on himself for not being more attentive to her. For allowing Halo's engagement to crowd her out. He'd had ten women approach him since noon, asking for dates. He'd been flattered, but passed. Eden had been on his mind ever since the bonfire. Since she'd eaten the burnt marshmallows he'd roasted. He had to admire a woman who got her fingers, lips, and the tip of her nose all gooey, and could still laugh at herself.

She'd been really nice to Eleanor, too. He liked that. Eden hadn't tried to draw his attention away from the older woman and onto herself. She'd listened intently when Eleanor outlined her future travels. She requested postcards from each locale, which pleased Eleanor greatly. Eleanor and Herman were willing to share their adventures.

Eden hadn't come looking for him today. He'd sought her out, catching her as she'd snapped and printed her last portrait photo, then locked up her shop. He'd invited her to dinner; she'd informed him of her wedding shoot. Scheduled at six, for an hour, no more. Then she'd be free. He decided to tag along. They would dine afterward.

"Who's getting married?" he asked her, as he chose a dry spot on the shoreline and dropped down. His light khakis were the same color as the sand. He bent one leg, rested an arm across his knee. "Family? Friend?"

"No one I know well," she told him as she walked along the compact sand at the water's edge. "A couple came into my shop last week, and had fun with their portrait shoot behind the bride and groom cutout. They asked if I'd photograph their vows. Nothing fancy. Stills, no video."

"Size of the wedding party?"

"Just the two of them." She smiled then. "Their officiant was ordained online overnight, just for the occasion."

"They're keeping it simple."

"Marriage is about two people committing to be one," she said. "Independent spirits can fly equally as high together."

He liked her philosophy. "The women I've dated made it all about me," he admitted. "They lost their personality in my popularity."

"You're in the spotlight much of the time. Do you perform best with eighty thousand fans shouting your name at the ballpark?"

He preferred one woman sighing his name in bed. He'd yet to find the right one. He evaded. "I don't mind the attention, although anonymity would be nice on occasion. I take downtime when I need it. Like tonight—you, me, the twilight. No hurry. No hassles."

She glanced toward the boardwalk, informed him, "Don't turn around then. We're not alone. There are dozens of people leaning against the railing, eyeing you. All wondering who you're with and what you're doing."

Landon blew out a breath. He'd hoped to lose his identity to the sunset, become no more than a blur on the beach. Not happening, he realized. They were seeking his autograph. Wanting to talk. While he was involved in another activity. They needed to keep their distance, and not crash the wedding. He had a way to move them on. People seldom interrupted a kiss.

He crooked his finger. "Come here, Eden."

She kinked her finger back. "You come to me."

So that was the way of it. He understood her position. She didn't want to appear to be coming on to him. So he went to her. He pushed up, got sand in his leather loafers. Sans socks. He shook out his feet. Some sand remained. Itched his toes.

Eden went still when he neared. She looked up, eyes wide behind her wire-rims. She seemed less self-assured. More shy. "What?" she asked, when he stared intently.

"An experiment."

"Why?"

Why, indeed? Because he found her interesting, unconventional, and sexy. He kept that to himself, and said instead, "My fans should disperse if I kiss you. They'll give us some privacy."

She scrunched her nose. Skeptical. "A kiss is your solution?"

He shrugged. There were holes in his theory. He just had the sudden urge to kiss her. "It's worth a try." He didn't allow her to question him further.

Her small Nikon hung on a strap around her neck, blocking him from getting too close. He gave her space, not wanting to damage the camera. Or push it into her chest, leaving an imprint on her breasts. He angled left, and their bodies touched. Awkwardly, but significantly. Satisfying him.

Sliding his hands into her hair, he cupped her face. The brush of his thumbs at the corner of her lips prepared her for his kiss. He leaned in, lowered his head. Experienced a sudden and unexpected physical jolt. Their kiss was strangely important to him. More than he'd anticipated. He took her mouth slowly, increasing the pressure when she kissed him back.

This was their first kiss, yet the romantic in him sensed both a newness and familiarity between them, as if they were meant to come together. To embrace each other at twilight.

Lingering, closed-mouth kisses were a turn-on, he found. Very soft and sensual, yet somewhat chaste and restrained. There was a different finesse to this kind of foreplay. Heightened sensation. Expectancy. Emerging feelings. Right there on the beach. Landon had never felt anything like it.

Apparently, neither had Eden. She clutched his upper

arms, as much to steady herself as to shift closer. Desire shivered through her, and into him. He absorbed her pleasure. Shared his heat. His sex pressed her hip. He was aroused and charged. Fortunately, he had his back to the boardwalk. He avoided a public erection.

He broke their kiss when it was about to get complicated. Their time together was limited. She had a wedding to shoot. He needed to catch his breath, bring himself under control.

She dipped her head, inhaled deeply. Then glanced over his shoulder. "Our kiss cleared the boardwalk."

Their audience had scattered. Privacy was theirs. For the moment. He waged an inner war. To kiss, or not to kiss her again. Her eyes were bright. Her face flushed. Her lips pouting, plump. Her breathing was uneven. Her breasts soft against his side. His thigh pressed between her legs. He was certain she was wet.

Her sigh whispered her own indecision.

He cleared his throat, came to his own conclusion. He stepped back. Disconnected. His hands itched to touch her again. He clamped them instead. Shifting his focus, he looked out over the Gulf. High tide. Heavy waves advanced on the shoreline. Retreated. He rolled his shoulders. Stretched his arms over his head. Kicked out each leg. Restored circulation to body parts other than his groin.

They'd separated just in time. "Eden, we're here." A woman's voice drifted to them across the sand. "Are you ready for us?"

Eden collected herself quickly. She motioned the woman, man, and officiant to join her at water's edge. She smiled warmly. "Perfect timing. We have an hour to work around the sunset." She next introduced everyone, by first names.

Landon met Zoey, Ayre, and their best friend, Wilson, who would preside over the ceremony. There was nothing formal about their nuptials. The bride wore a white tank top and shorts, a woven band of daisies in her hair. The groom was equally casual, wearing a blue T-shirt and ladder-ripped jeans. Wilson slung a tie around his neck, his blue button-down wrinkled and stuffed into a pair of navy walking shorts. All were barefoot.

Land sensed they were meant for each other. Ayre looked at Zoey as if she were the most beautiful woman alive. Zoey's gaze held his, deep and endearing. Her hands trembled, and Ayre brought them to his lips, kissing them reassuringly.

"I'm ready, whenever you are," Eden called to them. "Do what feels natural. Pretend I'm not even here." She took several steps back, circling them, standing on tiptoe, and then kneeling on the sand. She captured each expression from every angle.

They exchanged their vows on the sun's descent. There was a richness to the night as it fell in shades of gold. The Gulf rippled copper, as if cast with pennies. The sand shimmered medallion bronze. The horizon was gilded. A glowing backdrop for their wedding.

"Kiss her," Wilson soon told Ayre.

Free-spirited and spontaneous, Ayre picked up his bride, and carried her into the ocean. They kissed amid the toppling waves and waning twilight. Their laughter followed them back to shore.

"We're headed to the movies," Zoey said.

Marriage and a movie. Casual. Uncomplicated. Landon liked their lifestyle.

"Stop by my shop tomorrow," said Eden. "I should have proofs available by noon."

The couple waved as they ran across the sand. Wilson

trailed them more slowly. Zoey and Ayre went right once they reached the boardwalk. Wilson left. He ducked into Molly's Diner.

Eden stood at the waterline. Land walked to her. She smiled, happy in the aftermath of the wedding. He felt light-hearted, too. On impulse, he bent and kissed her on the forehead. As spontaneous as he, she kissed his cheek. Close to his mouth.

"What now?" he asked. "I promised you a meal."

"I like a man who keeps his word."

He hadn't made a reservation. However his status as a Rogue would get him a table anywhere in town. "Steak, seafood?" Her choice. He wasn't particular.

She made his life easy. "Let's take a walk, see where it leads."

He was willing. They held hands as they left the sand. He'd initiated the contact. She hadn't pulled away. Soft skin. Short nails. Solid grasp. She led him with hungry purpose.

Her idea of dinner was creative eating down the boardwalk. No fancy, five-star dining. No candlelight. No muted music. No after-dinner liqueurs. Instead, she enjoyed junk food. Lady had a sweet tooth. Caramel apples. A box of homemade fudge. Bags of penny candy.

She turned healthy at Vigor, a wellness spa around the corner from the boardwalk. She sipped an orange-banana smoothie. He ordered an organic carrot-apple juice.

He never took his eyes off her. She'd captured his attention without even trying. Her life was fun. Without drama. She was her own person. A woman of switch-ups and surprises. Honest. Cute, quirky, without pretense. Free. She embraced the night, hugging herself, and then him. He liked her spontaneity.

She also people-watched with a prescient eye. She recognized love between couples that had yet to be discovered, yet to be spoken. She was a romantic after his own heart.

The boardwalk was hosting the Spring Music Festival. Musicians set the night to dancing. Every kind of music from contemporary to reggae was performed. People stopped to listen. Some clapped, some danced, and the majority of tourists tossed a few dollars in the instrument cases.

Carefree and comfortable in her own skin, Eden danced down the boardwalk. Her moves were smooth, creative. Rhythmic. An unoccupied, upright piano was chained to the blue metallic railing. A block-lettered sign was propped above the keyboard: FREE PLAY. EXPRESS YOURSELF. She patted the bench, and he accompanied her. They pounded out a basic duet of "Chopsticks." A little off-key. Applause came with the last note.

Moments later, she took part in theater freeze frame, a boardwalk novelty performed by a local drama group. Still as stone, she became human art, alongside a pirate. People slowed and stared. She didn't blink, barely breathed for a considerable time. Impressive.

Landon had his own way of bringing her back to life. He leaned in and kissed her. Soundly. She lowered her eyelashes, and smiled against his mouth. He eased back, grinned, too.

"You've walked me home," she said. They'd nearly reached the end of the boardwalk. Her shop was two doors down.

It was only ten o'clock. He was having a great time and hated to see the night end. The air was warm. A half-moon climbed to meet the stars. He nodded toward a wooden bench. "Sit and share the moonlight?"

Silence from her, which didn't bode well for him.

Maybe she was ready to call it a night. Perhaps she wasn't as into him as he was into her. That would be unfortunate. Her letting him down. Then walking away.

She bit her bottom lip, thoughtful. "Or . . ." She weighed her words. "We could make out on my couch in the back room?"

He hadn't seen that coming. "I didn't know you had a back room." Totally lame. He tried again, "Kissing on a sofa, high-school style?"

"It's a foldout."

A bed. "You sleep here?"

"On nights I work late." She took a step toward him. Raised an eyebrow. "So . . ."

Dry humps and kissathons. Why the hell not? "Sixteen and horny."

She licked her lips. "Me, too."

He came up behind her as she unlocked the door, entered. The outside lights filtered through the main window, twinkling on the floor. She eyed him over her shoulder. "Feel free to drop quarters to find your way out, like you did on the path to the wedding chapel."

Heat crept up his neck. "You noticed?"

"I'm two dollars richer."

He followed her past the faceless cutouts to a narrow rear door hidden behind a tall metal cabinet. A flick of a switch, and a panel of lights ran the full length of the drop-ceiling. Her back room was more efficiency apartment than storage space. Small and compact and outfitted with a sink, refrigerator, and bathroom. A retro circular table and two chairs sat in the center. Customer portraits framed the walls.

She placed her camera safely on the kitchen counter. With an adjustment of the dimmer switch, the room softened. Taking his hand, she led him to the overstuffed sofa. Three wide cushions. Dark fabric. Comfortably folded.

She cut him a look from beneath her eyelashes. Licked her lips suggestively. Actually giggled. "My parents are playing cards at the neighbors. They won't be home for an hour. We can fool around, but no going all the way."

Lady had imagination. She also had rules. No sex tonight, which was fine by him. Foreplay had a dual edge. He had ways of winding her so tight, she'd never uncoil. She wouldn't be satisfied by anyone's hands but his own.

They came together. He sat, and she straddled his lap. A slow slide onto his thighs. A spreading of her legs. He curved his hands over her knees. Splayed his fingers. She was slender; his hands big. His fingertips wandered up her leggings. She covered his hands before he could tuck them beneath her bottom. She held him off. He let her.

As she looked into his eyes, her sexy side emerged. She tossed her hair, and her breasts bounced. Tilting her head, she asked, "Why'd you ask me out, Landon?"

He tugged one white-blond curl. Drawing her face closer to him, he played along. "I'm into girls with electric hair."

"I'm into popular boys. Especially jocks."

"I play baseball."

She flared her nostrils. "A turn-on."

"Are you turned on now?"

"I've been hot since you asked me out."

"That was three days ago."

"I know."

Land smiled to himself. She was good at their high school game. He felt a jolt in his belly. A stirring in his groin. Her sensual boldness aroused him.

She leaned in, finger-brushed his hair off his face. Then traced his eyebrows. Grazed his cheekbones. The blade of his nose. The symmetry of his jawline. Slow and intimate. Her gaze settled on his mouth. Eyes, deep blue and dilated. "You are fine," she admired, before nipping his bottom lip. Hard enough to twist his hips. Draw his moan.

Expectant, she waited for his kiss. With parted lips. A peek of her tongue. Instead of taking her mouth, he kissed her brow. The arch of her cheek. Nuzzling close, he licked the soft spot below her ear. Then blew softly. Goose bumps rose, visible at the vee of her button-down. He started to unbutton her top, but she stopped him. "Clothes stay on." Her rule, not his.

He could play dressed. It was very sexy. He also went with no touching. For the moment. He took her lips, only to pull back. Again and again. He kept his kisses light as breath. He savored her. Slow and lingering. Their closed-mouth kisses lasted forever, deepening their intimacy. Creating an emotional closeness.

"I heard you were a good kisser," she sighed against his mouth. "The girls were right."

"What girls?" He was curious.

"From my gym class. Susie, Linda, Danielle, Jody, Mary, Tammi."

He played along. "Ah . . . those girls."

"You've kissed many. Felt up a few. Gone all the way with the homecoming queen."

Gossip built his reputation. "I'm with you now."

"Are you liking me?"

Too damn much. "We're working it."

He wanted her. Bad. He went on to prove it. This time with touch and tongue. He French kissed her, long and deep. Mating with her mouth, mimicking sex. Until they were both breathing heavy. He wanted her hot. All worked up. When she gasped, needed a breather, he kissed her even more soundly.

She fanned her hands over his shoulders, curled her fingers into corded muscle. Her body had gone liquid. She clung to him as he grazed her chin, her cheek, with his teeth. Along with the pulse point at the base of her throat.

Her breath hitched, and her oversized shirt fluttered at her waist, revealing her belly. Her skin was as pale as the lighting. He felt her up; palmed her breasts. Her nipples poked the cotton cups of her bra. He wanted to flick the front clasp, but held back. Too much, too soon. He went on to trace her from cleavage to navel, then hand-spanned high on her legs. He stroked the crease between her thighs and torso, stopping short of her sweet spot.

She gave an involuntary shiver when he fingered the waistband on her leggings. Then strayed beneath the elastic. The rough pads of his fingers tipped her pubic bone. He realized that Eden shaved—everywhere. Her thigh muscles tightened, clenching his hips. An uncensored coming undone. He pulled out his hand. Cupped her butt.

Her heart pounded and anticipation took hold. Her own hands found their way beneath his blue polo. She saw his Rogues tattoo inside his left hip. The image of a sword with *Invincible* along the blade. She traced the edge. "A phallic symbol?" she asked.

"No metaphor needed." He sported seven inches.

"Then what?"

"Myths and legends," he managed. "I read *The Sword in the Stone* by T. H. White numerous times as a kid. Excalibur proved Arthur's lineage."

"I can picture you as a Knight of the Round Table. I have a cardboard cutout of Lancelot."

"I'd rather be king."

"Your Majesty."

She focused again on his body, as if he were royalty. Running her nails up his sides, she lightly scratched down his middle. He was six-pack cut. Her fingers followed his happy trail, dipping a fraction of an inch beneath the waistband of his khakis. Only to exit, and rub along his zipper. She squeezed his length. Wound him tight. He almost lost it.

The calculated shift of her hips made his palms sweat. His hands fist. His hips jerked. The muscles in his thighs contracted. She teased him without mercy. The slightest scoot forward, and she was centered over him. She must feel his every flex. His every inch of hardness. Had they been naked, he would've entered her.

The air was as heavy as their breathing. Their scents mingled. He was hard, and she was inaccessible. There'd be no skin-on-skin. Foreplay was killing him. He set his back teeth; a muscle jumped along his jawline. He couldn't collect himself. He was too far gone.

Their plan to make out on the couch like high schoolers was deceiving. Flawed. Teenage hormones didn't come close to adult libido. He'd long passed sixteen. Temptation rubbed him. Raw and urgent. Sex pressured him now. He'd never wanted a woman as much as he desired Eden Cates. His patience was stretched to the max. He needed to be inside her. To feel her wetness. To bring them to orgasm.

There was only one way out. He took it. He kissed her one last time, with passion and possession. A sinful tangle of tongues. Then breaking apart, he craned his neck and pretended to listen. "I heard a car door slam." His voice was deep, rough, forced.

"Y-you did?" she stammered.

"Your parents are home."

"T-they are?" Her face was flushed. Her lips were swollen. Another button on her blouse had come undone. The elastic of her waistband had rolled beneath her navel. Her femininity was outlined by the thin fabric.

He lifted her from his lap in one fluid motion. Set her beside him. He rose, stood with his arms at his sides. His heart hammered. His chest heaved. He felt as unsteady as she looked.

Turning aside, he adjusted himself. His dick twitched, felt betrayed. No action tonight. Another time, Land promised. He signed off with, "See you at school tomorrow."

"In algebra."

He made it through her shop and out the front door. He headed north on the boardwalk.

Stiff-man walking.

"How'd school go today?"

It was seven p.m., and Eden could barely hear Landon over all the barking. She sat on a long wooden bench in the fenced play yard at the no-kill animal shelter. She'd come to choose her four-footed companion for the Dog Jog, scheduled for Sunday. It was an event not to be missed. Worthwhile, memorable, tail-wagging fun.

She cut him a look. Appreciated the man. He wore a Barefoot William T-shirt tucked into worn jeans. He pulled off casual with style. Was male gorgeous. She was dressed similarly, in a pale blue tee with her store logo and cuffed jeans. "You cut algebra," she returned.

"I didn't finish my homework. I was preoccupied last night."

"Making out can be a distraction."

"I can always make up the assignment."

"Jocks need to maintain their grades."

"I carry a 'B' average."

He dropped down beside her, kissed her lightly, familiarly, on the lips. Then took her hand. "Thanks for meeting me here," he said. "We can pick our dogs together." He scanned the grassy area. "Any caught your eye yet? Do you have a favorite?"

She leaned her head against his shoulder. It seemed natural to do so. "Not just one, I love them all. A very tough decision." There were puppies and adult dogs. All sizes. All breeds. All worthy of adoption. All needing a forever home.

"I'm the last player on the team to pick a furry partner. The guys discussed the Dog Jog during warm-ups and scrimmages this morning. There are sixty entrants. Rylan's got Atlas. The lead Great Dane. Halo and Alyn will bring up the rear with Quigley. Zoo viewed the dogs yesterday. He went with a year old Rottweiler, Turbo. Our pitcher Will decided on a Chihuahua, Cutie Patootie."

She couldn't help but grin. "Love her name."

"Will's calling her Patoot. The man's six-six. The Chihuahua barely weighs four pounds. You can hardly see her over the top of his sneaker. He can carry her in his shirt pocket, if she gets tired."

"Her little legs may only last a block."

"He'll get her to the finish line."

They watched the dogs play, noticing that some interacted better than others. Eden was soon drawn to a shy male beagle who clung to the fence. He shook every time another dog approached, turning his head away.

Eden motioned to Betty Elroy. The shelter director hurried over. "Tell me about the beagle," she requested.

Betty told them what she knew. Which was very little. "That's Obie. Shelter-named. No background on him. He's been here a month. Someone dropped him off in a crate by the back door. No note. No care instructions. No aggression on his part. He just hasn't warmed up to anyone."

Eden's heart went soft and sad simultaneously. She released Landon's hand, stood, and slowly walked toward Obie. She stopped when he started to tremble. She lowered herself to the ground. Sat cross-legged. Allowing him to get used to her.

"Head's up," Land called from behind her. She glanced back, and he tossed her a dog treat. "I packed snacks. Came prepared."

Eden noticed that he had hunkered down, too. Presently, he began petting a reddish, long-haired dachshund. The weenie leaned against his ankle. Looked up at him adoringly. That was the effect he had on females.

"Her name is Ruby," the director told Landon. "She's eight. A real sweetheart. Sadly, her owner recently passed away. No immediate family wished to take her."

"Has she met Obie?" asked Land.

"She just arrived, and hasn't officially made the rounds."

"Introductions are in order then."

He pushed up, and Betty moved on. Scooping the dach against his chest, he crossed to Eden, then crouched again. He released Ruby. The dachsie sensed her purpose. She snuck the biscuit from Eden's outstretched hand, and delivered it to the beagle. She dropped it by his left front paw. Obie remained reluctant.

Other dogs circled, checking out Ruby. She allowed them a sniff or two, then barked them along. She stood guard, not letting them near Obie.

Eden pointed. "Ruby's gone belly-down."

"Not much of a drop," said Land. "She's two inches off the ground."

The dachshund scooted toward Obie. She didn't bark, only whined, offering canine sympathy. Obie hung his head. Whimpered back. The sound was pitiful. Utter dejection.

Tears filled Eden's eyes. The dogs were bonding. She'd never seen anything like it. She swore there was hope in Obie's eyes, a moment of trust. He did the unexpected. He nudged the biscuit back to Ruby. She ate it, then trotted back to Landon, demanding a second.

It became a game, Land handing Ruby a treat. Her tak-

ing it to Obie. The beagle ate one of three. Ruby confis-
cated the other two. Eden used her iPhone to take pictures. They were priceless.

"Stand up, and follow my lead," Land said. Eden did so.

"Ruby," he called, patting his thigh. "Come, girl." He
took Eden's hand, and they started to walk away. They
hoped Ruby would follow. And that Obie would come after her.

The dachshund grew dismayed. She whined. Her eyes
were on Landon, but she remained beside Obie. The director came to their rescue, providing a solution.

"A double-dog coupler," Betty said, holding dual
leashes, connected by a circular center link. "You can
comfortably walk two dogs of different breeds and sizes
without the hassle of tangled and twisted leashes. The coupler was donated to the shelter, but we've never had two
dogs leave together, so it's all yours."

"Ours?" Eden said slowly.

Betty waved her hand, was apologetic. "My mistake. I
jumped to conclusions. I assumed you'd be sponsoring the
beagle and dachshund in the Dog Jog. Helping to find
them a home."

"You'd be right," Landon assured her, accepting the
coupler. "We're also considering adoption. Joint custody."

Eden started. "We are?"

Land rubbed the back of his neck. "Give us five to collect our thoughts."

The director beamed. "Take all the time you need. A
permanent home is preferable. But a chance for them to
be showcased at the event is nice, too." She moved on.

Eden gave him the eye. "What are *we* thinking?" she
asked him.

"Pet parents. Any objections?"

She was truthful. "I barely know you."

"We've known each other since high school."

She laughed. A little. "Still, taking on pets is a huge responsibility."

He grew serious. Sensitive. "Too soon to adopt? You mentioned losing a dog and cat a while back."

"Their loss stayed with me a long time." She still had their food bowls. Their old toys. Their bedding. "I love being an owner," she admitted. "I miss having another heartbeat in the house. I'd planned on a future adoption. I just hadn't gotten around to visiting the shelter, until now."

Eden eyed the two dogs. "It's obvious Obie needs Ruby. They should be adopted together. I think they both need us." Somehow that felt right. Her heart warmed. Decision made.

"We have four days to familiarize them with the double-leash. They could enter the Dog Jog as a pair. Walk together."

"You'd help me train them?"

"I'm up to the challenge."

"It would mean seeing each other. Often."

He seemed relieved. "A means to an end. I have the dogs to thank."

"You want to spend time with me?" She wasn't fishing for compliments, merely needed assurance.

"I like you, Eden."

It was hard for her to accept. The man could date anyone on the boardwalk. Any woman in Richmond. Most any woman on the planet. Yet he chose to be with her.

She sat there, mind blown, until he nudged her with his elbow, asked, "You like me back?" His expression appeared more little boy than grown man.

"I feel sixteen."

"I'm feeling awkward. Answer anytime."

She considered. "Are you liking me to get me naked?"

He shook his head. "I've never told a woman I liked her to get her in bed."

"Liking me *will* lead to sex."

"It doesn't have to."

"So, you're fine with foreplay, nothing more?"

"More would be nice."

"Expect it." The when and where would come in good time.

"You're already making me sweat."

"I like making you sweat." Less apprehensive, she said, "I like you, too, Landon."

His smile came fast. Hot and sexy. "We're getting there."

Getting *where?* She was about to ask, but just then the director of the shelter returned. She clasped her hands before her and looked questioningly at the two of them. "I hate to interrupt, but the couple standing by the gate are interested in Ruby. I told them you were discussing—"

"She's adopted." Eden didn't let her finish.

"So is Obie," added Land.

"How fortunate for them." Betty was pleased. "Let me introduce the Fosters to another dachshund, and I'll start your paperwork. My office is through the side entrance, second door on the left. I'll meet you there."

Land hooked Ruby to the coupler, but Obie fought it. The beagle cringed. Despaired. Backed against the fence. Curled into a ball. Landon went down on one knee, placed his palm on Obie's shoulder. Gentled the dog. "No one's going to hurt you ever again. You're with us now. I protect what's mine."

Landon was their champion. He was kind and generous, a good man. Obie apparently thought so, too. He gave Land his paw. They shared a momentary truce, up until Landon tried to collar him. Obie panicked again, panting so heavily, Land released him.

He passed Ruby's leash to Eden. "I'll carry him," he decided. Obie went stiff in his arms. Fortunately, it was a short distance to the office. Land again set him down.

The director soon joined them. They signed the paperwork and paid the adoption fees. Then headed out. Ruby trotted along on her half of the coupler. Obie got carried. The dog buried his head in Land's chest.

They eventually stood in the parking lot between their Porsches, and went over their options. "My place," Eden assumed.

"No pets allowed at Driftwood Inn." Where the team resided.

"Follow me home?"

"Right behind you. I'll bring the dogs."

He didn't want to split them up. Eden was appreciative. The two were better together. "I'll drive slowly. Flash your headlights if they don't ride well."

"If for some reason we should pass you, and you see Ruby driving, be concerned. Very concerned."

She laughed. "That's a photo I'd stop and take." She helped him load the dogs. Ruby settled in on the passenger seat. Obie dove for the floor mat.

"Food," she said, once he was behind the wheel. "A stop at Quick Mart, and we're set."

He followed closely behind her. Eden glanced in her rearview mirror often. She saw Ruby's head pop up and her paws go to the window, as the dachshund tried to look out. She bobbed, but was too short to see much.

Once home, they allowed the dogs the run of the yard, then called them inside. They sniffed, explored. Obie became Ruby's shadow. They ate from the same bowl. Then took the hidden, narrow staircase located off the kitchen to the loft above the sanctuary.

Eden turned on a standing lamp just inside the door. The pink bulb provided soft lighting. Landon looked around her bedroom while she set out the dog beds. Two beds, but they settled on one. The excitement of a new home overtook Ruby, and she soon slept. Obie rested with one eye open. He breathed easier now, but wasn't fully trusting.

She next turned to Landon. They stood so close, they could've been one person. "Dogs are tucked in."

"It's our time now."

She was ready for him. The promise of sex filled the room. Invisible, yet tangible. Their silence became foreplay. The moments stretched out as awareness became arousal.

She kicked off her flip-flops.

He heel-toed his tennis shoes.

He curved one arm about her shoulders, the other beneath her knees, and lifted her. Still clothed. He moved the few feet to the double bed set in the middle of the room against the wall. Her bed was unmade. She'd left the house in a hurry that morning. The blankets and sheets twisted like lovers. Several pillows were scattered near the headboard.

He lowered her onto the mattress. She stared up at him, her hair as out of control as her heartbeat. Her lips were slightly parted. She slowly brought them together, licked them. She saw his body tense, as if she'd licked *him*.

Vulnerability lay with her, as he stood beside the bed. This wasn't high school anymore. She had an eye for visual composition. Balance and bone structure. Musculature. Landon was flawlessly handsome. She experienced a moment of panic. He belonged with a woman as equally attractive. Someone fit and feminine. With perfect teeth and soft skin. Not someone like her, who refused braces, and had no beauty regimen. Who binged on junk food, and believed chewing was an exercise.

He sensed her insecurity. Laid it to rest. "Don't question

how I feel about you, Eden. I have no words. It's all in here." He touched his heart.

She melted. Let the night unfold. The pull between them was poignant and strong, man to woman, and brought heat to her belly. She felt suddenly warm all over. Her breasts were heavy. The sexual ache between her thighs made her restless. She couldn't catch her breath. He hadn't even touched her.

Landon did the unexpected. His eyes darkened as he slowly stripped down. "I'm far from perfect, sweetheart," he said. "I have scars."

He showed them to her. One by one, as he took off his clothes. A show designed just for her. Off came his T-shirt, and he pointed to a laser thin line at his shoulder. "Rotator cuff surgery." Didn't detract from his appearance one single bit. She was far more interested in his sculpted chest.

"Appendix removed," he went on to say. Again, no more than a hint of a scar on his abdomen. She'd never seen a stomach so flat.

He unsnapped, unzipped his jeans. Dropped them. He stood in navy boxer briefs. He filled them out nicely. "Cleats to the calf," he continued. "An Atlanta Brave slid into me instead of the base." Barely a mark, yet she'd appreciated the tour of his body.

He lowered his boxers. His sex was impressive. She stared openly. He climbed on to the bed. The mattress dipped, as he stretched out beside her. Her hands itched to touch him. But he caught her wrists, stopped her. "Let me get a look at you first."

She wanted to close her eyes while he undressed her, yet remained brave. She watched his features for reaction, waiting for a narrowing of his eyes, a scrunch of his nose, his frown. Instead his eyes heated, his nostrils flared, and an appreciative smile curved his lips as he moved his hand beneath the hem of her cotton T-shirt and lazily dragged it up her chest. She lifted her shoulders, and he slipped it over her head. Next came her lacy bra. It was on; it was off. Her head again found the pillow, and her hair fanned her flushed face.

He moved his hand over her breast. Firm, round, and perfectly plump. Smooth and soft, and more than a handful. He liked the feel of her. She had freckles on her chest. And her skin was pale.

He wanted her out of her jeans, and took them off. Followed by her thong. Her waist was narrow. Her hips, perfectly shaped. The shaved, smooth skin between her legs made his heart slam; his dick throb. Misbehave. No other woman had ever stolen every thought from his head and made him forget to breathe. Eden was doing that to him now.

He wanted inside her. Bad. He managed to hold back, but just barely. He was twice her weight in muscle, and was easily twice as strong. Rising on his knees, he settled over her with a gentleness that made her stomach go soft. He hugged her to him, and buried his face in her hair. Then bit her earlobe, dragging his teeth along the plump flesh. She tensed under him, and her thighs pressed against his hips. He kissed her neck, felt the beat of her heart on his lips. Then lowered his mouth to hers.

"Are you on birth control?" he asked. "Or do I need a condom?"

"We're safe."

Landon tasted her further. He kissed her longer, deeper. Satisfying his craving for her. They explored each other with thoroughness. Each learned what the other person liked. Her heat wrapped around him. She absorbed his own warmth.

She ran her hands over his shoulders and down his back. She lifted her legs, offering herself, shifting until she was right where he needed her to be. Their bodies merged, molding together without any awkward motions or hesitations. They fit together as if they were created for each other.

Sensation hit him, which he hadn't expected. A sense of oneness settled in his soul. Eden was the woman he'd searched for all his life. The thought was clear. Powerful. He was overwhelmed by feelings for her that would never leave him. He needed to know if she felt the same.

He broke their kiss, and she blinked, her gaze heavy-lidded and lost in him. He saw her longing reflected in her dark blue eyes. The depth of her desire. Her commitment. She cared for him. Possibly even loved him. He was suddenly grateful. He silently counted his blessings.

"Land?" she questioned him. Her lips were swollen, well-kissed. Her chest rose and fell. Her nipples were fully puckered. Her pubic muscles clenched around him. "Is everything okay?"

His answer came in the slow rock of his hips. Followed by a rhythmic pace that heightened their pleasure. He whispered, coaxed her, driving her higher.

They were both suddenly there.

Both stiffening.

Both shattering.

Both boneless. Mindless. Replete.

He collapsed on her. Managed not to crush her.

Their breathing was heavy in the stillness.

Exhaustion had them moving slowly as they cleaned up. They could've lingered in the shower while Land gave Eden good loofa, but she wanted to ease back into bed, and sleep for an hour. He allowed her the luxury. Before he took her again.

He slipped back into his clothes, took the dogs outside, and was surprised that Obie stayed close to him. The beagle walked tentatively back into the house, while Ruby ran for the stairs. The dachsie already knew her way around. She was here to stay.

Land was glad that Eden had taken his idea of adoption and run with it. They both loved dogs. Another bond between them. He made sure Obie and Ruby were situated before returning to bed. Ruby lay with her chin on Obie's front paws.

Stripping down, he slid in beside Eden. She turned to face him, full on. He nuzzled his jaw against the top of her head. Kissed her brow. The warmth of her breath blew against his neck.

He felt comfortable with this woman. Compatible. He was at a crossroads in his life. At the end of the day, he'd chosen to come home to her. He had only to convince her to be there for him.

Eleven

"Who you trying to impress?" Left fielder Joe "Zoo" Zooker looked from Halo to Landon. Top of the fourth inning, and both men had returned to the home dugout. Halo after a triple; followed by Land airmailing a fastball over the center field fence. "What the fuck? We're playing a Saturday night exhibition game against local high school state champions. We agreed not to jack the score."

Halo side-eyed him. "One out. We're ahead by two, which we just scored. Barefoot William Hurricanes are playing hard. The guys are damn good."

"Underdogs do win," Land reminded Zoo.

"Not against us." Zoo was always cocky. "So who you doing in the stands?" He went back to his original question.

"The stadium's packed." With both major league baseball and high school fans. Families and local supporters of the Hurricanes sat on the edge of their seats, hoping their boys fared well. Rogues fans anticipated a night out with their team, as they eyed the season ahead. "Our contest winners are here, watching. We want to make a decent showing," said Halo.

"Bull-fuckin'-shit." Zoo wasn't satisfied. "Who are the babes?"

Zoo would dog them for the next five innings. He

could be damn annoying. Word had spread beyond Media Day that Halo had a fiancée. He'd received countless congratulations. Most were sincere; others, merely lip service.

Those who actually knew Alyn's identity kept it low-key. Anonymity worked for them, for now. People recognized his engagement. Accepted it. He didn't want her fully exposed to public scrutiny. He felt protective of her.

He'd accomplished what he'd set out to do. His life had improved for the better. He'd gotten the desired results from his engagement. Women sighed when they saw him, but no longer sought him out for sex. He and Alyn had yet to make love. They kissed, held hands, touched a little, but nothing more. He was a long way from a sleep-over.

"You misinterpreted my look," Halo said to Zoo. "I nodded to Danny Jayne."

Zoo snorted. "The boy or his sister?"

"My contest winner," brooked no argument.

"Land's gaze keeps straying to the Cates section, along the first base line. Shaye and Jillian are off limits, but the chick with the crazy hair has it going on. Nice boobs."

Landon stiffened, and Halo knew why. The two men had spent an hour talking in the locker room before the rest of the team arrived. Halo hadn't fully disclosed his relationship with Alyn; he'd skimmed over the business details. Land, however, had openly and honestly discussed Eden Cates. It appeared his best friend was taking their relationship seriously. They'd adopted dogs together. He was moving into her wedding chapel for the remainder of spring training. Which made Halo smile. He wanted his buddy happy. Eden damn sure put Landon on his game. He'd hit a home run for her.

Halo shifted the conversation. "Check out Rally Ball. Fans love him."

Rally Ball was the team mascot. Inside the big white

baseball costume with the red stitching was Charlie Bradley. Leg and armholes showcased long red-and-blue-striped sleeves and matching tights. Blue high-top Converses supported his movements. Rally had roll. He bobbed and bounced in the stands, meeting and greeting the crowd. Most mascots didn't come to spring training. Charlie was the exception. At sixty-five, he'd aged with the franchise. A widower, he considered the Rogues family. The team paid his way to Florida.

"Rally's talking to Danny. He's getting his picture taken with the boy." Land chuckled. "Danny's trying to hug him, but can't get his arms around the fuzz ball."

Top of the fourth played out. Zoo's solo shot over the second baseman's head landed him on first. The Hurricanes' pitcher had a gifted arm. His skills walked the next three batters back to the dugout without a hit. Zoo was left hanging.

The Rogues took the field. The leadoff batter for the Hurricanes popped the ball up. It arched toward third base, and landed in Landon's glove. Next, a fly ball to center—captured, out two. The right fielder for the Hurricanes took his bat. Eric Madison pounded a curveball to left field. Zoo charged, dove, slid on his belly. Missed the catch. Eric ran like a roadrunner, rounding the bases, scoring their first home run.

The crowd went crazy. Halo couldn't help himself. He stood in right and applauded Eric's ability. The hometown boy had placed the ball perfectly, just beyond Zoo's reach. Rylan in center joined the applause. Talent was talent, and needed to be acknowledged. Win or lose, the game wouldn't affect their preseason standing or stats.

The next Hurricane went down on strikes. Three outs. Halo and Rylan jogged toward the dugout together. "Tell me about Madison," Halo requested. "Dude's got instincts."

"He's one hell of a player," said Ry. "He was offered a

scholarship to Florida State, but turned it down. Family obligations. His dad got busted for drugs. Jail time. Eric has twin younger brothers and a baby sister. His mom works three jobs to keep food on the table. Eric's taken over parental responsibilities. He's pretty much raising the kids."

Eric's situation unsettled Halo. He kept an eye on the high schooler the remainder of the game. The Rogues worked through their batting order. There was one out in the count when Halo stepped to the plate. He knocked a fastball thrown down in the zone over the shortstop's head. He made it easily to first. Landon's short drive to third forced him to slide into second. A heartbeat before the throw. He dusted himself off. Zoo wasn't to be bested. He'd yet to make an impression. The time was now.

He went full count, three balls, two strikes, before launching a curveball toward center-right. No-man's land. It was a toss-up which outfielder would make the catch. *If* one of them even could. The ball was close to clearing the wall. Close to landing in the outfield stands.

Halo watched as two young athletes tried to save the home run. Damn if Eric Madison didn't make the play. He jet-packed at the wall, made the catch. Then had the reserve to fire the ball to the first baseman, who threw it to the catcher. Focusing on Eric, Halo and Landon were slow in crossing home plate. Landon hustled at the end. They earned two runs, with two outs.

Rylan Cates's fluid swing slammed a cutter down the right field line. The catch elicited Eric's skills once more. He scooped, powered the ball to first, and Ry was out, an inch off the base. Three down. Rogues went on defense. Halo grabbed Rylan's glove off the bench, took it to him. They connected in the outfield.

"Kid can field," said Halo.

"He's also a clutch hitter."

He had the knack for coming up with big hits in tight situations. "I'm impressed."

"You should be," said Rylan. "Given the opportunity, Eric could take your position someday."

"Just like I inherited right from Psycho." Psycho McMillan was legendary. No doubt the best right fielder of all time. He was front office now, vice president/general manager. Psycho kept his finger on the pulse of every player. He shook the skeletons in closets. No secrets were kept from the man.

Halo made a run at Psycho's stats every year. Had not yet succeeded. He still had time to accomplish his goals. He wasn't ready to hang up his jock. Not for a few years, anyway.

The game played out. The score was five to one in the middle of the ninth, when the Rogues went on final defense. Rylan had slam-dunked a homer over the left field fence moments earlier. He got a standing ovation.

A half-inning to play, and southpaw Andy Davidson was brought in to close, replacing Will Ridgeway. He played Triple-A, and was in town for daily scrimmages. The pitching coach had his eye on him. A possible candidate for the majors.

Davidson was all nerves. Halo could see him sweat from right field. Three consecutive outs should've wrapped up the game. Fifteen quick minutes. Instead three batters loaded the bases. Forty minutes later. No outs. What the fuck?

Eric Madison next took his bat. He made the walk from on-deck circle to home plate. Swinging his bat, then knocking dirt from his cleats, as he dug in, getting into position.

The kid had the balls to point to Halo. He was looking

for a grand slam to tie the score. The crowd was on its feet. Cheering, clapping, stomping. The kid was a favorite. The noise would carry miles.

Crap, Halo thought. Should the kid launch one his way, he'd be forced to make the out. Most situations needed heroes. For some strange reason he didn't want to be the one to steal the guy's thunder. He kicked himself for going soft.

Eric's previous at-bats had earned him a homer and a double. Rylan had warned him that Eric came through in the toughest times. Halo got into position. Ready, and waiting.

Intelligent and intuitive, Eric went two balls and two strikes, before he swung on a change-up, finding the sweet spot. Long, and possibly gone raced through Halo's mind. The wind could carry the ball that extra inch, over the wall.

His competitive instincts raged deep. Winning meant everything to him. He charged the warning track. As did Rylan Cates. Halo called him off. Yet Ry kept coming. His expression was hard, intent. A collision was imminent. Unless Halo backed off the ball.

Not the World Series, he muttered to himself. His sense of sportsmanship won out. There were different kinds of heroes. This time he gave up the run to let someone else shine.

"Gone," he hissed, when Ry was close enough to hear him.

Rylan staggered a step, and Halo jumped. High. He could've caught the ball. Would've had it, too, had he not tipped it over the wall with his glove. It landed in the stands. At the feet of a grandfather and his grandson. They were so surprised it took them a moment to scramble for the souvenir.

Halo and Rylan both bent over, caught their breath.

"Damn, Ry-man, you nearly took me out," Halo grunted.

Rylan straightened. "A bump to your arm, no more."

"No love tap, dude."

"I'm loyal to the team, but I also live here. It's all about community."

"Five-five. Let's hold them to a tie."

Eric's grand slam drew a fifteen minute celebration. The Hurricane players lifted him on their shoulders. Jostled him into the dugout. Gatorade was shaken; their uniforms splashed orange. Hurricane fans screamed themselves hoarse. The noise level went stratospheric. It took all four umpires to bring calm to the chaos. Security escorted people off the field.

The pitching coach, Zoo, and shortstop Brody Jones stood on the mound with the Triple-A pitcher. The coach would keep his cool. Jones would offer encouragement. Zoo would growl like a hellhound. He had the tattoo to prove it. He could be an ass.

Andy was shell-shocked. His expression grim. He allowed three further hits. Defense won the game. Landon caught a pop-up. Jake Packer, a lineout. Brody saved a bunt. Game over. Tied. No overtime.

Afterward, both teams formed two lines. They signed autographs and took photos with their fans. Up until the stadium lights flickered overhead, and the scoreboard shut down, thinning the crowd instantaneously.

Halo glanced toward the seats along the first base line, and noticed Alyn sat alone. It was late. Martha, Danny, and the contest winners had taken the commuter bus and returned to Barefoot Inn. She was waiting for him. A pleasant surprise.

He realized in that moment he wanted her with him at the end of every game. Meeting him in the parking lot for their own private celebration, win or lose. The thought of having one woman for the rest of his life didn't strangle him. Didn't give him heartburn. Didn't set his feet to running. It left him calm. Anchored. Alyn Jayne was the one.

He was the last man on the field, or so he thought. He called to her, "Hummer in twenty." A quick shower, and he'd join her.

She waved. Stood, and moved toward the nearest exit. It was then Halo saw Eric Madison, sitting by himself in the shadows of the visitor dugout. His head was bent. His hands wrapped around his grand slam bat. Halo approached him.

"Dude," was all he said. He didn't want to interrupt Eric if he was in prayer or doing some serious thinking.

Eric glanced up. His eyes were bright and he blinked several times. Halo understood the emotion that came with a major play. He'd been choked up himself on occasion.

The young man cleared his throat said, "Hey, Halo. You're late leaving the field."

"No later than you."

"I saw the woman in the stands waiting for you."

"Alyn Jayne, my fiancée."

"She's pretty."

Halo nodded. "And the nicest person I know."

"You're lucky, man."

"Sometimes life comes together when you least expect it." Halo paused, continued with, "I'm going to get personal. Tell me to back off if you'd rather not talk about your family, your scholarship, and your plans for the future."

Eric sat quietly, slow in responding, as if he was embarrassed. He squeezed the bat so tightly, his knuckles whitened. His words were choppy, his voice flat, when he told Halo about his college prospects, and how his life changed overnight with his old man's drug bust.

Halo wasn't good at giving comfort, but he could correct an unfortunate situation. He could remove obstacles. Project an opportunity. He made his offer of paying for the boy's education, along with supporting Eric's family until he signed a major league contract.

Eric was so stunned, he sputtered, "You think I'm good enough to play professional ball?"

"I know you are."

The boy's throat worked. "My dad didn't think so."

"I'm not your dad."

"Why me, Halo?"

"Because you pointed to right field and delivered."

"You laid glove on the ball."

"Almost had it, too."

"Almost . . ." Eric's voice caught.

Halo rose then, and Eric followed him up. "You'll need to contact my business manager," he said. "I'll follow up with the info tomorrow. I'll also stop by your house and give all the details to your mother."

"I don't know what to say."

"Say nothing. I'm doing this anonymously."

"Word always gets out. Barefoot William doesn't know how to keep a secret. We're all family, without being related. Good news will spread." He pursed his lips. "Any advice?"

"Play hard. Don't get complacent. Someday you may contract with the Rogues. I'd rather have you on our team than playing against us."

"I play right field."

"Switch to center. Rylan Cates will retire before me."

"Thanks, Halo." Eric gave him a man-hug. A thump to the shoulder.

Halo finished with a fist bump.

Eric took off, jogged toward the visitor locker room.

Halo leaned against the dugout rail. Silence separated

him from the team. The majority of the players would have already showered and changed, and headed out for the night. Alyn was on his mind. More and more she snuck into his thoughts. He heard a shuffle in the stands above the dugout. He peered around the corner, expecting to see the cleaning crew.

No one swept, no one picked up trash. The sound came from Alyn. She stood in the aisle, a tote in hand, and her eyes wide, as if caught in the wrong place at the wrong time.

"I didn't know you were still here," she apologized. "Or that you were talking to someone. I remembered my purse, but forgot my bag, and returned for it. I wasn't eavesdropping. It's quiet, and your voices carried."

"Not a big deal," he assured her. "I was talking to Eric Madison."

"Your conversation was life-changing. Hope is empowering."

"The kid is damn good. I've given him a chance. It's up to him to act on it."

"He won't let you down."

"I don't think so either."

They stared at each other. Neither wanting to move. "Come here," he said to her.

"How?" She'd have to crawl through the railing, and then there was a significant drop.

"Toss down your purse and tote," he suggested. She did so. "You're slender enough to squeeze through the rails sideways."

"What if I get stuck?"

"You'll spend the night."

He heard her huff, and smiled. "Try, you'll make it. I'm here to catch you when you jump."

"I'm wearing a sundress."

"Panties?"

She ignored him. "Don't let me fall."

Never would he let that happen. She slipped through without any problems, as he'd told her she would. Standing on the edge, she bent her knees, took a leap of faith. Her sundress billowed slightly, and her thighs were visible. It was too dark to see the color of her underwear. He caught her easily. Held her against his body. She didn't squirm, as he'd expected.

Instead, her long hair fanned his shoulders, and her dress flared as she curved her arms about his neck and wrapped her legs about his hips. He locked his fingers beneath her bottom. Cotton panties.

She turned his baseball cap around, so the bill faced backwards. Then rested her forehead against his. Her body was soft. Her eyes, liquid. "I like you, Halo Todd," she slowly admitted. An absolute first for her. "You're a good man."

"What brought that on?" Liking him was good, loving him, better. That would come with time.

"Speculation, only. I think you've been self-indulgent all your life. I find it very sexy that you're helping others."

"Sexy, huh." He'd write out checks every day for the rest of his life if she'd hold that thought.

"You're setting me up in business. You're sending Eric to college. There's more to Halo Todd than meets the eye."

"Don't look too closely." He didn't want to disappoint her.

"I want to be close," she breathed against his mouth, right before she kissed him. All on her own, without his prompting. He embraced his woman and the moment, in the semidarkness, behind the dugout.

He let her do the kissing. She kept it light, yet with feeling. Her innocence turned playful. Her tease drove him crazy. He needed more than her close-mouthed kisses. But when he snuck his tongue between her teeth, she bit down. Hard. The sting went straight to his groin. He stirred, swelled, and went all wood on her.

He groaned. "Damn, I'm horny."

"That's evident. You wouldn't need a baseball bat to play ball."

Halo grinned. She was right. "You still holding out on me?" he had to ask, on the off chance she'd relent and they'd have sex.

"It's best, Halo."

"For who?"

"For both of us in the long run."

"How about short-term, then?"

"There's a difference?"

"We need to take advantage of spring training. Short days, long nights. Regular season, it's reversed. I practically live at the ballpark." He nipped her bottom lip, sucked it into his mouth. Released it slowly. "You'd like us if you tried us."

"So you keep saying."

"I'll keep saying it, until we do it."

"Persistent man."

"I know what I want."

"Thank you for wanting me," said softly, appreciatively. Almost sadly.

He heard her uncertainty. Her inability to fully trust. She held back with him. They faced ten months together. He didn't want to push her further. She feared being let down. He wasn't going anywhere. He'd prove it to her.

He loosened his hold, and she slid down his body. "Late-date night?" he asked.

"Mom and Danny went back to the inn. They'll feed and walk Quigley. Danny's had a full day. He'll write in his school journal, go to bed. So . . ." She picked up her purse and tote. "I'm available."

Halo would make the most of their time together. They walked across the infield toward the exit tunnel. The cleaning and maintenance crews would arrive within the hour. But at the moment, the stadium was nearly deserted. He had her wait for him in the Media Lounge, where coaches and players met with the press after a game. She pulled her iPhone from her purse, checked, and answered messages. He headed for the showers.

He returned to her in twenty minutes. Unshaven, but wearing a clean gray pullover and charcoal slacks. He planned to take her to Saunders Shores, the city that shared the southern boardwalk with Barefoot William. That side of town was upscale and prestigious. A change from honky-tonk.

He parked off Center Street. Tucked her to him as they turned left into the world of the wealthy. The walkway shifted from cracked cement to cocoa-brown brick. Here, there were no in-line skaters, unicyclists, street singers, portrait painters, magicians, or vendors hawking hot dogs and churros.

There were no rickshaw pedicabs. No one wore swim-suits or walked around barefoot. The patrons shopping the main city blocks were dignified and well dressed. No one browsed; everyone bought. Customers carried designer boxes and bags. The boutiques and café owners flourished, even at this late hour.

Lantern-style lampposts stretched along the boardwalk. Tall pole lighting lit the sugar sand for walks. The ocean mirrored a thousand stars.

Alyn liked to window-shop. He smiled at her each time she pressed her face close to the glass. He could afford to buy anything that caught her eye. Ten times over. Alyn asked for nothing. She only wanted to browse.

They stopped before a formal dress shop and admired the fancy dresses and proper tuxedos, then inhaled deeply as they passed an outdoor Italian bistro. Wine, pasta, rich desserts.

Halo heard the catch in Alyn's breath as they passed the jewelry store. Diamond rings of every cut, clarity, and carat were presented on glass tiers. The display was blinding. She needed an engagement ring. It was time to make them official. He'd let her choose. A ring that represented them.

He took her hand, and walked her toward the entrance. He swore she dug in her heels, but he was stronger, and got her through the door. Wide-eyed, her cheeks pink, she stood beside him. She was too stiff for a fiancée. The women he'd known over the years would covet the rings in each glass-topped case. Wanting to try on the pricey and sparkling. Despite the cost to him.

A small man in a three-piece suit approached them. "Mr. Todd, I'm Ari LaMon, the jeweler," he introduced himself. "I recognized you right away. My son was at your exhibition game. He was excited over the tie."

"The high school team played well," Halo agreed.

America's pastime. Baseball brought people together. The Rogues had a wide spectrum of fans. The stadium filled with both the wealthy and the working class. They sat together, cheering. Everyone in the crowd carried the team's win home.

"What might I help you with?" LaMon politely inquired.

"An engagement ring for Alyn."

Could dollar signs flash in a man's eyes? If so, LaMon was already cashing in. Alyn, on the other hand, hadn't left his side. Shyness and uncertainty overtook her. Maybe he'd been misguided suggesting a ring. It had seemed right to him at the time. He wanted her comfortable with their arrangement. A ring seemed the natural next step.

"Our engagement rings are in the case near the far

wall," LaMon told them. "I'm happy to show you our latest designs."

Alyn had taken his hand in a death grip. Which Halo interpreted as her desire to look around without the man's hard sell. He squeezed her fingers in reassurance.

"We'd like to browse, first, if you don't mind," Halo requested.

"Most certainly." LaMon was cordial. He stepped back. He didn't want to lose a sale. He gave them space.

Halo led Alyn to the case of engagement rings and wedding bands. The selection was enormous. He felt her shudder, and looked down. "What, babe?" he asked. Something was wrong. No smile. Her expression was tight, pale. Her free arm curved about her stomach, as if she was sick.

She rose on tiptoe, whispered near his ear, "Please don't put me in this position."

"What position?" She'd lost him.

"Don't buy me a ring I'll be returning to you in ten months." She settled back down.

His gut clenched. He mentally thumped his forehead. Kicked himself in the ass. What had he done? He'd made her uncomfortable, hurt her, without meaning to. All because he wanted to prove his commitment to their partnership. To her. He'd done a damn poor job.

Alyn was smart, intuitive, a woman of foresight. She was already thinking months ahead, to their separation. He needed to fix that. He leaned down, kissed her lightly. "I'm sorry. I wasn't looking at tomorrow, only at tonight. I wanted to do something nice. Special."

She pressed her palm to his chest, right over his heart. "You're generous, spontaneous, and I thank you for that. You know our outcome, as well as I do. A ring isn't the answer. Now or later."

Halo had never felt more let down in his life. What he'd

thought a great idea had totally bombed. She had no clue how he felt about her. He wasn't ready to tell her. She wasn't ready to hear it. He wanted her to trust him first.

Uncertainty claimed him. His heart now raced, as it did at the ballpark, when he was in the outfield, running to save a home run ball, yet knowing it was beyond his reach. How could he fix their situation? He wasn't leaving the store without buying Alyn something that would tie them together. For the time being.

"No ring," he said, and her body relaxed against him. Lady was relieved. "But if you were to pick one, which one would it be?"

She gave him a small smile. "More *pretend* between us?"

"I can fake it if you can fake it."

"The aquamarine is lovely, with the circlet of diamonds."

She had good taste, Halo thought.

He turned to the jeweler, and off the top of his head, said, "Alyn wants something unusual for our engagement. Not necessarily a ring. What might you suggest?"

The jeweler swallowed his disappointment at not selling them an expensive ring, then suggested, "Perhaps an antique locket from an estate sale? Authentic, classic, memorable."

"Antique" caught Alyn's attention. "I'd like to see the locket, please."

LaMon walked them across the room to a smaller showcase, designed with jewelry box details. The black satin drawers pulled out to reveal broaches, cameos, bejeweled hat pins, strands of glass beads and pearls, monogramed rings and cuff links. Old, yet timeless. Pieces preserved from the past.

The jeweler slid back a glass panel, reached inside the case. He tapped a secret compartment on one of the boxes, and a side drawer opened. He removed a small heart-shaped locket on a delicate silver chain. He laid it out on a velvet rectangle for their inspection. "Filigree, gold filled," he told them. "The outer lacework is the finest I've ever seen."

The necklace left Alyn speechless. Her expression conveyed her sense of awe. She reached out to touch it, but her hand fell short. As if she were afraid. "It's incredible," she managed.

"I've determined the locket to be French, after a great deal of inquiry and research," he stated. "No doubt worn by a woman of class. Possibly even nobility."

Alyn could only stare, so Halo carefully picked it up, put it around her neck. The locket was delicate, like Alyn. The heart was meant for her cleavage, he thought. It complemented her breasts.

The jeweler produced a pedestal mirror. Placed it on the top of the case. He dropped his sales pitch. "I've had the locket for some time," he admitted. "It's been admired by my clientele, but never fully appreciated. You've fallen in love with it, my dear. I believe it was meant for you."

Halo thought so, too, but awaited Alyn's approval before making the purchase. The choice was completely hers. He'd make no further assumptions or mistakes with her. He stood behind her at the mirror, his face reflected with hers. The jeweler stepped aside, until they came to their decision. Halo took advantage of their moment alone.

He leaned close, kissed her on the neck, just below her ear. She shivered. "Beautiful locket, even more beautiful woman."

She fingered the fragile chain. Sighed. Then gently flipped the clasp, and looked inside the locket. It was empty. Waiting for her to decide which pictures or mementos should fill the heart. She closed it.

She met his gaze in the mirror. "*If* you truly want to

buy me something, *if* you persist in being engaged, then the locket seals our deal."

He had one final concern. "Promise me you won't turn around and sell it at your shop after ten months. That you'll keep it, no matter what goes down between us."

She turned to face him. "I won't ever part with the locket. I give you my word." She kissed him then. Right in front of the jeweler and a newly arrived couple, looking at watches.

He eased back, nodded to LaMon. "I'm ready to settle up. She'll wear the locket."

"I will get you the velvet bag and small box it came in, for when she takes it off."

Halo left Alyn, and followed the man to the back of the store. "I want to order an engagement ring." Halo kept his voice low. LaMon raised an eyebrow, questioningly. "Aquamarine, diamond circle." The jeweler gave a discreet nod. "It's perfect for us—she just doesn't know it yet."

LaMon's lips twitched, but he held back his smile. Didn't give a thing away. "Insured and delivered?"

Halo slid his wallet from the back pocket of his slacks, and passed the jeweler a Black American Express. "I'll pick it up tomorrow."

"Very good." LaMon extended his hand. Halo shook it.

Halo and Alyn left the store shortly thereafter. Happiness shone in her eyes, Halo noticed. Her heart was light. He was relieved. They stood on the boardwalk, gazing at the night. Laughter echoed to their left, as a group of people came through the door of Lavenders. The gourmet shop catered to the discriminating palate. Or so the sign read.

Halo tipped up her chin, asked, "Dessert?"

She was thoughtful. She looked through the window. "They specialize in sorbet."

"I've only had it once, but I'm game."

They entered through frameless glass doors etched with the letter *L*. The lighting was soft, and the French Mediterranean shutters were drawn against the darkness. Intimacy was served with the sorbet.

The hostess openly eyed Halo with interest and curiosity. Her gaze then touched on Alyn. She noticed the locket. "Lovely," she commented.

"Engagement gift," Alyn said softly.

"Lucky you." Her tone was envious.

The lady seated them at a linen-covered café table. The chairs were an intricate white wrought iron. Big man. Small chair. Halo shifted twice, trying to get comfortable. A server arrived with tall, fluted glasses of sparkling water. No ice. The crystal made the water dance. She then set a sheet of lavender parchment paper before each of them. The menu curled slightly and was as thin and delicate as tissue paper. He debated holding the menu, afraid his large hands might damage the paper.

"Elegant," Alyn murmured as she carefully ran her finger along the side and read the gourmet flavors. "Coconut-caramel, burnt sugarplum, cranberry-pear, and raspberry truffle. They all sound delicious."

"Fancy." He had no idea what else to say. He wasn't a fan of mixed tastes. He liked plain old vanilla ice cream. The occasional chocolate.

Their server returned. "Our three specialty flavors of the night are limoncello-mint, bittersweet chocolate-cherry, and white chocolate-chip mousse."

Alyn's lips parted on a sigh. She lightly tapped one corner of the parchment with her fingertip. "They have a sampler. Four flavors of choice. We could try a little of each." Her gaze was expectant. Hopeful. Tentative. Afraid he'd say "no."

He reached across the table, took her hand, and twined

their fingers. Reassured her, "Order a dozen samplers if you like."

"I'll bring two samplers," the server suggested. "Eight great tastes."

"Perfect," said Halo.

"Thank you," Alyn whispered.

"For what?"

"For being kind."

"I like being nice to you."

"And I appreciate it."

He had a history of doing what he wanted, when he wanted. He was doing his damn best to turn his life around. To think of others first. He stroked along the side of her hand with his thumb. "You could be nicer to me, you know."

She pursed her lips, feigned confusion. "How so? Should I buy you an engagement gift, too?"

"Not jewelry."

"Something personal?"

"You're getting warmer."

"Possibly sexual."

"On target."

"No."

Harsh. It had been worth a try. The mere thought of them having sex made his dick stir. Misbehave. The linen cloth only covered so much. He scooted his chair farther under the table. The pain of it all.

Alyn had the nerve to smile. They'd kissed several times, and she'd responded. Wholeheartedly. They would make love, he determined. Waiting wasn't all it was cracked up to be. The anticipation was killing him.

He was about to tell her so, when their sorbet arrived. The desserts came in small, frosted cut-glass bowls, placed on lacy ecru doilies. The portions were two bites. If that, Halo thought. He could easily eat the scoop in one. The spoons were sterling silver and tinier than a teaspoon. He felt like a giant at a doll tea party.

"Oh . . ." Alyn's eyes rounded. "Sorbet artwork. These are too pretty to eat." She was reluctant to spoil the arrangement, but equally afraid they'd melt.

Halo watched as she sampled the burnt sugarplum. The scoop was sprinkled with lavender-colored sugar, and framed by slices of plum. More a woman's dessert than a man's.

He picked up the tiny spoon, forced to hold it between two fingers. He went with the coconut-caramel, rich with flakes of coconut and shredded caramel. The sorbet melted on his tongue. Not bad. Unfortunately, he couldn't lean across the table and kiss Alyn. He'd like to mix their sensually smooth flavors. He would suck her tongue deep into his mouth. Taste her fully.

She ate slowly, savoring every bite. Her eyes closed and she sighed over the raspberry truffle. She licked her lips. And Halo hardened. A second bite of his coconut-caramel did little to cool his libido. The sweetness reminded him of Alyn. The sorbet was satisfying, but not nearly as good as sex.

She eyed him from beneath her lashes. A sneak peek, as if she had something on her mind, but didn't know how to approach the subject. "So . . ." He opened the door.

"I need to stop at Old Tyme Portraits before you take me home."

"For a cutout photo?"

"Don't ask, I'm not ready to tell."

"Secrets, Alyn? Really? Between fiancés?"

"I want you to wait on the boardwalk while I go inside."

"So many demands." He was curious about her request, but he'd do whatever she asked. "Fine, I'll give you ten minutes."

"It might take fifteen."

He'd wait for her, as long as it took.

They finished their samplers. Alyn moaned low in her throat as she finished the last of the white chocolate-chip mousse. Her hips rolled on the chair. He swore she had a sorbet orgasm.

He paid, left a big tip, and they moved to the door. The hostess touched his arm as Alyn passed ahead of him. "Come back anytime." What she meant was, "Come back *alone.*" He stepped around her without comment. The woman didn't see him as faithful. That bothered him a little.

They walked back the way they'd come. He held her hand. Kept her tight against him. They crossed Center Street, and the Barefoot William side of the boardwalk was ready to party. Shops remained open until midnight on Saturday. Energy charged the air. Laughter rose and fell like the tide.

Entertainment surrounded them. A unicycle troupe performed, riding everything from short cycles up to the tall giraffe. They moved forward and back, turning tight circles about Halo and Alyn, then making the bikes bounce in perfect unison. They had incredible balance. As did the stilt walkers and pogo stick jumpers.

Farther down the boardwalk, a magician turned a white straw into a red rose. He bowed and gave it to Alyn. The magic man's cape changed from navy to orange in the blink of an eye. Impressive. Halo slipped the magician ten dollars. He waved the bill on the air and it became a twenty. He'd doubled his money. Pretty cool.

They admired a caricaturist. The artist sketched in charcoal. A few quick flicks of her wrist, and she captured Alyn's likeness. Halo bought the drawing. For himself.

They reached Old Tyme Portraits just as a group was exiting, pictures in hand. Alyn slipped around them, entered. He wanted to peek in the window to satisfy his curiosity. Which would spoil her surprise. He lay low. Alone.

Until a blonde decided to keep him company. She split from her friends, approached him, hips swaying. She wore a belly shirt and low-rise jeans, flashing a lot of skin. Double-pierced navel. A tattoo of a middle finger etched her hip, with the words: *Flip-off.*

He knew the tat. He'd slept with her. After too many beers and a grinding slow dance. After an inviting smile and hearing she had an apartment within walking distance of the bar. He couldn't remember her name. She held no interest for him now. If anything, she made him uneasy. He didn't want a scene.

"Halo, hon." Her hands went to his hips. She pulled him close. Her thumb flicked the tab on his zipper. He clasped her wrists. He didn't need her hand action. She stuck out her lower lip. Pouted. "I heard a nasty rumor that you were engaged."

"Truth."

"Shit."

He released her. Expecting her to walk away.

She lingered. Walked her fingers up his chest. "We had an amazing night together. Any chance—"

He shook his head. Didn't let her finish. "Sorry, no."

"You plan to be faithful?"

"So he says." *Alyn.* She'd come up behind him.

Halo wondered how much she'd heard. If she even cared. Apparently, she did. She brushed his side, took his arm. Was competent, cordial. "I don't believe we've met," she said to the blonde. "I'm Alyn Jayne. Halo's fiancée. Thanks for keeping him company while I was in the store."

"Sharon Thomas," said the woman. "I haven't seen Halo for a year."

"Catching up on old times is always nice." Alyn kept

her voice even. "Did you need more time? Maybe have a cup of coffee? A beer?"

Sharon blinked, surprised and slightly confused by her invitation. Alyn was handing Sharon her man. "No," she slowly said. "We're done here." Sharon glanced one last time at Halo. "Good luck with this one. You're going to need it."

"I'm aware."

Sharon called to her friends, caught up to them.

Halo watched his past walk away.

Alyn came around to face him. "You dated her." More a statement than a question.

"Not a date-date. We met at a bar. Spent the night together." He was honest with her.

She tilted her head, eyed him speculatively. "She looks like your type."

"What type might that be?"

"Hot, sexy, out to party."

That might have been his type a month ago, but no longer. "I'm trying to get my act together."

"Who you were isn't who you are now."

"Not everyone sees the change in me."

"Actions speak louder than words."

"You handled Sharon like a pro."

"We have a business deal, Halo. I'm holding up my end of the bargain. I'll assume there are more Sharons to come."

He couldn't tell her how many.

He'd lost count a long time ago.

He had only one woman in his life now.

The one he planned to marry.

Twelve

It was Sunday morning, early, and people were gathering for the Dog Jog. The crowd was large at the starting line in the elementary school parking lot. With the firing of a cap gun, the walkers, joggers, and runners would proceed to Gulf Shore Boulevard, which ran parallel to the board-walk and beach. Fans and supporters would line the side-walks, cheering on the participants. The two-mile race finished near the pier. Trophies would be awarded, first through third place. There'd be canine treats and human snacks.

Alyn was as excited as she was apprehensive. Strapped in his wheelchair, Quigley stood on his front paws, his back legs secured in the stirrups, surrounded by all the other dogs. Number sixty, along with his name, was taped to the side of his handicapped cart. A blue bandana circled his neck, indicating he had a permanent home. A red bandana meant the dog was up for adoption. There were a lot of red bandanas.

Alyn held his leash loosely. She hadn't been sure how he'd react. He'd never socialized. Never had a playdate. Fortunately, he wasn't the least bit nervous. Only curious. He held his own.

"Ry-man, get a grip on Atlas," Halo called to Rylan Cates. Ry was standing a few feet away, conversing with his sister Shaye, organizer of the event. Atlas had the full length of his leash to sniff out Quigs. The Great Dane had nearly inhaled the pug.

Rylan snapped the leash, but Atlas paid him no mind. Ry came to them instead. "He won't hurt Quigley," Rylan assured them. "He's more interested in the wheelchair." Which Atlas was now nuzzling, rocking, with his nose.

"No tipping him over." Halo nudged the Dane aside with his knee. The big dog crouched down, wanting to play. He bounced left, right, barked. Then whined, until Quiggie responded. Not with a bark, but with a wag of his curly tail.

Alyn saw the quick, yet significant waggle. Had she blinked, she would've missed it. Her heart squeezed. She reached for Halo's hand. "Quigley's first wag since the accident."

"Nice going, Atlas," Halo relented. "He responded to you." Atlas had more expressions than a cartoon character. He looked quite pleased with himself.

"Joggers, attention, please." Shaye's voice boomed through a megaphone. "It's time to line up. Six rows across. Ten deep."

The majority of the Rogues decided on the last two rows, near Halo and Alyn. Rylan and Atlas would lead off. Hometown boy and legendary dog. Landon and Eden joined them soon after. Their two dogs were leashed together. Landon greeted them with, "Meet Ruby and Obie." The dachshund had her nose in the air, taking in every scent. The beagle was shy, and kept his head down. He tried to squeeze between Landon's sneakered feet.

Ruby would have none of Obie's hiding. She nipped his ear. Made unidentifiable sounds that only Obie could understand. He crept out in the open. She licked his face.

Pitcher Will Ridgeway and his Chihuahua Cutie Patootie found them next. "I'm betting six steps and you're carrying her," Landon said to the pitcher, who held her now.

"Every time I set her down, she cries like a baby," Will said. "She's easy to carry. She fits in my palm." A metallic blue ribbon wrapped the dog's neck. A bandana would've swamped her.

"Zoo's late," Halo noticed, as the left fielder sprinted onto the lot. An enormous Rottweiler was by his side. Another blue bandana.

"That's Turbo," Landon said. "Zoo said he's a chewer."

Turbo proved that fact shortly thereafter. Zoo came to the back of the pack. The dog was hooked to a leather leash; his teeth marks were visible all along the lead. The handle was worn thin.

"Sit," Zoo instructed Turbo. The Rottie dropped down, only to pop back up. "There's obedience school in his future."

"When did you adopt him?" asked Land.

"A few days ago."

"About the time we got our two."

"*We?*" Zoo was clearly in the dark.

"Eden and me."

"Whoa, dude, I hadn't heard you'd coupled." He cut his gaze to Halo. "Halo's got himself a woman. I'm wanting to meet his fiancée."

"Zoo, Alyn," was all Halo said.

"Your contest winner's sister? I should've known. You've been playing house for over a week now."

Halo's eyes narrowed. His expression dark. A warning sign. "Careful, dude. I've known her longer than you think. Several months, actually."

Zoo held up one hand, palm out. "I meant no disrespect."

"None taken," said Alyn.

Zoo took her in. A player fully checking out his team-mate's choice in women. His gaze held on her breasts, until Halo cleared his throat. "I was admiring her locket," he defended.

"My engagement gift," Alyn said.

"No ring?"

"The locket was my choice," she told him. "It's better than a ring. More visible."

"Nice display case." He referred to her cleavage. "What's inside?"

Alyn felt Halo tense beside her. His, "I just purchased it for her," covered up the fact it might be empty.

"So . . . nothing?" Zoo was smug.

"Something." Alyn broke her surprise. A careful flick of the clasp, and it opened. The inner gold rim circled two tiny photographs. One of her, one of Halo. Both photos were in profile, facing each other. A sepia shading aged the images. They looked as if they'd been in the locket forever. Very romantic.

She heard Halo release a relieved breath. His arm curved her waist, as he eased her back against him. He lightly kissed her on the lips, in front of everyone.

Zoo snorted. "Halo pictured in a locket? Never would I have believed it, had I not seen it." He and Turbo moved one row ahead. "Away from the couples," Zoo tossed back.

Halo whispered near her ear. "Where'd you get the photos?" he asked.

Alyn smiled. "From Eden, when we stopped at her shop. She took a lot of pictures at the bonfire. I was hoping she had one of us, which she could reduce to fit the locket."

Eden smiled. "It took a few minutes, but we got the job done."

"Just in time, too," Alyn reminded him of Sharon.

"Thank you," Halo's words encompassed both the photo and the save.

"Is everyone ready to start?" Shaye now stood on a ladder, scanning the group. "The Dog Jog route consists of one main street. The race ends when the last dog crosses the finish line."

Which would be Quigs, Alyn anticipated. Halo wore the front carry dog pack over his Rogues jersey. He'd offered to give the pug a lift should his front legs tire. Two miles was a long distance for a handicapped dog. They'd do their best.

"On your mark, get set, go!" Shaye fired the cap gun. It wasn't loud enough to scare the dogs. Merely to get the race started.

Halo craned his neck, chuckled. "Our line has yet to move. Atlas and Rylan are half a block ahead of us. A standard white poodle is keeping pace with them."

"Princess Pom-Pom," Alyn remembered. "She wears a tiara, and toenails painted pink. She wasn't from the shelter. A much pampered poodle."

"I'm hoping those dogs needing a home find one today," said Halo, as they edged forward. He took her free hand.

Quigley was alert. Expectant. He tugged against his leash. His front legs churned. Using up all his energy at the onset.

They soon cleared the parking lot and passed through the barricades that sealed off the boulevard. No street traffic was allowed. Several shop owners opened their doors, looked out on the race. It was the perfect day for the event, Alyn thought. A comfortable seventy degrees, with a faint breeze. Not a cloud in the sky. Enormous evergreens lined the two-lane road. Ancient moss clung to the cypresses. Royal Poinciana trees grew on each corner, shading the runners. A crowd gathered along the route. A huge turnout.

People called to their favorites. Atlas's name echoed back to them. Midway through the race, Quigley faltered. He progressively slowed. He began to pant. Alyn debated pulling him from the cart, and letting Halo carry him. But just as she was about to do so, the call out to Quiggie began. Low-rolling voices that turned into a rumble, as loud as any stadium chant.

Alyn was so surprised, she tripped over her own feet. Halo was there to steady her. "What's happening?" she asked.

"Seems your boy has a fan club."

The pug's ears twitched with the outpouring of his name. He came to a stop and listened. That's when Atlas appeared. Out of nowhere. Zigzagging through the joggers to reach them. No Rylan in sight. The Great Dane loped to the pug. Skidded to a halt. Ry showed a moment later, his expression set.

"Atlas slipped his lead," Ry explained. "We were just yards from the finish line when he spun, circled back around." He rubbed the back of his neck. "Winning's not important to my boy. He was more concerned about Quigley."

"We're getting there," said Halo.

"We're not that far behind Landon and Eden," Alyn noted. For every three steps forward, their beagle retreated one. Still, they remained in the race.

Atlas went belly-flat next to Quigs. He prodded the pug with his big nose. Atlas growled, but not menacingly. Alyn was certain it was his own canine encouragement. Atlas gave a lengthy rant.

Shortly thereafter, Shaye showed up on a bicycle. She held up her hands, questioningly. "What's going on? The

Dog Jog has come to a standstill. All participants are holding back, not one jogger has crossed the finish line."

Rylan was first to see the light. "They're waiting for
Quigley."

Alyn put her hand over her heart. "I'm not sure he'll
make it." Her voice was watery.

Halo pulled her close. "Quiggie's having muscle spasms.
His back legs are jerky. There's energy sparking along his
spine. Let him finish."

The pug was straining, trying hard to use his hind legs.
To straighten them out, only to have the muscles contract.

Quigley didn't wait for anyone's decision. His head and
shoulders stretched, and he pulled the cart forward. Atlas
nearly tromped him in his excitement. His bark became a
howl.

They had a mile yet to go. Shaye pedaled ahead and, as
they passed the other dogs, the participants fell in line behind them. Quigs moved from last to first in a matter of
blocks.

Even Zoo, always out to win, acknowledged their progression. Begrudgingly. He curbed his Rottweiler, allowing them to go ahead. Could dogs smile? Alyn wondered.
She swore Turbo grinned.

The cheers only got louder as they neared the end.
Alyn's heart swelled. Her throat tightened. She spotted
Danny and her mother on the corner, just beyond the orange tape that marked the finish line. Danny was jumping
up and down. Her mother clapping like mad. Even Eleanor Norris banged the rubber tip of her cane on the cement. Poor Herman, Alyn thought.

Atlas allowed Quigley to break the tape and cross the
finish line one paw ahead of him. Spectators rushed the
pug. Quigs was mobbed. Atlas barked people back, claiming the pug as his friend, and no one else's.

"Share," Rylan told the Dane.

Atlas grunted. A very rude sound.

Congratulations circulated. Alyn turned and gave Atlas a hug. "Thank you," she whispered near his floppy ear. Atlas licked her cheek. Halo used the sleeve of his jersey to wipe away the wetness.

A photographer snapped their picture. Shaye and the director of the animal shelter handled the interviews. Halo and Alyn kneeled at the same time. She unstrapped Quigs, and he positioned the dog in the mesh backpack. They stood. People stopped, praised, and petted Quigley.

Danny and her mother worked their way to them. There were hugs all around. Shaye announced the trophy presentation. She requested the winners come forward. Quigley took first. Atlas, second. Princess Pom-Pom, third. Alyn gave Danny the trophy to hold. Her brother held it high.

"I'm cutting out," Rylan finally said. "Any chance Atlas can get a playdate with Quigley once we return to Richmond?" he asked Alyn. "He lives with a golden and two dachs. A new friend might be nice."

"Why not get together sooner?" asked Halo.

"Contest winners and their families will be returning home in three days," Ry reminded him. "My schedule's maxed out at the moment. Local obligations. Once we get settled for the regular season, let's do it."

"We'd like that," Alyn agreed. "There's a park near our house."

"Team meeting before practice tomorrow," Rylan finalized with Halo. "Don't be late. Big hand on the twelve. Little hand on the eight."

"Funny, dude." He didn't smile.

"Do you often run late?" she asked him once Ry left.

"Not when something's important." His gaze had narrowed. His jaw was granite. A muscle jumped in his cheek.

"What's wrong?" she quietly asked as they followed Danny and her mother to his Hummer.

"You're leaving?" came out tight.

"We have to go home sometime."

"Danny and your mom, yes. You, no."

"I need to return and set up shop."

"I need you here."

"We'll only be apart a couple of weeks."

"Too damn long."

"The best time for estate and storage sales is early spring," she reasoned with him. "I don't want to lose out on great deals."

"You already have a ton of furniture."

"Not enough," she affirmed. "The store is five times the size of my living room. I want to offer large and eclectic groupings."

They walked half a block. His expression remained unrelenting. "Engaged couples spend time apart," she appealed. "Women admire a faithful man."

"I like how you keep the ladies off."

"I keep them off you, but who keeps you off me?"

His grin tipped then. "That's the challenge."

She slowed, looked at him then. At the big man strapped with a front carrypack, holding her dog. Quigley had fallen asleep. His head lolled to the side. His tongue hung out. One back paw twitched, as if he was chasing rabbits.

Halo held her gaze. He was a hard man to resist. But she had to think about her business. She had ten months to prove herself. To pay back every cent he gave her.

She shared her upcoming weeks with him. "I already have a floor plan. I've arranged the pieces in my mind. I'll hire a moving company, and open The Shy Lily in April."

"You're going to be busy."

"So are you. I saw the schedule for upcoming games.

You play more away games than at home. You won't have time to miss me."

"Maybe not you, but Quiggie Sparks."

She stopped, rose up on tiptoe, and kissed him. A nice, sound kiss. Not an easy feat with Quigs between them. The pug cracked his eyes, yawned, and zonked back out.

Alyn stroked her dog's head. "Quigley's had a long day."

"It's not even noon," he commented, as they walked on. "Let's hit the beach this afternoon. Danny wants to build a sand castle. The ice cream pontoon cruises offshore on Sundays. Near the sandbar. We'll wrap Danny's cast so it doesn't get wet. It's fun to swim out for cones. I've yet to see you in a swimsuit."

His mention of her swimsuit made her blush. No string or thong bikini, but it was break-out for her. It showed a lot of skin. She'd wanted to return to Richmond with a tan.

Halo drove them back to Barefoot Inn. Unloaded Quigley and his cart. Then left them for an hour so they could get ready for the beach. Her mother begged off, offering to pet sit Quigs. Alyn settled him on the dog bed. His soft snores made her sleepy. The room had a Mr. Coffee, and she brewed a pot. Drank two cups, and was wide-eyed when Halo returned.

The afternoon stretched sunny and warm, but not too hot. Tourists crowded the beach. Multicolored loungers and low sand chairs pressed together. Some sun worshippers preferred to lie on towels. They'd borrowed loungers from the inn, then purchased a sand castle building kit at Crabby Abby's General Store on the boardwalk. They located space near the turquoise lifeguard tower. The station would provide shade later in the day as the sun shifted. They would avoid sunburns.

Halo had wrapped Danny's cast in a small garbage bag covered with cellophane. A full roll. Leaving his fingers free. Her brother had freedom to play in the sand and salt water. He hated putting on sunscreen. So Alyn made him wear his white T-shirt. His swim trunks were baggy, hanging below his knees. Her brother was pretty well covered.

Danny bee-lined for the shore, seeking moist, compact sand. He opened his kit and, using a small shovel, began digging and piling sand. He was out to construct a baseball stadium. One that seated eighty thousand fans. He had a lot of building before nightfall.

"So . . ." Halo said, side-eyeing her, as he arranged the vinyl loungers. They hadn't had lunch, and he'd thoughtfully brought a cooler, filled with sandwiches, fruit, and soft drinks. Danny had peeked. Dessert would be an ice cream cone from the pontoon.

"So . . . what?" Alyn returned, knowing full well what he meant, but not admitting to it.

"You going to wear the cover-up all afternoon?"

Possibly. "We just got here."

"I'm waiting."

The man was insufferable. "You first."

He wore a gray T-shirt captioned with *I'm Not an Example, I Come with a Warning Label,* over black board shorts. "Fine," he said. He grabbed the hem, and drew the shirt over his shoulders and head. His hair got mussed, all sexy in his eyes.

She admired his chest, massive and muscled. His arms were strong. Black board shorts rode low on his hips. His abdomen was defined. His legs long, sinewed. She heard a woman sigh, close by, and realized Halo was drawing attention. Who wouldn't want to look at him? He was athletic perfection.

"Your turn." His green eyes flashed as wickedly as his dimples.

Alyn fiddled with her scrunchie, tightening her ponytail. She next fingered the top button on her purple-and-white maxi. The top was ruched and it had high slits on the sides. One button down, and she went for the second, until all were undone to her waist. She shouldered off the cover-up, let it fall, exposing her lavender crop halter top and high-cut bikini bottoms. A modest suit by Halo's standards. She braved his stare.

He gave her the once-over. The twice-over. His gaze heated, appreciative. His breathing deepened. His hands fisted at his sides, as he fought touching her. Her whole body blushed.

"You're hot," he finally said, his voice husky.

She'd never considered herself hot. Not even on her best days, which were few and far between. Despite his exaggeration, she appreciated the flattery. A fiancé should be kind.

She scooped up her beach bag, and located the suntan oil. Lowering herself on a lounger, she uncapped Hawaiian Hibiscus. Halo made his move. Unclenching his hands, he said, "Let me."

"I'm doing my front."

"I'm good with fronts."

She'd bet he was. "You can do my shoulders. I'll do the rest."

He hunkered beside her, and she passed him the bottle. He slickened his hands. She closed her eyes. He oiled her. Shoulders, arms, across her breastbone. His fingertips played along the edges of her halter top. Over, under, at the sides, applying to skin not exposed to the sun. Her nipples puckered. Her stomach softened. Sighing, she went lax. Lost to their surroundings, and the fact she lay in full view of the lifeguards and other beachgoers.

"All covered," Halo soon determined, squeezing her hip.

Covered? She blinked, lifted her head, and stared down her body. Shoulders to toes, he'd finished the task. Even her inner thighs glistened. His smile came, slow and sexy. Satisfied.

Danny took that moment to flag Halo down. "Come help me!" he shouted from water's edge.

"Be right there," Halo called back. He put on his Bulgari wrap-around sunglasses. "We need to move the stadium to higher ground. Otherwise, high tide's going to take the outfield."

Alyn watched as they moved up the beach. Closer to her. It didn't surprise her that Halo drew a crowd. A rather large gathering. He was fine to look at, and his sand castle skills were superb. Men dropped down, offered to help. Women stood back, eyed his tight ass and flexing muscles.

Her fiancé, Alyn thought. It was fun to pretend he belonged to her, for the moment. He looked up often, raised an eyebrow, grinned, and waved. He tightened their bond. Publicly.

Danny sent Halo to get him a sandwich while he stood guard over the stadium. No one packed a grain of sand without Danny's permission. Halo had made that clear from the start. The boy was in charge. And loving it.

Halo opened the iced cooler "Peanut butter and jelly, ham and cheese, or chicken salad?" he asked Alyn, giving her first choice.

"Chicken salad," sounded good.

"Pear, orange, or apple?"

"Pear."

"Iced tea, root beer, or grape?"

"Iced tea."

He gathered the remaining food and drinks and turned back to the sand stadium. "How's it coming?" she asked him, unable to fully view their project through all the people.

"We're at twenty thousand seats," he replied tongue-in-cheek.

They had a ways to go. She ate her lunch, read a book, and closed her eyes. Slept. For how long, she wasn't sure. A kiss wakened her. A man's mouth, firm warm lips and coaxing tongue. *Halo.* She'd recognize his kiss anywhere. Delicious.

"Ice cream, sis," she heard her brother call. "The pontoon's floating off-shore. Let's swim out."

Halo eased back. "You want to join us? Danny picked two people to guard the stadium while we take a break. We're good to get a cone or sundae. Fudgsicles."

Alyn sat up, squinted against the sun. The bright pink pontoon had anchored, and was easily accessible by a ladder, on the far side of the sandbar. The water didn't appear too deep. Halo could walk right to it. She and Danny would have to swim a short distance.

"Money?" she asked him. "Won't it get wet?"

He patted the pocket on his board shorts. "Waterproof."

He took her hand, and tugged her off the lounger. She brushed his side as they walked across the sand. He traced a finger over her shoulder and down her side. "I like my woman warm and slick."

Her skin was hot. The suntan oil slippery. The Gulf was pale blue and welcomingly cool. Danny went ahead of them. Bobbing in the water, until he couldn't touch the floor anymore. He paddled in a circle, splashing wildly, until Halo hauled him in.

"Hop on," Halo told her brother, bending slightly, and offering a piggyback ride. Danny climbed on.

Alyn lost her footing as the water deepened. She swam the breaststroke the remainder of the way.

Halo placed Danny on the sandbar. Her brother climbed the ladder onto the pontoon. Halo then took Alyn's hand and nudged her ahead of him. She was three rungs up the ladder when her foot slipped. She tipped sideways. Halo had her back, but could barely catch her. She was oily. His palm skimmed down her spine and slid inside her bikini bottom. His long, callused fingers cupped her bare ass. Fortunately, there was no one behind them.

"Sweet cheeks," he said, tightening his grip. Right before he squeezed. She nearly came out of her skin. He chuckled. Removing his hand, he patted her butt. Then gave her a solid push onboard.

Danny had gotten in line. The cabin served as a snack bar. There were outside tables on the main platform. "Banana split," he ordered at the window.

Alyn went with a Creamsicle. Halo had a Chipwich. They sat out on the covered deck and ate. Her brother's eyes were bigger than his stomach. Halo helped him finish the three scoops, banana, and toppings.

Danny burped, and Alyn raised an eyebrow. He remembered his manners. "Sorry." Pausing, "Burping's better than—"

She cut him off, knowing what he was about to say. "Neither one in public."

Halo sided with Danny. "Sometimes a man has to do what a man has to do."

Her brother found that inordinately funny. He started to laugh and couldn't stop. He clutched his stomach. "I like you, Halo. You're like a—" He gasped, unable to fully catch his breath.

A what? Alyn thought. Like a father? A brother? To him.

"My best friend," he finally managed.

Halo gave him a fist bump. "I'm there with you, buddy."

"Do you like me as much as Landon?"

"Landon is my adult best friend. You're my under ten."

Danny nodded, accepting Halo's answer. "What's Alyn to you, then?"

"My fiancée."

"Not for real."

Halo looked Alyn in the eye. "Reality is relative at any given moment. Your sister and I are together now. No telling what the future will bring."

Danny puzzled over his words. "So the future could bring something good? Like gifts at Christmas?"

Christmas was guaranteed, Alyn thought. Halo and she had a ten-month deal. She didn't want to disappoint her brother, so she said, "We'll see how it all shakes out, sweetie."

"I hope it shakes good."

She had started to cross her fingers, too, in hopes she and Halo might move beyond their business arrangement and have an actual relationship. Sex would figure into their equation. She wasn't quite ready for him, but soon. Making love to the man would be a life-altering experience. She would not deny herself. No matter the consequences.

Her previous boyfriend had hurt her. Halo's eventual departure would break her heart. But sometimes pain was worth it. When she had his memory to last her a lifetime.

The dolphin-shaped clock on the cabin wall claimed late afternoon. The air had cooled. A breeze rippled the water. The day had caught up with Danny. He leaned against her, his head drooping.

"I'll piggyback him to the beach," said Halo, rising. He cleared the plastic dessert dish; tossed it in recyclable trash. Then he prodded Danny. "Let's go, dude."

"I'm too tired to climb down the ladder."

Halo offered an alternative. "I could always toss you over the side."

Her brother made it down the ladder in record time.

Halo went ahead of Alyn, in case she slipped again. "Careful," he told her, as he cupped her left butt cheek until they reached the sandbar. She wiggled away the second her feet touched sandy reef. Then tugged down her swimsuit bottom, which had gotten pushed high on her tush. She showed a lot of cheek. Both sides.

She eyed him. "Really?"

"I had your back."

And her butt. His grin was pure sin. Her breath caught just looking at him. She needed to cool off. She dove into the water, headed for shore. She was a fairly strong swimmer, but not as strong as Halo, even with Danny on his back. A powerful free-stylist, Halo sliced through the water. They passed her halfway to shore. Danny's laughter echoed in their wake.

Shallow water landed them both on their feet. That's when Halo initiated a foot race. Knees high, she stomped more than ran, quickly lagging behind.

Halo got Danny to land, then returned for her. There was more in his expression than lending a helpful hand. She swatted water at him, discouragingly. It didn't faze him in the least. He was twice her size, and shadowed her from the shoreline.

The pontoon rang a bell, pulled away from the sandbar. Cruised farther down the coast. In the silence that followed, Alyn stared up at Halo. No man should look so good wet. He ran one hand through his hair, pushed it back off his face. Water droplets tipped his eyelashes. His gaze was hot, determined, and dangerously bright. A warning he was about to kiss her.

Still she hesitated. "I don't—"

"I do."

They did.

He trapped her close, and their bodies aligned. Her arms circled his neck. They were as close as two people could be and still have their swimsuits on.

Anticipation tingled and her knees went weak when he

walked her backwards, to a greater depth. Where the ocean played beneath her breasts, and fully covered his groin.

His mouth descended. A man ready to claim his woman. He'd chosen her. He teased and tasted, and courted her with hot, deep, moist kisses. He bit her bottom lip and sucked the plumpness. She moaned.

Her resistance floated away.

The strong beat of his heart collided with her own. The hard ridges of his abdomen flexed against her belly as he breathed in and out. Roughly. More rapidly.

His hands slid lower, to cup her butt, lifting her against his sex, settling his erection into the vee of her thighs. She arched her back, raised her hips, and deepened their contact. She rocked and rubbed the full length of him. The man was large. Very large.

His hand moved beneath the water, rounding her hip, and grazing her inner thigh. The callused pads of his fingers eased between her legs. He stroked her through the lavender bikini bottom. The abrasive rub of his fingertips was erotically sensual. His unrelenting attention taxed every nerve ending in her body.

A craving took hold, and she moved against his fingers. He increased the pressure. Her lungs compressed. Her heart beat too fast. Her inner muscles contracted. She tensed to the point of snapping. He took her to climax. Sensations, tremors lingered.

Her low moan broke their kiss. Their breaths connected in short pants. He rested his forehead against her brow. He now knew her body far better than she knew his. She'd found release, and he remained hard. Her cheeks grew warm. She was afraid to look at him.

He was the one to tilt up her chin with his thumb, to meet her gaze. Her chin felt a little tender. Whisker burn.

Halo hadn't shaved in several days. He was all sexy rough-
ness and soul-stealing. He'd captured her heart.

He released her slowly. Let her slide off his body in one
fluid motion. His erection poked her all the way down.
She licked her lips. "What about you?"

"What about me?" His tone was amused.

"I—" she faltered.

"Had an orgasm," he helped her.

"You—"

"Didn't."

"What now?" She wasn't sure how to handle the situation. How to handle the man.

He didn't have time to answer. Danny ran to the shoreline, waved to them. "Halo," he shouted. "I want to do
the fan walkway outside the stadium. Come help."

"Two minutes," Halo called over his shoulder.

"Maybe I should go ahead, and you can follow," she
suggested.

"I need to deflate."

"I'll start the walkway."

Alyn was on her hands and knees, forming a sidewalk
when Halo returned. His gaze was steely, and he walked
stiffly. No one seemed to notice, and if they did, no one
commented. He crouched down across from her, and next
to Danny, on the opposite side of the stadium. The sand
castle was detailed and enormous. It would've taken first
place in any contest. The builders were focused, intent,
squaring off angles and rounding edges.

The building continued until twilight. Until her brother
clapped his hands and declared it finished. People rose,
backed slowly away, as if letting the sand castle breathe.
Fully come alive. Awaiting the shout of "play ball."

The waning sun scored the stadium in shades of red and
hints of purple. The fan walkway was tinged orange. Halo

retrieved his iPhone from his backpack, took group and single pictures. Alyn captured one of boy and man, both smiling, both content and proud with the day's activity.

"Be sure you check out the Rogues' Facebook page and website when you get home," Halo said to Danny. "I'll have Jillian post a few pictures on one or both." He glanced at Alyn. "You can track updates on spring training, home and away games, and future events on-line, too."

Danny frowned. "Wish I was staying."

Halo ruffled his hair. "So do I, dude, but you need to get back to school, and I need to focus on our upcoming season."

"You're ready." Danny was positive. "You'll hit a home run every game."

"Maybe not every game."

"I'll be counting."

Alyn wouldn't be counting his at-bats; instead, she'd be marking off days on her calendar until he returned to Richmond. She'd gotten used to having Halo in her life. She would miss him. More than she cared to admit.

Their time in Barefoot William came to an end. Far too quickly. Private time with Halo was limited. A few kisses. Nothing more. Flying home with the pets wasn't an option, so Halo hired a limousine service to drive them back to Richmond. One with a television, Wi-Fi, and mini-fridge.

On the day of their departure, they strolled the beach one last time. High tide and foot traffic had leveled the stadium. Only one small section of the fan sidewalk remained.

Shortly thereafter, they stood on the sidewalk outside the inn, each taking a turn hugging Halo. Danny was sad. Halo fist bumped the boy until he smiled. Martha thanked him profusely. The vacation had done her mother a world of good. Then came Alyn. Her arms wrapped his waist and she laid her cheek on his chest. The beat of his heart was steady and strong, and would travel with her.

He stroked her hair, tipped up her chin, and kissed her deeply. Leaving her breathless. She climbed into the black stretch limo, and settled beside Quigley in his child car carrier. Then clutched her locket and stared out the window. Her gaze held Halo's until they turned the corner. The professional driver got them home safely. No detours this time. The ride home wasn't nearly as much fun as their initial trip south.

Thirteen

Alyn had never been so busy in her life. She was living her dream. The Shy Lily was taking shape. A moving company hauled every piece of heavy furniture from her home to downtown, then up a flight of stairs to her shop, where she arranged the groupings. She further cleared out the storage unit. Adding even more pieces. Mirrors, lamps, clocks, and other smaller items created the perfect ambiance.

The store's interior was as old as her antiques. Indoor red brick walls. Soft blue cottage-style shutters on the windows. She had a view of city hall, a historical building restored over time. Quigley came with her to work. They took advantage of a nearby park. The pug was able to stretch his hind legs without contractions, and paw-tap the floor. Their veterinarian was pleased by Quigs' progress. Alyn hoped he'd be walking by Halo's return. Or soon after.

When late afternoon came, she would join Danny and her mother for supper. She missed spending time with them, but there were only so many hours in the day. Most were spent at her store. Jacy Kincaid, owner of the corner coffee shop, had come upstairs and introduced herself. She was married to Rick Kincaid, managing general partner/ co-chairman of the Rogues. Jacy had heard she and Halo were engaged, and offered her congratulations, delivering a caramel latte and box of butterscotch scones. Alyn had liked her immediately.

Today, Alyn closed the shop at five-thirty, loaded Quigley in her car, and drove home. She carried her pug inside, settled him in his cart, let him wander. There was lots of open space now, since she'd moved the antique furniture to her shop. Quigs made wide circles around the coffee table. Then followed her to the kitchen.

She found her mother standing before the stove, preparing baked chicken. Alyn stopped inside the doorway and stared, absorbing the color and fragrance of the room. A bouquet of magenta orchids was collected in a milk glass vase on the table. A potted orange bromeliad along with two smaller African violets decorated the countertop. The arrangements reminded her of when her father was alive. He'd brought her mother flowers daily.

"Kitchen looks pretty, Mom," she said.

Martha glanced over her shoulder. "Eleanor Norris dropped by today," she told Alyn. "The woman still drives. It appears she and Herman get around town just fine. We enjoyed tea and butter cookies. Eleanor is a curious sort. She asked to see the greenhouse. I was reluctant at first, but gave in. We spent two hours together, tugging back vines and organizing planters. I sent her home with two containers of bare root hybrid tea roses, which she intends to revive. Eleanor hinted at us going into business together. Something small. Part-time. I have the greenhouse, and she has the floral know-how. She worked beside her husband for sixty years. She stays in touch with all her old customers. I'm giving it some thought."

"Definitely worth considering," said Alyn. The venture could benefit both women. Give them a sense of purpose. "Should you move ahead, I'll place my order now. A weekly delivery of lilies for my shop."

"Lovely," her mother agreed. Only to dip her head, and sigh. "After Eleanor left, I sat down on the sofa and cried." Her voice broke even now. "The loss of your father weighed heavily today. I hurt. He was the other half of my heart. My life. I kept looking around the greenhouse, expecting to see him. To hear his laugh. I missed him sneaking up behind me. Kissing my cheek. Wrapping his arms about my waist. I felt so alone. So lost. To think I will never see him again—"

Alyn crossed to her mother, hugged her tight. Sadness embraced them both. "I understand, Mom. I miss him every day, too."

They stood holding each other, until Martha eased back slightly, and grabbed tissues off the counter. They wiped away tears, blew their noses. Her mom cleared her throat, said, "I want you to know the same love I had with your dad. Halo Todd is a good man. I only wish he was more than your business partner."

Alyn wished so, too. "Time will tell."

Her mother patted her cheek. "Make the most of your ten months with him. Don't let time pass you by."

Alyn nodded. She would make every day count. "Where's Danny?" she asked.

"Playing on the computer in his bedroom. Ten minutes, and we eat."

Alyn went to see which game was distracting him from his homework. Quigley remained in the kitchen. She found her brother on the Rogues' Facebook page, scanning posts and photographs.

He bounced on his chair, grinned at her. "Halo hit a home run today against the Miami Marlins!" He was beyond excited. He motioned her to view fan photos. "Rogues won, six to four."

Alyn looked over his shoulder. There, before her on the screen, was Halo, crossing home plate. His expression was smug, as if he was doing his job, and he was good at it. Very good, Alyn thought. She read fan praise for Will Ridgeway. The pitcher was throwing heat, and drawing strikeouts. The team had scored a runaway preseason.

"Halo and Landon have more photographs on Facebook," said Danny, locating Landon's official fan page. "They're having a party. Read to me," he requested.

Alyn obliged. "Landon got engaged to Eden Cates, the photographer," she said with a smile. "They're getting married at her home, a restored wedding chapel. Friends and family are pictured, celebrating their announcement."

"Where was the party?" he wanted to know.

A neon sign hung over the bar. "Lusty Oyster."

"What's 'lusty'?"

She went with, "Healthy and strong."

"An oyster that lifts weights."

"Funny image, don't you think?"

Her brother laughed. Then squinted at the screen. "Halo's sitting at Landon's table." He touched his fingertip to the man's face.

Halo's presence was unmistakable. Seated and smiling with Landon on his left, and—she blinked, *Sharon Thomas* on his right. The woman from the boardwalk. The one who'd come on to Halo while Alyn was inside Olde Tyme Portraits having their pictures reduced for her locket. Alyn had intervened on his behalf, and Sharon had moved on. But not for long, it seemed. She was with him now.

"Halo looks happy," Danny noted.

Way too happy for an engaged man. Alyn was pleased for Landon and Eden. They made a solid couple. She and Halo were unraveling. In less than a month.

She crossed her arms over her chest, took several deep breaths. Her fault? Maybe. She would partly shoulder the blame. He'd asked her to stay in Barefoot William. She'd declined. He'd seemed disappointed when she left.

Apparently, he'd recovered. In record time. Sharon had reappeared, and now kept him busy. Him and his blue balls.

She and Danny scanned the remaining party pictures. The shadowed lighting couldn't hide the empty beer bottles on the table, the couples dancing in the background, and the shared kisses. Sharon's lips brushed Halo's cheek, near his ear. She might've bitten the lobe, for all Alyn knew. The blonde's hands were under the table. Touching Halo? His thigh. Groin.

Her stomach twisted. Was she misreading the situation? Hard to conceive. The evidence stared her in the face. He was having a good time with his buddies. Them, and their women. All without her. The realization left her cold. Hurt. She'd trusted him. Mistakenly. He'd let her down. Ten times the fool, she thought. She was a slow learner when it came to men. Halo in particular. Pain took hold. Gripping her so tightly, she broke. She wasn't certain she could pull herself together again. She was that shattered.

Her mother called them to supper. Danny shut down the computer. They walked to the kitchen together. Alyn fed Quigley, then took a chair at the table. Not the least bit hungry. She pushed her food around on her plate. Making pathways with her fork through the mashed potatoes.

Her mother looked worried. "Problem, dear?" she asked.

Her mother seldom went on-line, only twice a month to check bank statements and balance the household budget. She hadn't seen the photos that confused Alyn. Her mom was fond of Halo. Alyn didn't want her involved in a situation beyond their control.

She nudged Danny with her foot under the table, a request that he keep quiet. He side-eyed her, reached for a second piece of chicken, and kept right on eating.

She fingered the corner of her napkin before saying, "I'm fine, Mom. Just tired. I'm calling it an early night."

Her mother didn't press, merely appeared sympathetic. She corralled Danny to clear the table and load the dishwasher. Her brother dragged his feet, but got the job done. Alyn left the table to walk Quigley. They strolled around the block. Quigs kept a steady pace. Once back at the house, she went to her bedroom, readied the pug for bed. He soon snored.

She showered, slipped into a T-shirt and cotton tap pants. Crawled into bed. She slept fitfully. Morning came too soon.

Three weeks later, and spring training wrapped. The Rogues headed back to Richmond. The city welcomed them. The team had done preseason proud, winning twenty-five of thirty games. Bull's-eyes marked their backs. They were the team to beat.

It was late afternoon, and Alyn would soon be seeing Halo. He'd texted and called every day. Sometimes twice. She tried to keep her own texts light, informative. When they talked, her voice level. Smooth, as if she hadn't a worry or problem in the world. Or a broken heart. She even managed to laugh a little. The sound of his voice made her stomach soft. So deep and sexy. She forced herself to stand back, to stay strong, and to imagine life without him. It was difficult to do. Over the past few days, she slowly began to limit, then to avoid all communication. The toughest decision of her life. Pride was all she had left.

She wore the locket, never taking it off. It felt cool against her skin. The thought of removing the necklace, placing it in a jewelry box, represented another failed relationship. She'd had plenty of disappointment in her life—what was one more? They still had a business deal. Which she was about to break.

She'd recently designed an internet website, and The Shy Lily had branched out overnight. Flourished, actually. The hits were numerous. The requests for private showings of the merchandise were continuous. She'd sold several pieces before going public. Large, lucrative sales. She was close to reimbursing Halo. Paying off her loan was her top priority.

Alyn paced her shop now. The hardwood floors had a worn patina. She went to the window, saw Halo's Hummer pull to the curb. A jerky stop, as if he'd hit the brakes hard. His vehicle hogged two spaces. She noted his exit, and tried to collect herself. No time. He glanced up, as if he knew she watched him. He stared back. He was coming for her.

He had his game face on. She barely recognized him. His shoulders were squared. His expression hard and unrelenting. Scary, yet sexy. Her pulse jumped. Her stomach knotted. Calm eluded her. He gave her chills.

He crossed the street, dodging traffic. The closer he got, the harder his expression. He'd gone long between haircuts, she noticed; the ends brushed his collar. He wore a rugby pullover, dark brown with a navy stripe. Jeans. Athletic shoes. He carried a manila envelope.

She'd been expecting him, and dressed up a little. She was about to break up with him, and wanted to leave a lasting impression. She would greet him in a white eyelet tunic top belted over a tiered sage skirt. Then show him the door.

She bit down on her bottom lip. More than anything, she wished their situation was different. That they would hug and kiss, and he'd take her on the new brass bed, ac-

quired at an estate sale, and recently delivered. She'd positioned the queen-size heirloom with the railed head and
footboards and new mattress near the front window. The
natural light enhanced the fine linen bedding and lacy pillow covers. She'd had an offer of ten grand, but had held
out for fifteen. It would sell to the right person. Someone
who'd appreciate its ornate beauty and history as much as
she did.

Quigley had sniffed the bedframe, decided it wasn't a
chew toy. Having grown tired of her arranging furniture,
he was presently napping in the small storage room. Door
closed.

She now stood behind a chesterfield armchair, clutching
the back for support. Her fingers dug into the rich bur-
gundy leather. She awaited Halo, wishing for an escape.
No backdoor.

The buzzer sounded below stairs, announcing his arrival. He came through the door, and she heard him set
the dead bolt. Loud in the silence. She wasn't going anywhere.

He was up the steps before she could catch her breath.
All tall, dark, and intimidating. He stopped on the landing,
glaring with an intensity that nearly knocked her backwards. He flared his nostrils, and the corners of his mouth
pinched. Widening his stance, he slapped the envelope
against his thigh. A dull, angry sound.

His voice was hard when he said, "You've gone silent
on me."

That she had.

"I found you."

Not too difficult. "You had two choices. Home or here."

"I stopped by your house first."

"You've seen Danny?" Her brother would've been
thrilled.

"He was glad to see me. You, apparently, are not." His lips pursed. "Woman, we need to talk."

Talking was what she'd had in mind before he'd arrived. His accusatory stare left her apprehensive. As if she'd done something wrong, and he was calling her out. Their meeting was all about him. Not her.

He cut his gaze to a table in one corner. A French inlaid rosewood oval designed for a formal dining room. He motioned her to take a chair. Sitting made her vulnerable. She'd have preferred to stand. She went ahead and joined him. Sat three seats away. Distance was her friend. Too close, and she might do something foolish. Like kiss or hug him. Tell him how much she'd missed him. How her heart was glad to see him.

He placed the envelope on the table, slid it toward her. "Danny was on the computer when I arrived at your house. Checking out the Rogues' Facebook page."

"He's a loyal fan. He believes in the team."

"I wish you believed as much in me." His voice sounded as accusatory as it did defeated.

She was unable to speak. She wouldn't have known what to say if she could. So she let him continue.

"I hadn't seen all the practice and game photos posted on the website. Your brother and I went through each one. Including a few party pictures on Landon's page. Danny pointed out the photos that made you sad. I immediately saw how they would affect you. How you would've jumped to conclusions."

He leaned his elbows on the table, steepled his fingers. "Time to hit the reset button, babe. What you didn't take into account was that only part of the pictures were visible. You had to double-click on the photograph to enlarge each one. To get the full impact. Especially those with me and Sharon. I had Danny print them out. Kid's got computer skills."

He tapped the envelope. "Take a look, Alyn. Land's my best friend. We've always had each other's back. He wanted to go to the Oyster for drinks. To celebrate his engagement. I went. Alone. The place was packed. Twelve people sat at a table for four. We were sitting atop each other. I stayed for one hour. Cut out."

Alyn's hand trembled as she opened the clasp. Removed two photos. These showed a much wider view of those gathered. Sharon was seated on Halo's right, snugged close. On her opposite side was Zoo. The left fielder had his arm about her shoulders. There weren't enough chairs to go around. She half-sat on Zoo's lap.

Alyn moved to the second photo. The one where Sharon had her mouth on Halo, near his ear. "She's thanking me for setting her up with Zoo," he said. "The bar was loud, she leaned in close. I didn't catch everything she said. Other than she was hot and horny for him. She's met her match in Zoo."

"Not you . . . Zoo." She had to say it out loud. To hear it with her own ears. A deeper look at the photo showed Sharon's hands positioned on her lap beneath the table. Not on Halo.

She sat back, took it all in. Then slowly returned both photos to the envelope. Closed the clasp. Relief flooded her. Normal reclaimed her life.

His jaw worked. "I'm ticked you doubted me."

"Can you blame me?" She stuck up for herself.

"Communication," he stated. "You should've asked me."

"Maybe I should have."

"No maybes, babe. We're engaged—"

"We're pretend."

"What if I wanted to make it real?"

"You don't love me."

"You don't know that."

"You haven't indicated otherwise."

"Neither have you."

"I . . . care." She gave him that much. Afraid of sharing too much too soon.

"Care enough to accept an actual engagement ring?"

"I'd consider it."

"Consider this, then." He reached into his jean pocket, and removed a small, square black box. He held it on his palm, admitted, "I'm not a traditional down-on-one-knee kind of guy."

Which she already knew. She'd never ask him to change. He was her kind of perfect.

He rose slowly, and approached her. He curved one hand about her upper arm, and lifted her to face him. "I never planned to love you, Alyn Jayne. Our time came quickly. I fell fast, fell hard. You're with me, even when we're apart. You never leave my thoughts. Marry me."

Her heart opened. Tears fell. "Here I was about to re-pay my loan. To walk away. And miss you forever."

"No missing me. I'm right here. Going nowhere."

"I'm going nowhere, too."

He handed her the ring box. "Yours."

"Mine," she said on a sigh. It took her two tries to open the lid. She was that shaken by what he'd said. Halo was the man she wanted. The man she needed. He'd just offi-cially proposed.

Her engagement ring brought another rush of tears. He'd purchased the aquamarine with the circlet of dia-monds, the one she'd admired in Barefoot William. It was beautiful, feminine, and slid on her finger as if made for her. "Oh . . . Halo," she said softly, thankfully, lovingly.

"Can I take that for a 'yes'?"

"Ten times over."

"I have something else to show you," he stated, reach-ing for his wallet. He cracked the leather, pulled out a yellow feather. One left from her chicken costume. "I saved it, to remind me never to do another game show. In the end, it reminded me of you. I kept it safe."

"I want a piece of it for my locket," she said. "Another memento."

"You got it."

He was about to kiss her when he caught sight of the brass bed. His eyebrow spiked. Words weren't needed— Alyn knew his intention. She was in agreement.

Closing time had come and gone.

The door was locked.

The shop was empty.

Sex was waiting to happen. They both knew it. Both felt it.

Halo hadn't been with another woman since he'd met Alyn. She'd been waiting for him. He would take her for the first time on the antique bed. She had old-fashioned values. He was bold as the brass. They were meant to come together.

The time was now.

His pulse picked up as he looked down on her face. Really looked at her. Saw her with his eyes and his heart. She was beautiful, inside and out. Her eyelids were shuttered, her brown lashes long. Her ponytail shadowed one cheek. Her lips were inviting, sweetly curved, and generous. The insecure flick of her tongue aroused him.

"Want me, Alyn." His voice was deep, raw.

"For longer than you know." Tilting her head, she raised her chin. On a heart-warmed sigh, she wound her arms about his neck, went smooth against him. She initiated, seeking his mouth with her own.

Need embraced them both. His mind shut down and his body turned on. The light brush of her lips made him instantly hard. The softness of her breasts pushed into his chest. Their hips came into line. His erection prodded her belly.

Never breaking their kiss, he unbuckled her wide leather belt, slid his hands under her tunic, and up her sides to cup her breasts. He delved beneath her bra. His thumbs rubbed across her nipples, drawing them to points. He scrolled his knuckles down her ribs, then circled her navel. He went on to caress her lower spine, her bottom, the crease of her ass through her skirt. The cotton bunched high on her thighs. He stroked the smooth backs of her bare legs.

He wanted her naked. Needed to touch her. His body was hyped. His balls tightened. He was about to take her with the passion of a man long without his woman.

His experience had her undressed in seconds. Her tunic crowned her head, and he tossed it aside. He unclipped the barrette from her ponytail, and her hair fell long and loose. He unsnapped her bra, and let it slide off her slender shoulders. Her breasts spilled onto his palms. Brown-tipped and puckered.

She stepped out of her ballerina flats, and he undid a row of side buttons on her skirt. It shimmered over her hips. She had great legs. Off came her satin panties. Bikini wax and sweet ass. She was perfect for him.

Nude felt natural with Halo. No shyness. No embarrassment. Alyn could wait no longer. She went to work on him. She shoved his rugby pullover up his chest and stared. He was all solid muscle and six-pack cut. Her fingers played over his ribs. She brushed his nipples. His breathing deepened. His top came off easily. She tossed it on the back of a chair.

Mesmerized by the width of his chest, she took advantage of his bare shoulders. She nipped him, leaving her mark. She flicked her tongue to the pulse point at the base of his throat. He closed his eyes and growled. Primal.

She kissed her way to his jawline. His evening stubble was dark and rough against her lips. His maleness, potent. She kissed the soft spot beneath his ear. He lost it when she bit his lobe. He grew sexually impatient.

She tucked her fingers into the waistband of his jeans, flicked the snap with her thumb. Then lowered his zipper and reached inside, found him stark and stiff. Gently, purposely, she rubbed her thumb over the head of his penis, then down the underside of his shaft. Sensitive to her touch, he swelled in her grasp. He groaned when she squeezed him.

Male urgency had him removing his sneakers, then shucking his jeans. No underwear. He ruffled in a pocket, and snagged a condom. Palmed it.

The air between them grew hot. Explosive. Her face flushed, and her lips parted. He drew her full against him. They kissed again.

Halo was an exceptional kisser. His warm tongue thrust into her mouth, tangled with her own. Mated. She grew lightheaded.

She dug her fingers into the corded curve of his biceps and clung to him. Her hips angled toward him unconsciously.

He clutched her bottom, lifted her. Fitted her to him.

She inhaled his scent and absorbed the man. Soul deep. The plump swell of her naked breasts pressed his hard chest. He carried her to the bed. Laid her on the linen. Then tore the silver packet with his teeth. Sheathed himself. Lowering over her.

He kissed up her body, then back down. Tasting her. His fingers moved between her thighs, stroking her deeply. Her nerves tingled and her spine strained. Her fingernails traced the crease of his thigh and his muscles twitched in response. She tilted her hips, and he entered her. A slow slide until she rocked her hips, fully accepting him.

Streamlined, he began to move. Tense heat. Burning. He claimed his mate. He took and gave. Stretched time. Pushing her to the edge.

Blood thrummed. Desire throbbed.

Sensation came in wild currents. Their climax built.

Her orgasm shook her.

A hard shudder convulsed him.

A sated, sensual ease brought them back to reality. Satisfaction settled in her bones. Deep and forever. Halo was here with her now. He'd promised her a future together. Always.

He rose, walked naked to the small bathroom at the back of her store. She admired him going. He disposed of the condom. She appreciated his coming back to her. He resettled beside her. He rested his forehead against hers. He kissed the curve of her cheek, the tip of her nose. "You were amazing. Worth waiting for," he said, his voice husky.

"It's the bed."

"It was the woman in the bed."

"It's for sale."

"You just found a buyer, babe. Me."

"I could never make you pay—"

"The price is right. The pleasure, ours."

"Sold, to the man who gives good orgasm."

He took her again, just to show her how good.

It only got better between them.

An hour later, there was a scratching at the door to the storeroom. "Quigley," Alyn said, rising on one elbow. "I was moving furniture around, and he got tired. I took him out of his cart. He's up now. Wants out."

Halo sat up on the bed. Swung his knees over the side. "I'll get him." He pulled off the mattress, drew on his jeans. Bare chest, bare feet, he crossed the room. The man definitely had a great ass.

He cracked the door, peeked inside. Quigs barked his welcome. Halo took several steps back, knelt down. Patted his thighs. "Come here, speedster."

Alyn propped herself up to watch their reunion. The pug nearly came out of his fur, he was that excited to see Halo. Quiggie scooted toward him. He was wagging so hard and fast, his body bounced, twisted, and his back legs scuttled beneath him.

Time stopped, and healing took hold. Wobbly and weak, Quigs pushed up. Supporting his weight for a moment before collapsing. The dog tried again. Even more successful this time. He held his own for several seconds, took a tentative step toward Halo, before sitting back down.

"He walked!" Alyn jumped off the bed. She threw on her tunic, which covered part, but not all of her. She didn't care.

She reached them, dropped down. Relief overtook her. Quigley had stood on all fours. Attempted a step. He would recover. Shaky, trembling now, he panted. She hugged her dog so hard he grunted. Sadness over his accident left her. She couldn't stop smiling.

Halo's arm went around her, snugging her against him. He kissed her forehead. "Your boy's going to make it."

"*Our* boy," she said. "He was glad to see you."

Quigley did something he hadn't done for a long time. He used his back legs, and pushed himself onto Alyn's lap. Cuddled close. Both she and Halo praised and patted him. The three of them sat together on the floor for a long time.

Halo angled his head toward her, grinned. "I fell in love with a chicken," he said, referring to their first meeting. "You had me at cock-a-doodle-do."

"I'll have you again once Quigs sleeps."

The pug's soft snores soon sent them back to bed.

Read more Kate Angell next month in

THE COTTAGE ON PUMPKIN AND VINE

National Bestselling Author Kate Angell

Jennifer Dawson

Sharla Lovelace

This Halloween, love is the sweetest treat . . .

Welcome to Moonbright, Maine . . .
Where the scents of donuts and cider waft through
the crisp night air . . . with just a hint of magic.

It's time for the annual Halloween costume party at the cottage on Pumpkin and Vine, the perfect place to celebrate the pleasures of the season. Guests return to the picturesque B&B year after year to snuggle up in its cozy rooms, explore the quiet, tree-lined streets, and enjoy all the spooky fun of the holiday. But local legend whispers that it's also a place where wishes have a strange way of coming true.

For three unsuspecting revelers, it's going to be an enchanted weekend of candy corn kisses and midnight black kittens, along with some *real* Halloween surprises—the kind that make your heart skip a beat—for many more celebrations to come . . .

And look for even more Kate Angell this October!

THAT MISTLETOE MOMENT

New York Times **Bestselling Author Cat Johnson**

USA Today **Bestselling Author Kate Angell**

Allyson Charles

As the holidays descend, three single women take a thoroughly modern approach to good old-fashioned romance and wonder if the best—and most complicated—gift of all is just a click, tap, or swipe away . . .

MADE UP

Like a Christmas miracle, the Build a Boyfriend App lets you simply input the stats of your dream man, and witty texts, passionate emails, and hot Instagram pics start flooding in. No more awkward questions or pitying looks as you face the holidays alone!

MIXED UP

But even the best technology has its glitches. When real-life emotions come into play, this trio of twentysomethings find themselves in a tangle of crossed signals, flying wrapping paper, disastrous Christmas parties . . . and surprising kisses.

MATCHED UP

Yet despite the confusion of their mistletoe misadventures, when the New Year dawns, these very satisfied women just may find themselves waking up with true love beside them.

Connect with

Visit us online at
KensingtonBooks.com
to read more from your favorite authors, see books
by series, view reading group guides, and more.

Join us on social media

for sneak peeks, chances to win books and prize packs,
and to share your thoughts with other readers.

facebook.com/kensingtonpublishing
twitter.com/kensingtonbooks

Tell us what you think!

To share your thoughts, submit a review,
or sign up for our eNewsletters, please visit:
KensingtonBooks.com/TellUs.